A
STORM
OF BLOOD
AND
SWORDS

ALSO BY MARION BLACKWOOD

Marion Blackwood has written lots of books across multiple series, and new books are constantly added to her catalogue. To see the most recently updated list of books, please visit: www.marionblackwood.com

CONTENT WARNINGS

The Oncoming Storm series contains quite a lot of violence and morally questionable actions. If you have specific triggers, you can find the full list of content warnings at: www.marionblackwood.com/content-warnings

A STORM OF
BLOOD AND SWORDS

THE ONCOMING STORM: BOOK SIX

MARION BLACKWOOD

First edition

ISBN 978-91-986387-5-2 (hardcover)
ISBN 978-91-986387-4-5 (paperback)
ISBN 978-91-986387-3-8 (ebook)

Editing by Julia Gibbs
Book cover design by ebooklaunch.com

www.marionblackwood.com

For everyone who does not bow

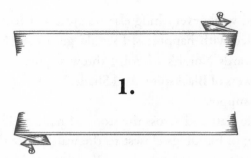

1.

Coming back after a life-changing journey is strange. You've been through all of these incredible experiences that have shaped you into something different, into someone who isn't quite the person you were when you left. In your heart and soul, you know that you have changed, and for some reason that makes it feel like the world around you should've changed too. But then you come back. After all that time and everything you've been through, you look at the city you left behind. And everything is just... the same.

A warm night wind swept through the city. I took a deep breath. The air in Pernula still smelled like spices on a warm summer day and the colorful awnings and flowers still swayed in the gentle breeze. Just as they had before I left. Shifting my weight, I adjusted my position on top of the city wall.

For a long while, I just sat there atop the battlements and went through the motions. A lot had changed. But a lot was also the same. Warm feelings that had nothing to do with the heat of summer spread through my chest as I watched the city while the night wore on. I smiled at the familiar view before me. It was good to be back.

Soft thuds echoed into the night as I jumped down the last few steps from the city wall. Despite the strange feeling that I had changed while everything else was just as I had left it, my heart sparkled with happiness. I would get to see Liam again. Starting towards Norah's school, I threw a quick glance at the obsidian towers of Blackspire. And Shade. I would get to see him again too, I supposed.

A pebble clattered across the stones. I had barely made it to the first ring of buildings closest to the wall before dark shapes began appearing from the shadows. Yanking my hunting knives from their sheaths, I slowed to a walk. When the street before me and behind me, as well as all the side alleys in between, were blocked by silent people, I came to a halt on the smooth stones.

"This is quite the welcome," I called into the night.

The unmoving sentries around me remained quiet. For a moment, only the wind rustling fabric and kicking up dust clouds disturbed the peace. Then, the mass of bodies up ahead parted. A slim man stepped out of the darkness, flanked by two muscled ones. I squinted at them.

"The Oncoming Storm," the skinny man said.

That voice. I recognized it from somewhere. As the mysterious man closed the distance between us, his features became clear. Graying hair and dark beady eyes shone in the moonlight. I let out a chuckle.

"The Rat King," I said.

Since I had already come to the conclusion that my two hunting knives would be useless against the army of people surrounding me, I stuck the blades back in their holsters. The gang leader known as the Rat King, the one that I had pissed off back when we were manipulating the Pernulan election, was still advancing on me as I drew myself up and crossed my arms.

"How did you know I was back?" I spun a hand in the air. "All I've done is sit atop the city walls."

"I know about everything that happens in the Underworld." His beady eyes glittered with satisfaction. "This is my city now."

The Rat King and his two bodyguards had stopped so close to me that I could have easily shoved a knife between his ribs. How careless. However, since I wasn't sure what the armed people surrounding me would do if I did that, I decided to wait and see how this played out.

I snorted. "That right?"

My head snapped to the side and pain shot through my jaw. Blinking, I wiped blood from the corner of my mouth before turning back to the man who had struck me.

Drawing my eyebrows down, I glared at the muscled bodyguard on my right. "Ow."

"Show some respect when addressing the King of the Underworld," he growled in response while lowering his fist again.

"The King of the Underworld, huh?"

"Yes," the pompous king replied. "All the gangs in this city answer to me now. And you will be no exception." A smile filled with malice twisted his lips. "Kneel and swear your allegiance to me."

A baffled chuckle escaped my throat. "Yeah, I don't think so."

Pain shot through my cheek again.

"You will submit," the Rat King announced with deadly menace while his goon raised his fist again.

I spat blood onto the dusty stones before leveling a disinterested stare on the man who had hit me. "The next person who lays a hand on me... loses the hand."

While the muscled bodyguard drew back for another strike, I reached deep into my soul. Anger burned like wildfire in the blackened pits. I yanked it out.

His fist faltered in the air and he retreated a half step as black eyes filled with death and insanity now met him instead. Dark smoke whipped around me.

"I'd back off now, if I were you." A feral grin spread across my mouth. "Unless you want to meet the God of Death, then we can arrange that."

Clothes rustled and weapons clanked as the mass of people crowding the streets around me drew back slightly. None of them appeared to be in any hurry to die. Pity. Shutters slammed closed somewhere up the street.

"Ah, yes. Ashaana." The Rat King ran a bony hand through his graying hair. "I've researched that quite a bit since I met you last. There wasn't all that much to know, but apparently, there have been a lot of reports about Ashaana passing out after using their powers." He shot me a challenging smirk. "So, go ahead and use them. I will just wait until you're unconscious then."

A haughty snicker dripped from my lips. "Oh, you know nothing."

I slammed a hand forward. Startled yelps echoed into the silent night as the wall of people blocking the street in front of me were pushed back by a strong wind. Feeding the rage inside me, I raised my arms. Black clouds billowed around me.

The Rat King and his goons stared in shock at the people now scrambling to get back on their feet. Lightning crackled over my skin. The self-proclaimed King of the Underworld backed away as the darkness around me grew. I flashed him a mad grin before throwing my arms out again.

More screams bounced off the stones as the crowd standing in the mouths of the side alleys were hurled backwards. I kept the dark clouds to my sides so that the Rat King and his crew could see me. See the death and insanity they were playing with. Thunder boomed around me.

"You want me to bow to you?" I squeezed my hand into a fist and yanked my arm down.

Lightning zapped the gray stones in front of the Rat King. He yelped and jumped back.

"I bow to no one." Madness played over my lips as more lightning crackled around me. I jerked my chin. "You'd better run."

Black smoke shot out all around me and blanketed the whole area. Lightning bolts lit up the dark haze and thunder claps echoed between the buildings, mingling with the screaming that rose from the Rat King's gang as they bolted. I kept the storm out until the last man had scurried back into the shadows. When I pulled the darkness back, tiredness washed over me. But thanks to the months and months of grueling training under the sharp eyes of Morgora, I still had lots of power left to use if the Rat King decided to give it another try.

He didn't. Once I was sure that the ridiculous fool who now called himself King of the Underworld wouldn't be coming back, I started out towards my initial destination again. Norah's school. I blinked at the empty road before me. Wait. Liam was an upperworlder now. He would most likely be sleeping. Because that was what normal people did in the middle of the night. By Nemanan, being normal was so boring. I shook my head and adjusted my course towards another destination. After climbing onto the roof of the nearest building, I took off at a run.

So, the Rat King controlled the Underworld now? I hadn't seen that coming. Ever since I bought Silver and rode out the gate in search of the Storm Casters over a year ago, I had barely been back in Pernula. After my disastrous stay in Travelers' Rest and the awful months I'd spent with the star elves in the City of Glass, I'd only made a short pit stop in Pernula before heading off to the White Mountains and then to Sker. And then I'd left again and spent even more time in the hidden Ashaana camp. Apparently, the Rat King had used that time to carve out an empire.

I blew out a breath as the city of Pernula flashed past below me. Okay, so maybe not everything was just as I had left it.

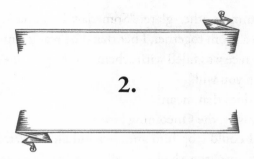

2.

Darkened hallways of black and red lay silent as I snuck across the obsidian floor. A grand door waited at the end of the corridor. Keeping to the shadows, I closed in on it. Something creaked behind me. I threw a quick glance over my shoulder but only an empty dark red carpet and grand paintings stared back at me. A soft hiss escaped my teeth as I turned back around and found reddish-brown eyes looking down at me from only a stride away.

Malor's lips twitched in amusement. "Did I startle you?"

I glared up at the tall man I had helped rescue from Sker last year and who now worked as Shade's senior advisor. "Of course not. I knew you were there the whole time. I'm a cat burglar, remember?"

"Naturally." Malor crossed powerful arms over his broad chest and peered down at me with amusement still twinkling in those strange red eyes of his. "Morgora hasn't killed you, I see."

"Well, to be fair, it wasn't from a lack of trying." I shook my head at the memory of the grueling training she had put me through in those mountains. "But I have a lot of experience with people trying to kill me so..." I shrugged.

"I can't imagine why."

I shot him another glare. "Someday, I wanna see you and Morgora in a room together. I bet that'd be really amusing."

Malor's face was filled with schemes as he gave me a knowing smile. "Soon you will."

"What does that mean?"

"Goodnight, the Oncoming Storm."

Before I could stop him and demand an answer, Malor had glided back into the shadows. Flicking my eyes to the dark ceiling, I blew out a deep sigh and shook my head. One day, I'd get to the bottom of all the secrets he and Morgora kept. One day. But not tonight. Tipping my head back down, I continued down the empty hallway. Tonight, I had another mission.

The grand door at the end rose before me. I studied the intricately detailed handle before pulling out a pair of lockpicks and getting to work. A soft click sounded. Edging the door open, I slipped inside.

The room before me was still as I shut the door again and snuck towards the lone figure bundled in covers on the double bed. Stopping next to the sturdy wooden frame, I grinned while reaching for a knife. Oh, he was about to get the awakening of a lifetime. With gentle fingers, I lifted the cover from his head.

A black pillow stared back at me. I blinked at the fluffy decoy right as the cold edge of a sword grazed my neck.

"The Oncoming Storm," a smug voice said.

I let out a chuckle. "General Shade."

Ducking, I twisted under his sword and threw up my hunting knife to meet it. He saw it coming and instead grabbed my wrist and used my movement to whirl me into the closet next to the bed. Wood rattled as my back connected with the tall piece of furniture. Still keeping his grip on my knife hand, he pinned it to the wood above my head while moving his sword back to my throat.

Shade smirked at me from across the sharpened blade. "It's actually High King Shade now."

Surprise flickered over my face for a few seconds before I let out an exasperated chuckle. "Of course it is." Shaking my head, I flashed him a sly smile. "So, you finally managed to subvert democracy, huh?"

"Democracy is overrated anyway."

Stepping back, he released my wrist and sheathed his sword again. I stuck my own blade back in its holster while the High King of Pernula lit the candle on the nightstand. Flickering flames danced over the smooth room decorated in black and red. I ran my eyes over his body while his back was turned.

He must've really been asleep when he heard me breaking in because he was only wearing a pair of black pants. No socks. No shoes. And no shirt. I watched the light play over his lean muscles as he turned back to me. Narrowing his eyes, he closed the distance between us in a few quick steps. While I was busy trying to figure out if he was reacting like this because he'd caught me staring at him half naked, he placed soft fingers on my jaw.

"What happened to your face?" he asked.

Oh. *That*. I blew out an amused breath but didn't slap his hand away.

"The Rat King wanted me to bend the knee to him."

A chuckle shook his muscled chest as he let go of my chin. "I imagine that turned into a pleasant conversation."

"Right." Since he hadn't stepped back after releasing me, I had to tilt my head back to meet his eyes. "You let the Rat King take the Underworld?"

"My focus was on becoming High King." He lifted his toned shoulders in a shrug. "I can't run both worlds, and as long as *someone* controls the Underworld and doesn't get in my way, I don't care who."

"How did you even become High King?"

Shade flashed me a smile. "Let's just say that after Sker fell, it was much easier to convince the good people of Pernula that they needed a strong and efficient leader."

I raised my eyebrows. Did that mean that his reason for going to Sker had actually not been to take it over but to make sure it fell so that he could rise to power here? Or had he just used the situation to his advantage after the fact? Blowing out a sigh, I shook my head. Nope. I wasn't even going to try to untangle the nest of snakes that was Shade's schemes and motives. Taking a step to the side, I skirted around him and flopped down on the bed.

The piles of covers and pillows he'd used as a decoy dug into my back so I twisted and pushed them back to the other side before stretching my body across the foot of the bed. Raking my fingers through my hair, I blew out another sigh. The mattress groaned as Shade lay down next to me.

For a few minutes, we just lay there on the double bed filled with black silk sheets and pillows. I glanced at him from the corner of my eye. When his muscles shifted as he rested his arms above his head, I had to resist the urge to trace my fingers across his abs.

"So, you're back," Shade finally said into the quiet room.

"Yeah."

"You've mastered your powers?"

"I mean, I'm not nearly as good as Marcus and some of the others, but yeah, Morgora has declared that she's now taught me everything I need to know. I'm now a real Ashaana." A dark chuckle slipped my lips. "You should've seen the stunt I pulled on the Rat King and his gang."

The mattress vibrated as Shade let out a dark laugh as well. "I'm sure it was quite the show." Silence fell for a few moments before he spoke up again. "So, what are you going to do now?"

"I don't know." Sitting up, I pushed off from the bed and took to pacing the room instead. "I mean, I'm staying in Pernula. But the Rat King clearly feels threatened by me after I challenged him and made him look weak back when we were messing with the election. And now he's out for blood and submission." I blew out a breath. "I've only been back for a few hours and I've already been pulled into another damn power struggle."

The bed creaked as Shade rose as well. "Do you know what your problem is? What your problem always has been?"

I frowned up at the assassin as he stepped right into my path and forced me to stop pacing. "What?"

"You want to be free to make your own decisions, to do what you want, to live life the way you want it, but you don't have the means to make that happen. You're a small player stuck in bigger players' game."

"Hey, I'm not..." I began but trailed off when Shade took another step towards me.

"Yes, you are." The Master Assassin traced gentle fingers over the bruises on my jaw. "The other players do stuff to you, or make you do stuff, and you have to do it because otherwise they'll crush you. Most people don't care that they have to answer to others because that's part of life." A lopsided smile drifted over his lips as he let his hand drop. "But you're not most people."

Damn straight. I grinned at him but before I could say anything, he pressed on.

"You want to be free to live life in any way you choose. If you truly want freedom, at least the kind of freedom you so desperately crave, you have to become a big player."

Outside the window, a warm night breeze blew a gust of fragrant air into the room. The wind made the candle flicker, and light from the quivering flame danced across Shade's handsome face while I considered his words. I didn't want to admit it, but there was a lot of truth to what he'd said. How many times had I been forced to do things for other people just because they were more powerful than me and could hurt me or my friends if I refused? Maybe it really was time that I became a big player too.

"Is that why you want it so badly, then?" I asked. "Power, I mean. Because of the freedom it gives you?"

"It's part of the reason." A smirk tugged at his lips. "I also really enjoy it when people obey my orders without question."

I snorted. "Bet you do." While gesturing vaguely at the open window, I nodded. "Alright, tomorrow I'm gonna buy a place of my own and see about becoming a bigger player."

"See, you're obeying my orders." Shade's black eyes glittered. "Just the way I want it."

Rolling my eyes, I swatted his chest with the back of my hand. "Shut up."

Amusement played over his lips before his features turned serious again. "Where are you staying tonight, then?"

"Don't know yet. Liam and Norah are sleeping like normal people so I don't want to disturb them."

"You could stay here."

"Here?" I flicked my eyes between Shade's bare chest and the bed of black silk behind him before asking the question that had been on my mind since I set foot in his room. "What would the High Queen say about that?"

Shade let the silence stretch for another few seconds. I had the strangest feeling that he was studying my expression so I made my features as neutral as possible. At last, he replied.

"There is no High Queen."

Relief and satisfaction flowed through me. The feelings surprised even me, so in the shock of realizing that the emotions had been mine, I was a fraction too late to stop them. When I returned my gaze to Shade's face, I wanted to kick myself. The corners of his mouth were twitching in a way that told me he had seen right through me. Damn assassin.

"And I meant *here in Blackspire*." Shade's lips drew into a sly smile as he ran his eyes over my body. "But you can interpret it any way you like."

Heat flushed my cheeks. I opened my mouth to... call him a bastard? To tell him that I wanted to interpret it as *here in his room*? I wasn't sure. And I was never able to find out because a sharp knock sounded from the door before it was yanked open.

"My King," a thin man panted as he swept into the room. "There have been reports of an unnatural storm out by the..." He trailed off as he took in the scene.

Suddenly acutely aware of how close I was standing to Shade's half naked body, I took a step back and crossed my arms while glaring at the intruder.

"Yeah, I know." The High King of Pernula tipped a hand in my direction. "She's already here."

"Oh, I apologize. I..." the man stammered.

"I accept the offer to stay in a room here in Blackspire tonight," I cut him off before he could ask any of the no doubt numerous questions that the situation he had blundered into had raised.

He glanced at his king, who gave him a nod, before pulling himself together enough to motion at the door. "Of course, please follow me."

I ignored the amusement playing over Shade's face when he watched me stalk towards the door. Boots thudded against the obsidian floor as the thin man disappeared into the hallway. I followed him. Right as I was about to step across the threshold, Shade's voice stopped me.

"I'm glad you're back, Storm."

Twisting around, I met his eyes from across the bedroom. "Me too."

He gave me a slow nod, that lopsided smile tugging at his lips. I sent one back at him before pushing the door closed behind me and hurrying to catch up with my guide. A whole cacophony of emotions swirled around inside me. Casting a glance at the now closed door, I let out an amused breath and shook my head. Yeah. It really was good to be back.

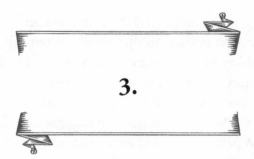

3.

The pale light of dawn trickled in through the windows. I swept my gaze over the neatly arranged kitchen and the large wooden table before me while I leaned back in the sturdy chair and crossed my ankles. Footsteps thudded on the stairs out in the corridor.

"If you get the eggs started, I'll cut up some bread."

"Of course. Are you sure you have time, though? If you have to find a substitute teacher before the kids get here."

"I'll manage. I think the–"

A gasp echoed. Pots clattered to the floor as the two people rounded the corner and stepped into the kitchen to find a woman covered in knives sitting at their table. Norah brandished the pan she had snatched up like a weapon while Liam just gaped at me.

"Storm?" he finally blurted out.

"Hello, Liam." I smiled at him before turning to the gorgeous black-haired woman beside him. "Norah."

While the frying pan-wielding teacher lowered her weapon, Liam closed the distance between us in a few long strides. His body was warm against mine as he wrapped his arms around me and drew me into a fierce hug.

"You're back."

Holding him tightly, I smiled. "Yeah, I'm back."

After another few seconds he withdrew, but kept his hands on my shoulders while locking eyes with me. "For real this time? Not just a short visit, you're actually here to stay?"

During the seven months I'd spent with the rest of the Ashaana in the White Mountains, I'd thought a lot about where home was. A part of me would always consider Keutunan home, with Bones and everyone else in the Thieves' Guild, but it also felt more like a piece of my past. After everything I'd been through these last few years, how could I just go back and be a normal member of the Thieves' Guild again? I had changed too much for that.

In Pernula, on the other hand, I felt like I could be the new me. The real me. Be the person I had evolved into without people trying to shove me back into a mold I no longer fit in. I glanced at the sparkling blue eyes in front of me, looking at me with such hope. And besides, I had family here.

"Yes, I'm here to stay." My smile widened. "Permanently."

Liam beamed at me and squeezed my shoulders. "I'm glad to hear that."

"Me too." Norah sent me a smile while picking up the pots that had fallen from the counter when she yanked out the frying pan. "And you're always welcome to stay here until you find a place of your own, you know that."

"Thank you." I nodded at the both of them.

The fallen kitchen equipment produced dull thuds as Norah returned them to their proper places atop the sturdy wooden slab. Glossy black curls fell across the soft lines of her face as she bent down to pick up another pot. When the beautiful teacher straightened, her dark eyes had a mischievous glint.

"Though, the next time you show up after being away for so long..." She placed the final pan on the counter. "Maybe try knocking first."

I flashed her a grin. "I don't knock."

Amusement bounced off smooth wooden surfaces as both Liam and Norah laughed at that. While the teacher and the hat merchant got ready to make breakfast, I strode towards the door. Eggs and pork sizzled in the pan and filled the room with heavenly scents while I draped a shoulder against the doorframe.

"That's actually why I'm here," I said.

Liam flipped the pork. "Because you don't knock?"

I answered his grin with an eye roll and a mock glare. "No. I need your help finding a place of my own. You both know a lot of merchants and people like that. Anyone selling any property?"

Norah and Liam exchanged a glance. "The apartment by your store?" the teacher asked.

"No, they sold it last week."

"Hmm." Bread crunched as Norah cut another slice. "What's your budget like?"

A wicked smile spread across my lips while I lifted one shoulder in a lopsided shrug. "Money's not an issue."

Once I had decided that I was going to stay in Pernula when I got back from the White Mountains, I'd sent word to Zaina and enlisted her help in shipping my rather considerable fortune here from Keutunan. Ordinarily, I would never have trusted anyone to move my assets and store them for safekeeping until I returned but Zaina was... well, Zaina. And besides, I'd paid her handsomely for her trouble too.

"Right." A soft laugh shook Norah's narrow chest. "Underworlders."

Faint hisses and pops came from Liam's frying pan as he stirred it absentmindedly. "I can't think of anything off the top of my head but I'll ask around." He pushed brown curls out of the way and wiped his forehead with the back of his hand. "Meet me after work?"

"Sounds good." Peeling my shoulder off the doorframe, I straightened. "See you later, then."

"You're not staying for breakfast?"

"Can't." I grinned at the two upperworlders. "I've got places to break into and money to find." Lifting a hand, I sauntered off into the corridor. "See you after work."

Laughter echoed between the wooden walls as the two of them called out goodbyes and teasing reprimands. A smile spread across my face as I moved towards the side door. They were good together, those two. I was very glad that they had found each other. As I stepped into the warm summer morning, I couldn't help thinking about what my life would look like when I was finally done. Maybe one day soon, I would find out. Setting course for the buildings across the courtyard, I took off across the stones. But first, I had a fortune to find.

A TALL THREE-STORY building made of dark wood towered before me. Cocking my head, I studied the area. We were in the Inner Ring, so everything was made of high-quality material. The planks weren't cracked or weathered and the front door had been carved with sweeping patterns.

"What do you think?" Liam asked.

The short blond man next to him cast nervous glances between the building and me. Or rather, the knives strapped to my body. I gave Liam a slow nod before shifting my gaze to the blond man.

"I wanna see the inside," I said.

"Of course." Pulling out a key, he hurried towards the front door. "Right this way."

Liam shot me an encouraging smile while we followed the short man across the threshold. A wide room filled with tables and chairs met us. The front half of the room held an assortment of freestanding seating arrangements while at the back, booths made of dark wood lined the walls. I moved my gaze along the bar and past the door to the kitchen before studying the carved staircase that spiraled towards the second floor.

"Well?" the nervous man asked.

"The rest too." I jerked my chin at the winding stairs.

"Of course, of course."

As we made our way to the upper floor, Liam swatted my arm with the back of his hand and whispered, "Be nice."

"I'm always nice." I grinned at him.

"Uh-huh."

The second and third floors held a series of smaller rooms that the blond man explained had been rented to travelers who wished to stay at the tavern. They all appeared to be in good condition and could most certainly be used for... other stuff. Equipment, assets, and training rooms that an underworlder might need, you know. My grin widened as we reached a large room on the top floor. A double bed, a desk, chests and drawers. Plenty of open floor space. And windows with easy access to the roof. This would most definitely make a great bedroom for me.

"Well?" the blond man said again while fingering a button on his shirt sleeve.

Suppressing the scheming grin on my mouth, I shifted my gaze to meet his eyes. "I'll take it."

A small sigh of relief sounded before that nervousness was back on his pale face again. "As I mentioned, given the location and the size of the property, it is quite expensive." He flicked his eyes between me and Liam. "But Liam has assured me that you are able to pay the full amount today."

Since I had found my fortune intact at the locations that Zaina had specified, I nodded at the seller. He wiped a hand over his brow.

"Splendid." Motioning towards the stairs, he risked a small smile. "Then this way, please."

Liam took it upon himself to inspect the kitchen while the previous owner and I settled matters of payment and transfer of property. When the final paper had been signed, the blond man looked slightly less nervous. He nodded before striding towards the door.

"Hey," I called before he reached it. When he turned back to me, I waved a hand at the tavern around us. "Does it have a name?"

"The Black Emerald."

Frowning at him, I let out a short chuckle. "That doesn't make any sense."

"I know. That is why I didn't put it in the sales papers." He flashed me a quick smile before disappearing out the door.

Liam strolled out of the kitchen and took up position next to me. "That went well."

"Yeah." I gave his arm a short squeeze. "Thanks for setting this up."

"Anytime."

My heart beat like a steady drum in my chest as I watched the tavern made of dark wood. This was mine now. A sense of stability, a sense of having something permanent in my life, flooded through me and filled me with calm. I had my own place now. A tiny part of the world that I owned. The Black Emerald. My home.

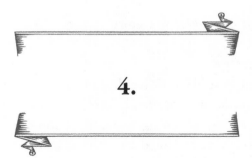

4.

A low whistle echoed off the dark wooden surfaces. I placed the final cushion on the bench of the last booth before tearing my gaze from the rich emerald fabric and shifting it to the two people who had just walked through the front door.

"You really have done well for yourself," a man's voice said.

Two pairs of blue eyes met me from across the spotless floor. My mouth drew into a smile.

"Yngvild. Vania. It's been a while."

"Yeah, it has." The tall brown-haired warrior grinned at me while striding across the wooden planks. He held out a muscled arm. "It's good to see you again, Storm."

I clasped Yngvild's tattooed forearm. "Same."

Vania threw her long blond hair back behind her shoulder before offering a toned arm as well. I took it. After we broke apart again, she glanced down at me with perceptive blue eyes.

"We heard you've challenged the Rat King for supremacy of the Underworld," she said.

"What?" I let out a baffled laugh. "I haven't challenged him for *supremacy of the Underworld*. I just wanted him to back off."

In the week since I arrived, I'd been busy transforming the Black Emerald into the home I wanted it to be so I hadn't paid much mind to the rest of the world. The Rat King and his minions had left me alone during that time so I figured he'd taken the hint that I wasn't going to bow to him. But apparently, my actions had been interpreted differently by others.

A rumbling laugh shook Yngvild's broad chest. "That's putting it mildly. I wish I'd seen it. And especially the look on the Rat King's face as you sent lightning after him."

"Me too," Vania filled in. "After that show, the whole Underworld has been buzzing with the news that you've challenged him for control."

A groan made it past my throat. Great. As if the target on my back wasn't large enough already. I had no intention of ruling the Underworld, I just wanted people to leave me alone. Huffing, I shook my head. Oh well, if I didn't go after him, maybe he'd steer clear of me too.

"Yeah, I'm not planning on going to war against the Rat King." I narrowed my eyes at the two tall warriors in front of me as suspicion crept into my mind. "Not that I'm not happy to see you, but why are you here?"

Yngvild shrugged, making the huge battle axe across his back shift. "We've come to join your gang."

"I don't have a gang."

"You do now."

When Vania backed him up with a nod, I blew out an exasperated sigh. "I'm not a gang leader."

"Call it whatever you want." Yngvild grinned at me. "We're still here to join you."

The blond warrior next to him brushed a hand over the sword on her hip. "We don't like how the Rat King runs the Underworld but he's crushed all opposition. All other gang leaders have bent the knee to him so no one else with any chance of winning will challenge him." Her piercing eyes locked on me. "You're our best bet."

How many power struggles had I been involved in by now? I didn't want to get stuck in yet another one. Wood scraped against wood as I pushed the chair next to me a bit closer to the table.

"Look, I don't–"

"Just come with us and see for yourself," Vania interrupted. "See how the Rat King rules and you'll quickly realize that there's no middle ground. You're either with him or against him."

Turning slightly, I glanced at the moonlight streaming in through the windows. It couldn't hurt to at least see what I was up against. If Yngvild and Vania could show me how he operated, then I might at least get some kind of advantage to use against the Rat King if it really came down to a full out war. Straightening, I blew out a deep breath.

"Alright." I flicked my gaze between the two of them. "I'm not making any promises, but yeah, let's go see how this new King of the Underworld rules his domain."

Vania and Yngvild exchanged a look while grins tugged at their lips as if they had already won. Shaking my head, I went upstairs to strap on all my blades. I wasn't sure what they thought was going to change my mind. I mean, it was the Underworld. People were already pretty shady. How bad could it be?

"THIS IS BAD."

"I know," Vania whispered back.

Keeping low, I crawled forward on my stomach until I reached the very end of the roof. The tiles were warm beneath my body. Raising my head slightly, I peered down at the scene in the courtyard below.

A tall brown-haired man and a sinewy woman with dirty blond hair were circling each other in the middle of the square. Boxing them in were a whole mass of people with weapons out. The Rat King sat in a high-backed chair atop a boarded-up well while the two muscled bodyguards I'd met a week ago flanked him. Even from this distance, I could almost see his eyes gleam with malice.

Red flames from the burning torches danced over their faces as the two people in the middle flew at each other again. The man swung a fist at the sinewy woman's head but she ducked and slammed a hand into his chest. He staggered backwards. Stepping forward, she tried to press the advantage. Her head snapped to the side as the man's backhanded strike connected with her jaw.

Resting my chin on the back of my hands, I continued watching the scene. The fight continued until the brown-haired man managed to land a blow so hard that his opponent dropped to the ground. He kept hitting while she lay on the ground until she raised a hand in surrender. The crowd around them were utterly silent as they parted to let the fighters out.

"What happens now?" I whispered.

Vania was clenching her jaw so hard I feared her teeth might crack. "Watch."

The woman who had lost tried to wipe the blood from her face when she staggered towards the Rat King but she only managed to smear it further across her cheeks. A vicious smile spread across his face as she dropped to her knees in front of him. I stared in mute horror as the blond woman bowed down to the stones and begged. Begged the King of the Underworld for mercy.

He left her prostrate on the ground for a good minute before he finally deigned to flick his hand and utter the word that would seal her fate. Tears streamed down her face as she struggled to her feet and disappeared into a darkened alley, bloody and alone.

"What the hell just happened?" I flicked my eyes between Vania and Yngvild.

The blond warrior on my left still looked like she was going to break her own teeth so it was Yngvild who answered.

"Every day, the Rat King has the other gang leaders report which one of their members has contributed the least to that day's earnings. Then, he picks the two worst ones and has them fight each other." Yngvild waved a calloused hand at the square below. "The one who wins is safe. The one who loses has to grovel at his feet and beg him for another chance. Sometimes, he lets them stay and sometimes, like tonight, he dismisses them."

"What do you mean *dismisses them*?"

"He kicks them out of their gang." Yngvild shook his head. "As you know, for most of us, our gang is our family. To be kicked out... it's the worst kind of punishment."

Dark clouds blew across the moon and cast the area in shadow for a moment. I stared at the now empty alley that the blond woman had disappeared into. By Nemanan, what a cruel way of ruling. I knew firsthand how awful it was to be branded an enemy to one's own guild and I wouldn't wish it on anyone.

"He does this every day?"

Vania gave me a tense nod.

"And because of this," Yngvild continued, "loyalty to the people in your own gang is disappearing. Since someone from each gang has to be in the report each day, members have started ratting each other out, stealing from each other, and ruining each other's work because no one wants to risk getting kicked out." Sadness filled the warrior's blue eyes. "It's tearing the Underworld apart."

By all the gods. If there was one thing that was sacred, it was your own guild. Or in Pernula's case, your own gang. I was all for people pulling their weight but to turn members against each other in this way, it was despicable. Loyalty to your own should be the cornerstone.

In the courtyard below, the gathered people were dispersing while a somber mood hung over the gray stones. The Rat King had already left a few minutes ago but everyone still seemed tense. As if they were being watched.

That was when I realized why Vania had said that there was no middle ground. The whole Underworld lived in fear of being forced out of their gangs. Out of their families. That meant that if the Rat King told them he wanted my head on a platter, every single one of them would come after me with swords if it kept them from being kicked out of their own gang. Damn. Every underworlder was now a potential enemy. If I wanted to live a life in the Underworld on my terms without swearing allegiance to the Rat King, I would have to go up against him. Hard. And win. No middle ground, indeed.

Tearing my gaze from the now empty courtyard, I turned to the two warriors next to me and blew out a deep sigh. "Alright, then. I guess I'm officially challenging the Rat King for supremacy of the Underworld."

"Good," Yngvild said with a wide grin on his face.

A wicked glint crept into Vania's blue eyes. "When do we start?"

Placing my palms on the tiles, I pushed myself up and climbed to my feet. The night lay dark and still over the roofs of Pernula as I strode to the edge with Yngvild and Vania close beside me.

I flicked my gaze towards the blackened horizon. "Right now."

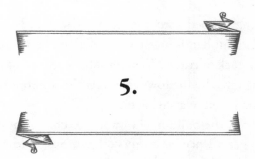

5.

Boats creaked as waves pushed the sturdy hulls against the wooden planks of the pier. Every soft breath filled my lungs with air smelling of saltwater and seaweed. I followed the two tall warriors in front of me into the deep shadows of a warehouse.

"The Rat King has a lot of property around the city," Vania said. "But we don't know exactly where. Apart from his headquarters, this is the only place we know for sure belongs to him."

"Yeah." Yngvild lifted a large hand to point at a single-story building made of dark wood. "He sent us here on a job sometime back so we know it's his."

Light flickered in the windows of the warehouse as if someone was still inside, and two guards were positioned outside the main entrance. I squinted at the flames dancing inside but couldn't make out anything useful.

"What's inside?" I asked.

"Don't know." Yngvild lifted his broad shoulders in a shrug. "We were ordered to stand guard outside for a couple of nights."

Vania glared at the building. "It was a week, Yngvild."

"Right, yeah, for a week. We couldn't exactly refuse so we did it. We weren't allowed inside but we think it's one of the places where he stores all the stuff he smuggles."

Clattering echoed into the night. The guards at the door tensed up and put hands on their swords right as two cats darted away from a stack of crates. Their dark fur streaked past us before disappearing into the shadows again. At the warehouse entrance, the two armed men relaxed again.

I nodded at the building. "I wanna go check out the inside." Shifting my gaze, I peered at my companions. "How are you at sneaking and breaking into houses?"

"Yeah, uhm..." Yngvild reached up and patted the huge battle axe across his back. "I'm more of a bash-people's-heads-in-with-an-axe kind of guy."

Vania shook her head at him but then turned to me and nodded. "Same. But with a sword."

A soft chuckle escaped my lips. "Alright. Then, uhm, just follow my lead."

The two warriors might not be adept at breaking into houses, but at least they knew how to move quietly, so we managed to skirt around the warehouse and approach it from the back of the docks without anyone noticing. A small wooden door was set into the back wall. We snuck towards it on silent feet.

"How do we get inside?" Vania breathed as we reached it.

There was a metal handle sticking out but no lock. Moving carefully, I pushed it down and pulled the door towards me. Nothing happened. Was I really standing here pulling on a push door like an idiot? I stifled an annoyed curse and pushed on it instead. The door didn't move that time either. Okay, so I wasn't a complete moron at least.

Motioning for Yngvild and Vania to remain where they were, I slunk towards the window. Flames flickered inside. After positioning myself at the far corner of the window, I edged my head upwards and peered through the cracks in the shutters.

Stacks upon stack of crates crowded the room beyond. I swept scrutinizing eyes across the area but found no people moving on this side of the building. Twisting further, I threw a glance at the door. A heavy bar was lodged across it. No wonder it hadn't moved.

"The door is barred from the inside," I whispered to my two companions. "Wait here. I'm gonna sneak in and get it open for you."

Once I'd seen them nod, I braced myself on the edge of the window and climbed up. For a moment, I remained sitting on the windowsill. If I had missed someone during my initial inspection, I'd be able to see them now before I became trapped in a warehouse with the doors barred. When no one showed up to ambush me, I stuck a lockpick through the gap between the shutters and lifted the latch. They opened on silent hinges. Climbing through the window with practiced moves, I lowered myself to the floor on the other side.

Somewhere deeper inside the warehouse, glass clinked faintly, followed by wooden thuds. I snuck towards the back door. The monstrosity of a beam was much larger than it had looked from outside. Sending a quick prayer to the fickle Goddess of Luck, I put my shoulder underneath it and heaved upwards. It let out a loud groan.

"*Really, Cadentia?*" I mouthed while glaring at the noisy slab of wood.

Seconds ticked by. My heart thumped in my chest as I waited for people to come rushing towards me to see what the sound had been. But no one came. Putting my shoulder back under the log, I shoved it upwards again. Another groan echoed into the warehouse but after that it remain silent. I tilted it on its head and carefully leaned it against the wall before pulling open the door.

Flicking his eyes towards the heavy bar, Yngvild gave me an impressed nod as he and Vania snuck inside. I grinned at him while we moved towards the closest stack of crates. After motioning between the three of us, I pointed at different lid-covered boxes. Both of them nodded their understanding and drifted off to check the contents of their containers.

Rows of bottles met me as I edged open the one closest to me. I frowned but stuck a hand inside and pulled one out. A label with elegant lettering covered the bottom half of the dark glass. Huh. Alcohol. I swished the liquid around while perusing the text. Very high-quality alcohol, too.

"Rum," Vania whispered as she closed the distance between us after studying her own crate.

Yngvild nodded his agreement too. So, the Rat King was smuggling fine rum? My mind went back to the two guards outside this rundown nondescript building. Smart move. Hiding something this valuable in plain sight instead of drawing attention to it by using lots of guards and a conspicuous location. Or maybe he was just that certain that no one in the Underworld would dare make a move against him.

I glanced around the tall wooden stacks. If all these boxes contained that expensive liquor, the contents of this warehouse must be worth a fortune. A malicious grin stole across my lips. It would be a shame if something were to happen to it.

Another faint clink sounded. Jerking my head, I motioned for us to move further in while I pulled two hunting knives from the small of my back. Vania drew her sword and followed me, with Yngvild and his battle axe close behind.

We followed the sound of clinking glass until we reached a desk towards the middle of the building. A bespectacled man sat on the rickety chair behind it. He pulled up a bottle, inspected it, made a mark in a ledger, and then returned it to the crate before lifting another one. Candlelight flickered over sagging cheeks and tired eyes.

"Anyone else working here?" I asked.

He sucked in a sharp breath between his teeth and jerked around. Glass shattered next to him. With panic flashing over his face, he flicked his eyes between us and the dark green shards that now lay scattered on the floor.

"Oh, no, no, no, no," he stammered and dropped to the ground. His hands trembled as they hovered over the expensive rum now soaking the floor. "He's going to kill me." Desperation colored the man's eyes as he stared up at us. "Who are you? Did the Rat King send you? Please don't tell him about this..."

"That bottle's gonna be the least of the Rat King's problems before the night is over." I waved a knife towards the main entrance on the other side. "You should get out of here."

"What are you going to do?"

I answered him with a wicked grin.

Wood creaked to our left. Vania whipped around and pointed a sword in the direction of the sound.

"Don't even think about it," she warned.

A tall blond man stepped out from behind a crate. The raised bottle in his hand shook slightly as he held it between us and himself as if that delicate piece of glass could save him from the lethal weapons we brandished.

"Is there anyone else?" Vania asked.

Both men shook their heads.

"Leave," I repeated and tipped my knife in the direction of the door again.

Placing the bottle on the desk, the blond man snatched at his friend's sleeve and pulled them both towards the main entrance. They walked backwards and kept suspicious eyes on us until they rounded a tower of wooden boxes. After that, feet smattered against the floor as they ran.

"What now?" Yngvild asked.

"Now we just need to convince the guards to leave too." I followed the fleeing workers towards the door. "This should be fun."

The muscled warrior chuckled as we made our way towards the unsuspecting guards. Wood banged as the door was thrown open further ahead. Startled yelps followed it.

"Hey!" a man's voice snapped. "The hell do you think you're doing, huh? Get back here. What? Whaddya mean there are people...?"

Right as we rounded the final stack, two heads peered in through the doorway. The guards jerked back and blinked once they noticed the three armed strangers striding towards them. I flashed them an evil grin. Metal clanged as the two surprised guards scrambled to pull their own weapons before barreling into the warehouse.

"What's the meaning of this?" the dark-haired one demanded.

"I'm afraid your job has become superfluous." I tipped my head from side to side. "Or it will be. In a minute."

He lifted his sword with a steady hand. "You're making a grave mistake. Do you have any idea whose warehouse you're robbing?"

"Oh I'm quite well aware that this is the Rat King's smuggled rum." Sticking my knives back in their sheaths, I flashed him a smile dripping with malice. "And who said anything about stealing it?"

My eyes went black. Tendrils of dark smoke snaked around my arm as I raised my hand and squeezed it into a fist before yanking it down. Lightning crackled and struck a pile of ledgers by the door. The two guards yelped and jumped to the side.

"Ashaana," the long-faced one on the right breathed while staring at me. "You're the Oncoming Storm."

"Yeah, I am." Shifting black eyes filled with rage and insanity between them, I jerked my chin towards the door. "Now, as I was saying, the Rat King won't be needing your services at this particular location anymore." Lightning crackled over my skin. "Get out."

Even though his hand trembled, the dark-haired guard raised his sword. I rolled my eyes. Work ethic. Seriously? I shoved a hand forward.

A strong wind shot out and slammed into his chest, sending him flying backwards. His back struck the wall with a loud thud. The guard with the long face gaped at me before turning worried eyes on his friend, who remained standing completely stunned by the wall I'd just pushed him into. I raised my arms. Black clouds billowed around me.

"Leave," I ground out.

"I don't get paid enough for this," the nervous guard announced before slinking out the door.

The steadfast one opened his mouth to protest but his friend was already gone. For a moment, it looked like he was about to fight all three of us on his own but then he just snarled at us and disappeared as well.

Flames hissed next to the wall as the fire from the lightning strike continued devouring the heap of ledgers. Vania and Yngvild turned to glance at me.

"You can set fire to stuff now?" Yngvild said and nodded at the flaming stack.

"Yep. And do you know what else burns easily?" With eyes still black as death, I grinned at the two warriors. "High-quality rum."

A rumbling laugh shook his chest. "I like the way you think."

While the two of them went about lighting papers, ledgers, and stray straw on fire using the candles still burning on the tables, I practiced my ability to direct lightning. Crackling bolts zapped the room where I wanted it. Morgora would've been proud.

Once we were satisfied with our pyromancy, all three of us beat a hasty retreat and darted out the back door before the quickly spreading fire could melt the glass bottles and set the alcohol vapor aflame.

Light flickered in the windows as we watched the warehouse from a safe distance, until finally, a *whoosh* sounded and the fire burned blue. The first crate of rum set off a chain reaction. Satisfaction coursed through me as flames licked the walls and reached for the darkened heavens as the building burned to the ground.

"There is no going back now," Vania said. "This is as good as a declaration of war. The Rat King will come at you with everything he has now."

"I know." Flames danced over my face. "Let him try."

The Rat King's power came from his fortune and his reputation. If I wanted to cripple him, I would have to gut his business, empty his coffers, and drag his name through the dirt. Of course he'd be gunning for me now, but you see, here's the thing. People had been trying to kill me my whole life. And I was still here. Schemes swirled in my mind. *Bring it on.*

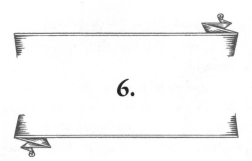

6.

The Black Emerald was bustling with activity. Pots clanked in the kitchen and men grunted as they hauled crates filled with supplies up the stairs. I glanced up from the letter I'd been reading. From the booth at the back that I had chosen as my table, I could see the whole bottom floor of the tavern, as well as the stairs and whoever walked through the front door. It was the best seat in the house.

Lounging back against the dark green cushions that covered the wooden sofa, I studied the two chairs on the other side of the table while deciding whether I could be bothered to pull one closer. My desire for comfort triumphed over my laziness. I leaned forward and drew the chair forward until I could swing my legs up on it. Crossing my ankles, I picked up another letter. A wide smile spread across my face as I read it.

"Good news?" Yngvild asked as he lumbered over.

"Very." I looked up at the tattooed warrior. "We just got confirmation. Our final piece is in place. Soon, the Rat King can kiss his grand smuggling empire goodbye."

"If I'd known you were this connected, I would've suggested this before he even rose to power."

"It wouldn't have made a difference." I scratched the back of my neck. "I had some stuff to work out before I was ready to put down roots."

"But you've put down roots now?"

A wistful smile stole across my lips as I swept my gaze across the tavern I now called home. "Yeah. I guess I have."

It had been two weeks since we'd set fire to the Rat King's warehouse and more people arrived outside the Black Emerald every day, asking to join my gang. Despite me insisting that I wasn't actually running a gang, they'd stayed. Most of them were people who'd been forced out of their original crew but some of them were ordinary gang members who just really disliked how the Rat King ruled. Among them were Kildor–the brown-haired man who I'd met two years ago and who had been part of the same group of independent underworlders as Yngvild and Vania–and most of their other friends. I'd made it very clear from the start that this wasn't a charity and that they all needed to pull their weight. To my surprise, no one had complained.

The ones who were adept at their chosen trade continued plying it and contributed money as compensation. Those who were less skilled had chosen to cook, clean, or tend the bar here at the tavern. In a matter of a few weeks, I suddenly had a fully operational headquarters and people who paid me guild rates. Well, not guild rates. Or gang rates. Because I was not running a gang. Oh no. I was *not* a gang leader.

While I'd been busy not being a gang leader, the Rat King had done... nothing. I kept waiting for the other shoe to drop but he never retaliated for my rum-soaked fire. Maybe the two guards had run off before informing him that I was the one responsible for it. Or maybe he was just taking his time planning a really nasty revenge.

The door was flung open. Heads turned and stared at the tall blond woman striding across the floor. I smiled. Vania. Smart, capable, and commanding respect. She was a natural at helping me run the gang. I mean the Black Emerald. Not the gang. Because I was not a gang leader.

"I just got word of another one," Vania said as she came to a halt next to Yngvild. "There's a shop called *Antiquities Empire* here in the Inner Ring that sells a lot of the Rat King's smuggled goods."

"Is it still open?" I cast a glance at the moonlight streaming through the windows at the front of the room.

"Yes."

Swinging my legs off the chair, I jumped to my feet. "Then let's go pay them a visit."

The two blue-eyed warriors exchanged a look and a satisfied smile. Gathering up all my business papers, I stalked upstairs to lock them up in a secret cabinet. Just because the people at the Black Emerald had come to join me didn't mean that I had to automatically trust them. Distrusting was one of my core traits, after all.

After locking everything away and strapping on my full arsenal of knives, I joined Vania and Yngvild outside the tavern.

Warm night winds full of fragrant spices and blooming flowers ruffled my hair as we jogged towards the shop and the blissfully ignorant owner who was soon about to find out that he had sided with the wrong underworlder. Vania led the way.

"Give me that," a man hissed from the shadows of a side alley.

"No, I'm the one who stole it," a woman snapped back. "Find your own."

"But I need it more. You don't want me to get kicked out from our gang, do you?"

"I don't want to get kicked out either! If you–" A scuffle broke out. "Stop! Give me back... Get back here!"

Feet smattered against stone as the two of them disappeared out of earshot. Disgust crawled up my throat. Underworlders stealing from other underworlders. And from members of their own gang, no less. This was not at all what the Underworld was supposed to be like. Our world in the shadows might be full of thieves, killers, and every kind of shady profession you could think of, but it was also built on loyalty and respect. For our gang and for the Underworld as a whole. Or at least it should be. I shook my head. Someone should do something about that once the Rat King was gone.

"It's that one," Vania said and nodded towards a building halfway down the road as we rounded the corner of yet another darkened street. Lights flickered inside it. "He has no guards inside the shop."

The night lay still around us as we surveyed the area around the Antiquities Empire. Colorful awnings that someone had forgotten to take down at the end of the day flapped in the breeze but other than that, there was no movement around the store. I flicked my eyes to Yngvild and Vania, who nodded in response to my silent question. We started forward.

Once we were almost at the polished wooden door, the hair on the back of my neck stood up. I threw out my arms and screeched to a halt, making the two tall warriors beside me stop as well. They cast curious glances at me but said nothing. Up ahead, the road was still clear. However, I couldn't shake the feeling that something was wrong.

Figures slid out of the shadows. Yngvild yanked the battle axe from his back while Vania drew her sword and turned in a slow circle. The horde of people materializing in the darkness now blocked the street on both sides, as well as the alleys we'd passed. Dread drew its freezing fingers down my spine. The other shoe was about to drop.

Without taking my eyes off the ambushers, I lowered my voice and addressed my two companions. "You need to get the hell out of here. I will buy you some time. When I say run, you run."

The wall of people in front of us moved forwards. Weapons clanked as the ones behind advanced as well.

"If you think we're going to leave you..." Vania began with steel in her voice.

"You wanted me to be a gang leader," I hissed at them both. "That means you follow my orders so do as you're bloody told. Now, when I say run, you run back the way we came. You run straight and you don't stop. Is that clear?"

I knew it was a cheap shot using the gang leader angle but I needed to get them to leave. This was happening because I had decided to burn down the Rat King's warehouse and I couldn't let other people get hurt because of a war I started.

Vania and Yngvild locked eyes for a moment before shifting their gaze back to me and giving me a reluctant nod in acknowledgement. The ambushers kept advancing from both sides. My heart slammed against my ribs. I would have to calculate this just right, otherwise we'd all die.

"Good." My fingers twitched as I turned towards the wall of people behind us. "Now get ready." I slammed my arms forward. "Run!"

Winds hurtled towards the attackers who had come up behind us and before the force had even struck home, Yngvild and Vania was sprinting after it. I yanked my arms upwards. Black clouds shot out around me right as cries of terror rang out from the ambushers who were flung away by my storm winds. With the route temporarily cleared for my two companions, all I had to do was keep the rest of the Rat King's minions busy while they escaped.

Feet smattered against stone on the other side. Hoping that Vania and Yngvild had made it out, I returned my attention to the battle descending on me. Screams rose as men barreled towards me through the dark haze. Thunder shook the buildings and lightning danced around me as I fed the burning rage inside and expanded the black cloud blanketing the street. As long as I used my powers wisely, I'd survive this without blacking out afterwards.

Most of the attackers staggered to a halt when the darkness grew around them but a few stupid ones continued charging towards me even though they couldn't see me. I pulled out my hunting knives and crouched into an attack position.

Incoherent yelling assaulted my ears as the small group of morons closed in. Twisting through the black smoke, I sliced. Blood sprayed into the darkened night. I continued my dance of death until the last idiot had bled out on the street around me.

Yngvild and Vania should've gotten clear by now so it was high time for me to slink back into the shadows too. Wiping my blades, I stuck them back in their sheaths.

"All sides!" someone called from up ahead. "Charge. Now!"

My breath hitched. Boots thudded against stone from every direction as the whole damn force attacked me all at once. I spat out a frustrated sigh. Damn. This complicated my escape plan.

Raising my arms above my head, I drew them around and around in a sweeping pattern until I was certain the blast would be strong enough. Shouts echoed between the buildings as the armed men closed in. I unleashed the storm.

Hurricane winds flew in every direction as I turned and snapped my arms in a circle above my head. The battles cries were replaced by shrieks as the force slammed into them and sent them flying backwards. I had to get away.

Right as I was about to start my sprint to safety, feet smattered against stone again. I whipped my head around. The first row of attackers who had fallen had already shot to their feet and were charging towards me again. I shoved my hand forward. A strong gust flattened them with the ground again but no sooner had the thuds stopped than another section was back on their feet once more.

A frustrated howl tore from my throat as I raised my arms and made the black clouds spread further. Balling my hand into a fist, I yanked it downwards. Lighting zapped the closest attacker but the others kept coming. I swept my arms around my head again before releasing the wind on the final snap. Yelps, clanking weapons, and dull thuds echoed as the ambushers were flung backwards again.

Tiredness washed over me. I was using too much power too quickly. Banking the fury inside, I let the black clouds shrink a little to save energy. If I kept this up, I would run out before I made it back to the Black Emerald and then I'd be as good as dead anyway.

Raising my arms again, I got ready to focus the next blast on one particular section. Once it hit, I was sprinting through that opening no matter what. I drew a deep breath.

Something whizzed through the air. I jerked around just in time to see a whole swarm of small darts speeding towards me from the side. Throwing my arm out, I sent a gust of wind to knock them off course. They smattered against the walls. Panic rose in my throat as I heard another wave of projectiles buzzing through the night air. Whirling around, I snapped out my arm again but this time I'd had less time to aim.

A sharp needle embedded itself in the side of my neck, followed shortly by another one in my upper arm.

"Shit," I swore.

I yanked them out and threw them on the ground while raising my arms for another blast of hurricane winds. My body tilted to the side. Taking a quick step, I tried to steady myself but my feet refused to move at the speed I had requested.

Pain shot up my hip as I tipped over and slammed into the stone street. The darkness snapped back into my soul. I tried to push myself up but my hands wouldn't obey. A blackness that wasn't mine pressed in from the corners of my vision. Intense panic flared up my spine but I could do nothing as my sight grew foggy and boots closed in around me until finally, the world dropped away completely.

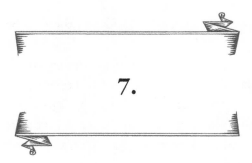

7.

Blurry faces stared down at me. I tried to blink past the fog and the alarm bells blaring in my head. When I worked my tongue around my mouth, I swore I could almost taste whatever drug had been in those darts. Still trying to clear my vision, I reached up to rub my eyes. Dread washed over me. I couldn't move my arms.

"Wakey, wakey," a taunting voice jeered.

As the haze cleared, my surroundings finally came into focus. Shelves overflowing with trinkets and antique bits and bobs covered every wall, while tools and a whole stack of knives crowded the table in the middle. I recognized the rather impressive pile of blades straight away. It was mine.

Pushing down the flash of irritation, I flicked my eyes over the rest of the room. There was no chair by the table but I assumed that was because I was currently tied to that particular piece of furniture. And then there were of course the five men leering at me.

"All this just for me?" I said. "Wow. I'm flattered."

The ropes digging into my forearms and keeping them trapped against the armrests were an inconvenience but if I got my hands on a knife, I could fix that problem.

A man with dark blond hair and bulging muscles took a step towards me. "I'm so glad you chose to go for this shop so that I could be the one to deliver you to the Rat King."

Aha. So this had been one of several ambushes planned for me tonight. And I'd walked right into it. Was I getting sloppy?

"You don't remember me," the blond man continued, "but I was there two years ago when you put on that first show in the square we trapped you in. And then again by the city wall a few weeks ago." Hatred crept into his eyes. "Do you have any idea what the Rat King did to me for letting you escape?"

"I don't see how that's my fault."

If I could just knock them out, then I could drag the chair over to the table and get a knife to cut the ropes. The blond man took another step forward. Right now, they were all positioned in front of me so if I was going to do this, it would have to be now. Drawing a shallow breath, I reached for the burning anger in my soul and flicked my palms upwards.

Panic flashed through me. Sheer, utter panic. Nothing happened. I reached deep inside my soul again, looking for that fiery rage. Nothing. The blackened pits were empty and cold. Confusion and dread seeped through my bones like cold poison.

Rough laughter rippled through the room.

"You looking for your magic? Wondering why it doesn't work?" A malicious grin slashed across his face as the muscled man studied me. "That's because it's gone."

That cold dread and flaming panic combined into a truly horrible feeling that threatened to consume me. My powers were gone? It had to be some kind of trick. I reached for the darkness again but it was like sticking my fingers into an empty black hole.

He leaned his hip against the table and picked up one of my knives. "Apparently, there's this ritual that can be performed to strip someone of their magic." Looking up from the blade, he shot me a challenging stare. "Who knew?"

The star elves' ritual. Had these lowlifes really been able to perform that ritual and strip me of my magic? Was that what the Rat King had meant when he said he'd been researching a lot about Storm Casters since we last met? The pounding alarm bells in my head grew louder. I had only just mastered my powers and now they were gone?

Still gripping my blade, the blond man closed the distance between us. The other four stepped closer as well. With that wolfish grin still on his face, he placed his hands over my forearms and leaned down over me. Malice glittered in his eyes. Pulling back slightly, he lifted the knife.

"Hans," one of his companions hissed. "What are you doing? The Rat King will be here in a couple of minutes."

I blinked as Hans cut the ropes tying me to the chair. Ignoring his friend's question, he stepped back and spread his arms.

"Come on then." He raised his chin with a superior smirk on his face. "Don't believe me? Try it. Blast me with wind." The leering smile grew wider. "Do your worst."

The four men behind Hans moved their hands to the swords swinging at their hips as I pushed out of the chair and took a step forward. This was just a trick. Feeding all the anger I had gathered throughout my life, I bared my teeth at the smirking man and slammed my arms forward.

Nothing. Not a single breath of wind or puff of cloud. Fear fluttered its poisonous wings in my chest.

Another harsh laugh ripped from his throat as Hans shot forward. Pain vibrated through my ribcage. I stumbled to the side as his fist connected with my chest. My mind was still so scattered from trying to accept that my powers were gone that it was incredibly difficult to mount any kind of defense. Hans grabbed the front of my shirt and pulled me towards him before throwing me backwards.

Wood rattled and metal dinged as I slammed into the shelves behind me, sending antique items clattering to the ground. The five men advanced on me like wolves. I flicked my gaze across the room, looking for a way out. There was only one door that led out of this storage space but it was on the other side. My captors hadn't drawn their swords yet but there were still five of them and one of me. And without my powers...

A hand shot out. I yanked up my arm and gripped his wrist but it was too late. Hans had already closed a large hand over my throat. Metal containers dug into my back as he pushed me further into the shelves while lifting the knife he had taken from the table. He traced the tip down my cheek. My heart thumped in my chest.

"You're pretty when you're scared." Hans leered down at me while tightening his grip on my throat. "How does it feel to be helpless?"

Scared? Helpless? A truly staggering amount of irritation shoved out the fear and panic that the suddenly gaping void in my soul had created. What was I doing? I was deadly long before I knew I was a Storm Caster. My whole life I'd dealt with people like this and I most certainly didn't need my powers to kill them. I was lethal. With or without the darkness.

Casting my gaze around, I searched for something that would give me an advantage. Fallen antiques littered the floor around me after I'd accidentally knocked them off the shelves when I slammed into them. Silver cups, plates, a collection of wooden figurines. And *that*. Schemes formed in my mind.

"Please, I'm sorry. Don't give me to the Rat King." I dropped my eyes so that he wouldn't see the smirk hiding behind the scared façade. "I'm begging you."

"Begging, huh?" I could feel his eyes roaming my face but I didn't meet them. He let go of me and took a step back. "Then do it properly. On your knees."

Stopping a cackle from slipping across my lips was a considerable feat, I'll have you know. So I bit the inside of my cheek to stave it off while getting down on one knee. Carefully, I moved my hand as if to steady myself on the floor.

"Both knees," Hans demanded.

My fingers brushed the item I had aimed for. I snatched up the decorated letter knife and rammed it into the side of his calf. Once. Twice. Three times. A howl reverberated through the air as Hans staggered backwards. His left leg wobbled. I shot to my feet just as it finally buckled and the muscled man fell towards me. Still gripping the letter knife, I shoved up through his chin. Warm blood spilled down my hand.

"Who's helpless now?" I whispered sweetly.

And then all hell broke loose. The four men behind Hans screamed and drew their swords from their scabbards. While yanking the blade out of Hans' chin, I ripped his knife, *my* knife, from his hand and slashed it across his throat. I shoved his corpse forwards and threw the letter knife just as the other attackers reached me.

Since I wasn't accustomed to its weight, the letter knife flew slightly off course. It missed my target's throat and buried itself in his shoulder instead. At least the dead Hans collapsed onto the friend behind him as planned. I grabbed the tall shelf on my left and pulled with all my strength. Wood groaned but then it moved. I darted to the other side as soon as I was sure that it would tip over.

Priceless antiques rained from the shelves in a smattering of wood and metals as the shelf fell. Shouts rang out. While the falling furniture attacked the two closest men, I sprinted towards the table.

A sword whizzed through the air. The man who had swung it bellowed as it got caught on the side of the collapsed shelf. Just as I had predicted. Fighting with swords in this tight space definitely put them at a disadvantage. I snatched up a throwing knife from the table and hurled it at him right as another man reached me. The blade struck the bellowing man in the throat while I twisted and slid under the table.

Chips of wood sprayed through the air as the sword meant for my head slammed into the table instead. Flicking out a hand from under the tabletop, I slashed his hamstrings. His cries of pain as he fell were interrupted when I rammed my knife through his windpipe.

The two remaining attackers had finally finished their fight with the shelf and were advancing on me as I popped up from underneath the table. Releasing the blade I was holding, I instead snatched up two throwing knives and hurled them across the room.

Surprise flickered in the men's eyes as they struck home. With metal sticking out of their throats, they both collapsed on the floor in a thudding of weapons and body parts. A wicked smile drifted across my lips as I surveyed the carnage. Yes, I was still deadly.

My chest heaved while I retrieved all of my knives but I couldn't afford to slow down. The Rat King was still coming and I needed to get out before then.

Once I was fully armed again, I darted out of the storage room. The rest of the Antiquities Empire lay deserted as I sprinted towards the front door. Though I had already come to the conclusion that it would be, because if there had been others here, they would've most certainly heard the ruckus we made and come to investigate.

Neat shelves filled with expensive trinkets stood like silent sentries in the main room of the shop. I drew myself up against the wall and peered through the shutters. My heart leaped into my throat.

A skinny man with graying hair, accompanied by two muscled bodyguards, stalked down the street towards the door. *Shit*. The Rat King was here. I raced back through the shop and into the hallway beyond.

The door to the storage room was located at the end of the corridor but there was no way out there. Instead, I set my sight on the staircase leading upwards. Taking the steps two at a time, I ran towards the top floor. Another hallway met me. I darted into the closest room just as I heard the front door being pulled open.

"They should be holding her in the back," a man's voice said.

As soon as they walked into the storage room, they would realize that I'd escaped. I had to get out before then. Lifting the curtains aside, I gently edged open the shutters. I braced myself on the sides of the window and climbed onto the windowsill.

Shouts of outrage echoed from downstairs.

Night winds smelling of warm spices caressed my face as I swung myself out and reached for the top of the roof. Rough tiles met my fingers. I pulled myself up and rolled over the edge. Intense relief finally flooded through me as I sprinted across the rooftops and disappeared into the darkness.

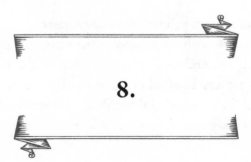

8.

"Two late-night visits in my bedroom in only a few weeks." A sly smile spread across Shade's lips as he ran his eyes up and down my body. "One could almost think there was a particular reason for that."

I snorted. "Don't flatter yourself. It's just because it's so easy for me to sneak in here."

Candlelight danced over the tidy room and the neatly made bed while Shade strode across the obsidian floor. The flickering flames played over his lethal body. At least the damn assassin was wearing a shirt this time.

"Yes." Shade magicked a knife from somewhere in his clothes and used the tip of it to tilt my head up to meet his eyes. "One of these days you're going to tell me where your secret entrance into Blackspire is."

With a smirk on my face, I shot a stiletto blade into my palm and pushed his knife away. "Make me."

A dark chuckle drifted through the black and red room. "Careful now. Or I will take you up on that."

I threw him a light smile but I could feel him searching my face. When his perceptive gaze found the fuming irritation I had hidden behind the mask of carefree banter, he took a step back and narrowed his eyes at me.

"What's wrong?"

"Do you know anything about..." I trailed off. "Anything about the star elves' ritual? If it can be completed without consent?"

"The ritual? I think you know more about it than me. Than anyone in Pernula, for that matter."

"Yeah." I lifted my shoulders in a shrug. "I just figured that you with all your *being prepared for every eventuality* stuff... That you might know something."

For a moment, Shade just continued holding my gaze. A warm night breeze blew in through the window, making the candles on the table splutter. Realization dawned in the assassin's eyes.

"You've lost your magic," he breathed.

"Yeah." I shot him a sharp look. "But no one can know that. If they do, they'll just come at me even harder."

"By Ghabhalnaz, how did that even happen?"

"That's what I'm trying to figure out."

Worry flickered in his black eyes. "Are you okay?"

Pausing for a second, I considered his question. Was I okay? I had just lost my powers but how did I actually feel about that? At last, I met his gaze head on and nodded.

"Yeah," I answered honestly. "Yeah, I'm okay."

To be honest, I thought that I would be more devastated. After all, I had just spent the past seven months slaving under Morgora in order to master my powers and now I couldn't use them anymore. I thought that would break me. Send me into another spiral of heartbreak and loss of identity like the one I'd experienced in Travelers' Rest.

But that hadn't happened. Instead, I had just put those feelings on the pile of shit I would deal with once my life was a bit less chaotic. Which would probably be never. Maybe it was *because* I had lost myself in that hopelessness and despair once already, and had managed to drag myself out the other side, that I could just shrug it off. I might be more resilient now. Or maybe just a lot more jaded.

Of course I resented the fact that I couldn't use my powers. I wouldn't deny that. But truth be told, I had been a knife-fighter for far longer than I had been a Storm Caster. The darkness had always just been an added bonus. Not what I relied on to survive. I still wanted it back, though.

"Good," Shade replied in response to my confirmation that I wasn't going to spiral into another self-destructive cycle. "Then we'll figure this out."

A smile tugged at my lips. *We.* "Yeah, I don't think it's really *gone* gone. I just need to figure out how to get it back."

"Elaran and the others are on their way here to train the army now so you could try asking them when they get here."

"You made him the commander of the joint forces?" When the assassin confirmed it with a nod, I let out a soft chuckle. "I can think of no one better."

With Elaran drilling the armies of Pernula, Keutunan, and Tkeideru into one cohesive fighting unit, the star elves wouldn't stand a chance. I cast a glance at the dark night outside the window. There were now two wars on the horizon. The great battle against the star elves that loomed like a dark shadow over all our futures. And my own personal one against the Rat King. Well, *personal* probably wasn't the right word since we had dragged the whole Underworld into it. I just had to make sure I settled the battle for the Underworld before the real war reached our gates.

As if he'd heard my thoughts, Shade waved a hand over my body. "You challenged the Rat King for control of the Underworld. That's why this happened."

It had been a statement and not a question but I nodded anyway.

The Master Assassin closed the distance between us and placed his hand on my jaw. With glittering eyes locked on me, he tilted my head up and leaned down until his lips were close enough that they almost brushed against mine. "Shall I kill him for you?"

His hot breath against my lips sent lightning crackling through my body and I barely managed to suppress a satisfied shudder. Letting him keep his hold on my chin, I stared into his intense black eyes. "You do know that wouldn't actually solve anything, right? His Second would just continue running his empire."

"I could always kill them all for you," he breathed against my mouth.

I grabbed the front of his shirt and pulled his lips the final bit towards mine. Who in the world would ever want flowers and pretty jewelry from rich noblemen when you could have the Master of the Assassins' Guild offer to kill your enemies for you?

Shade drew his hand along my jaw and towards the back of my neck until he could knit his fingers through my hair. With a steady grip, he pushed me tighter towards his muscled body while his greedy lips roamed mine. Firelight flickered over us as we lost ourselves in a hungry kiss.

When we at last drew back, I sucked in a starved breath as if I hadn't breathed at all in the last few minutes. Tipping his head back, Shade let out a long exhale and raked his fingers through his hair. A satisfied smirk tugged at his lips. I put a hand to his chin and tilted his head back down again.

"As much I appreciate the offer..." Sincerity burned in my eyes as I locked them on his. "This is my fight. And I will see it through. I will take apart his empire piece by piece until there is nothing left." Dropping my hand, I let a feral grin spread across my lips. "And then, he will meet the God of Death."

A dark chuckle escaped Shade's lips. "Oh I have no doubt he will. And you're right, we can't just kill the Rat King and his top people. It would leave a power vacuum that would send the Underworld into chaos and civil war." He locked serious eyes on me. "The Underworld needs an undisputed leader."

I knew where he was going with this but I didn't want to hear it. Yes, the Underworld would need an undisputed leader but it was not going to be me. As soon as I had removed the Rat King from the equation, I would just hand over that position to someone else. Someone who was actually fit to lead.

Papers rustled by the desk as another night breeze ruffled the stacks that Shade had no doubt been poring over before I'd snuck up on him. When he looked back to see if they'd blown off the desk, I saw my chance to escape before his intense gaze and serious implications kept me trapped in this room forever. I threw a quick look at the silk sheets. Or before something else happened.

Slinking away, I made it all the way to the door before his voice stopped me again.

"Oh, and Storm?"

Glancing back over my shoulder, I found him watching me with a hint of amusement playing over an otherwise serious face. "Yes?"

"I will let you handle this on your own, as long as you have the Underworld under control before the star elves make a move."

A wicked laugh slipped my lips. "Oh you will *let me* handle it, will you?"

"Yes, I will *let you*." His mouth drew into a smirk.

"Good luck with that."

The teasing smile disappeared and seriousness descended on his handsome face. "We can't afford to have a divided city when the war starts. If you don't have it completely under control by then, but the majority of the Underworld supports you, then I will step in and kill the Rat King and all his people for you and hand you the crown." Eyes dripping with authority locked on me. "But if the Rat King still controls the majority of the Underworld, you will back off and bend the knee to him. Understood?"

Turning back to the door, I pushed down the dread building in my stomach and instead threw him a challenging grin over my shoulder. "I think you have forgotten the part where I don't take orders from you."

Some of the tension left his body as he let out a breathy laugh. "Keep telling yourself that."

After sending him one final eye roll, I stepped across the threshold and slipped into the darkened hallway beyond. That damn assassin might be infuriating and arrogant and bossy but he was right about one thing. If I hadn't settled this war with the Rat King long before the star elves made their first move, I would be putting all my friends at risk. And that, I would not allow. So right now, defeating the Rat King was the priority.

Soft carpets muffled my footsteps as I slunk through the empty palace and towards my secret entry point. I would send a letter to Morgora and ask if she knew anything about my current magic problem, and I would keep searching for ways to get my powers back, but my main focus right now had to be on tearing down the Rat King's empire. And I had already set my plans in motion. I let out a malicious chuckle as I slipped into a forgotten doorway. That beady-eyed little man would never know what hit him.

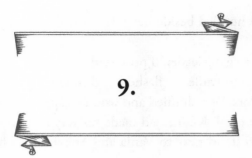

9.

"What's going on?"

Stopping halfway down the stairs with my hand still on the railing, I frowned down at the mass of people who filled the whole tavern. Most of them were the ones who'd already asked to join my non-existent gang but many were people who had never been at the Black Emerald before. Like the woman with dirty blond hair who I'd watched being kicked out of her gang by the Rat King two weeks ago. She gave me a small smile from where she stood by the wall.

"We heard what you did for Yngvild and Vania," Kildor said from the middle of the room.

When I'd gotten back last night, I'd only let people know that I was back and unharmed before locking myself in my room. After the Storm Caster fight, the drugging and the beating, the knife fight and the escape, and my intense meeting with Shade in Blackspire, I had needed a long sleep to recover. Apparently, word about my actions had spread during that time.

"Okay?" I replied tentatively.

The two blue-eyed warriors pushed to the front of the crowd and looked up at me on the stairs with serious eyes.

"You sacrificed yourself so that we could get away," Vania said matter-of-factly. "Without even a moment's hesitation."

Yngvild nodded beside her. "That's what a *real* gang leader should do."

"I'm not a gang leader," I protested.

Knowing smiles flashed through the gathered underworlders. Feet shuffled and wood scraped against wood as the crowd stirred. Kildor had made his way from the center of the room to stand next to Vania and Yngvild. His brown eyes flicked up to me again.

"The Rat King throws his people into harm's way to save himself," he said. "You throw *yourself* into danger to save your people. Protection, somewhere to belong, knowing without a doubt that your people will back you up." Kildor lifted his arms to motion at the packed room. "That's what we're looking for in a gang."

Yngvild squared his shoulders. "And the way you lead brings all of that to the gang." His piercing blue eyes locked on me. "*You* are what we're looking for in a gang leader."

Completely lost for words, I just stared at them all in bewildered silence. What in Nemanan's name were they talking about? I was *not* a gang leader. I was just a selfish arrogant thief who had challenged the King of the Underworld for control because I stubbornly refused to bow to anyone.

However, before I could once again remind them of that, the crowd moved again. My mouth dropped open. Clothes rustled and weapons clanked as the whole room got down on one knee and pulled out a blade. I had to grip the railing to keep from falling down the stairs in shock.

"No. Wait. What are you doing?" I stuttered.

"I hereby swear loyalty to you," Yngvild said. His words were echoed by the rest of the room. "To obey you, protect you, and keep you safe. The way you will protect and keep us safe. To put our gang's needs before my own. To protect our people from anyone who would do us harm." He drew a shallow cut across his palm. "By this blood oath I so swear."

"Wait..." I began again.

The very air in the room seemed to vibrate as the promise was repeated by the others. More steal glinted in the candlelight as people drew shallow cuts across their palms.

"By this blood oath I so swear," echoed between the walls.

"What are you...?" I flicked desperate eyes across the room. "Stop..."

Squeezing their bleeding hands together, the gathered underworlders held them out in front of their chests. Muted dripping sounded as blood fell from their clenched fists.

Putting a hand to my forehead, I shook my head in disbelief. "And now there's blood on the floor..."

Yngvild's rumbling laugh resounded throughout the tavern. "There will be a lot more blood on the floor before all this is over."

"Yeah, I guess there will." Dropping my hand, I let out a tired chuckle.

Vania's serious eyes found mine. "Do you accept our allegiance?"

Sweeping my gaze across the kneeling crowd, I took in the determination and hope blazing in their eyes. By Nemanan, I didn't really have much of a choice, did I?

After a soft exhale, I drew myself up. "I accept your allegiance."

Smiles spread across the faces of everyone in the tavern as they climbed to their feet.

While the room stood back up, I motioned at the bar along the wall.

"Drink are on the house tonight." A wry smile tugged at my lips. "Because after this, *I* need a drink. Or ten."

Excited cheers rose. As everyone moved to take advantage of the offer, I staggered down the final steps to the ground floor.

Yngvild and Vania remained waiting for me there. Both tall warriors stood with their arms crossed and satisfied smiles on their faces. I narrowed my eyes at them.

"This is quite the thing to suddenly spring on someone, you know," I grumbled.

Yngvild's eyes twinkled. "We thought you needed a push."

"And we meant what we said," Vania filled in. "We like the way you run things. The loyalty it brings to the crew." She locked eyes with me. "Thank you. For yesterday."

I scratched the back of my neck. "Anytime."

"Now let's go get those drinks you promised," Yngvild said and released another rumbling laugh.

People cleared a path for us as we moved towards the bar.

After grabbing a mug of ale, I slunk away to my table in the back.

While the sinewy woman with dirty blond hair–whose name I now knew to be Helena–continued serving drinks to the parched people in the tavern, I watched the room.

All these people had just knelt on the floor and sworn a blood oath to me. To *me*. By all the gods, did they have any idea what kind of selfish scheming bitch they had just pledged loyalty to?

I shook my head. But they had. And if there was one thing my self-serving underworld ass always did, it was to protect my people.

Blowing out an exasperated sigh, I downed my drink. Yep. Apparently, I was a gang leader now.

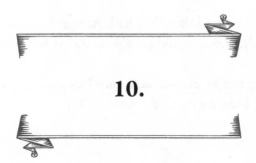

10.

Seagulls squawked as they raced past in a flapping of white wings. Raising a hand to my brow to shield it from the sun, I squinted at the figure swaggering down the pier. High cheekbones and a jawline as sharp as the black eyes above it met my gaze.

"How's the pirating?" I called.

"Not nearly as lucrative as the smuggling." Zaina drew a hand through her curly black hair. "Which is why I was pleasantly surprised when you sent me that letter."

With a hand on her cocked hip, the stunning smuggler came to a halt before me and threw me a wide grin. I matched it.

"It's good to see you, Zaina."

"You too." Her tanned face beamed down at me even as she narrowed her eyes slightly. "Why did you never tell me you were friends with a jewelry forger of that kind of rank? We could've done a lot of business together for years."

"Sorry. I didn't think about it until now."

"Well, I forgive you. Since you're giving me the exclusive smuggling contract for your new business." Her eyes glittered as she grinned at me. "And that Lady Smythe. I like her. A lot."

A soft chuckle escaped my throat. "I can see why."

As soon as I'd decided to mess with the Rat King's monopoly on smuggling, I had taken inventory of my contacts. I knew straight away that I would need a supplier and a runner. Someone who could manufacture whatever I wanted to sell and someone who could transport it. Luckily for me, I happened to know both a world-class jewelry forger and a smuggler.

Lady Smythe and I hadn't been in contact since I hired her to create the counterfeit pearls we'd used to save Keutunan from being taken over by Marcellus, but she had been happy to get into business with me again. After all, the market over here was much bigger. The fierce noble lady from Keutunan was a force to be reckoned with, as was Zaina, so I had a feeling that their acquaintance would turn into a deeper relationship before long.

Wooden planks creaked as two men lugged a crate down the pier. The black-haired smuggler threw a look over her shoulder. Since the midday sun was beaming down on us, I shielded my eyes again as I shifted my gaze to watch them as well. Waves lapped against the docks.

"Over here is fine," Zaina said and motioned at a spot at the edge of the pier.

The two dark-haired men deposited their burden in the indicated place before nodding at their captain and disappearing back to their ship. Zaina nodded as well before turning her attention back to the crate. Taking a firm grip, she pried the lid off.

Between the straw used as padding, smaller boxes made of fine wood were visible. Brushing off the lid of the topmost one, she opened it. Jewelry glittered in the sunlight. I lifted an exquisite necklace made of gleaming silver and emeralds and held it up to the light. After a thorough inspection, I returned it to the case and met Zaina's gaze.

A satisfied grin spread across my mouth. "You know what, I like that Lady Smythe too."

Zaina chuckled and nodded towards the open crate. "They're stunning, right?"

"They're perfect."

During my career as a thief, I had stolen a lot of jewelry. After a few years of accidentally stealing fakes that my fences informed me weren't worth anything, I'd become somewhat adept at recognizing forgeries when I saw them. But these... I *knew* these pieces were counterfeit but I still had a hard time believing it.

My smile turned wistful as a memory flashed by in my mind. Me, twirling a knife in my hand while leaning against a closed basement door, asking an elegant lady in an orange dress whether her husband knew that she was one of the best jewelry forgers in town. And Lady Smythe, with her observant dark eyes, replying by letting out an indignant huff and informing me that she wasn't *one* of the best jewelry forgers – she was *the* best.

A soft chuckle escaped my lips as I studied the glimmering necklaces before me. *Well, Lady Smythe, you weren't wrong.*

"I've never unloaded smuggled merchandise at the main dock before." Zaina cast wary glances around the area. "It feels weird."

"We need to convince our future buyers that this is a legit enterprise." Closing the lid to the small necklace case again, I shrugged. "And besides, being friends with the High King of Pernula helps with not getting busted for smuggling."

"*Friends*," she replied with a pointed emphasis on the word. Her dark eyes glittered as she gave me a quick rise and fall of her eyebrows. "Right."

"Shut up."

"Do you really think I didn't see what happened on my ship after I fished you out of the water outside the City of Glass?" The satisfied smirk on her lips widened. "How he pushed you up against the wall and then—"

"Alright, alright," I huffed and gave her upper arm a shove. Crossing my arms, I glared at the amused pirate. "Enough, or I'll fill in Lady Smythe on *your* feelings."

That glint still present in her eyes, Zaina ran her tongue over her teeth. "Now why would I wanna stop that?"

Thudding feet saved my flustered self from coming up with an appropriate reply to that. Turning around, I found a gorgeous girl hurrying towards us. Her white skirt fluttered in the warm summer winds.

"Zaina!" Norah called before wrapping her arms around her sister.

"Hey, sis."

"I'm so glad you decided to take this contract because that means you'll be back in Pernula a lot more, right?"

Zaina drew an affectionate hand over Norah's loose curls. "Yeah, I'll be focusing more on smuggling for a while now so we'll see each other more."

"Good."

While the two sisters hugged each other fiercely, I occupied myself with brushing nonexistent pieces of straw off the topmost jewelry cases. It was good to see the two of them back together again. Ever since Zaina received the Pernulan warship from

Shade as payment for her help two years ago, she had been trying her luck at pirating. But she had missed the steady stream of income that smuggling brought. I studied the contented expression on Zaina's face. And apparently, she had missed something else too.

"Liam and the others are on their way," Norah said when they at last stepped back from the embrace. "They'll be here any minute."

"I'd better make myself scarce then." Zaina swung an arm over her sister's shoulders while shifting her gaze to me. "Just signal Samuel on the ship when you're done and he'll move the crate back."

"We'll wait for you at the Lemon Tree Café," Norah added.

"Alright." I nodded. "See you there."

Raven strands gleamed in the sunlight as a gust of wind snatched at their hair while the two of them strolled back towards the city. Norah swatted Zaina's arm in response to something she had said while the smuggler threw her head back and laughed. A smile tugged at my lips. It was *really* good to see the two of them together again.

Wood groaned as boats shifted in the water behind me. I pushed a few rogue strands back behind my ears before bending down over the open crate again to make sure that the jewelry cases inside looked presentable. Once I was satisfied, I flicked my gaze over my body.

Nondescript black and gray clothes, no visible weapons, and a braid holding my hair back. I didn't exactly look like a rich jewelry merchant but it was the best I could do. And besides, I hoped that the merchandise would speak for itself.

Chatter rose from across the harbor. I glanced up to find Liam leading a procession of very well-dressed men towards me. Their colorful clothes gleamed in the bright sun. Man, I definitely didn't look like a merchant. Oh well, too late to change that now.

"Gentlemen," Liam said as the six of them came to a halt on the other side of the crate. "May I present Storm, the business associate I was talking about."

The five merchants looked me up and down with scrutinizing eyes. While the black-haired one on the right gave me an acknowledging nod, the blond one with the thick mustache narrowed his eyes at me.

"That doesn't sound like a real name," he observed. "And you don't look like a merchant."

I barely managed to suppress a snort and an eye roll. *As I was saying...*

"I know." I let a friendly smile drift across my lips. "I have chosen to go by that name for the same reason I'm wearing such bland clothes." With a knowing look on my face, I motioned at the open crate between us. "When you are in the business of selling items as expensive as these, it is best to draw as little attention to yourself as possible."

For a moment, the five well-dressed merchants pondered my words. Then the suspicion cleared from their brows and they gave me nods of approval. I stifled another chuckle. *Amateurs.* On the far left, Liam's lips were twitching.

"And the merchandise...?" the dark-haired one said.

Shooting them another brilliant smile, I lifted the first case and opened the lid. A series of low whistles echoed over the creaking pier and the crashing waves as the merchants inspected the stunning pieces of jewelry I showed them. While they continued passing the necklaces between them and assessing the quality, Liam's dark blue eyes met mine. *Nice*, he mouthed. I threw a quick grin in his direction before a question from the man with the mustache pulled my attention back.

Once the five gentlemen were satisfied with the quality of the merchandise, I returned the polished cases to the crate and put the large lid back on. "Now that you have seen what I have to offer, are any of you interested in selling my jewelry in your shops?"

The man on the right drew a hand through his shoulder-length black hair. "Yes, I would be very interested in such a partnership."

"Indeed." The blond man stroked his moustache. "I will have a contract drawn up and sent over to you."

Murmurs of agreement rose from the rest of the party as well. I nodded at them.

"Well then, gentlemen," I said. "I look forward to a long and fruitful partnership."

"As do we."

The dark-haired jewelry merchant shifted his gaze to the man on the far left. "Liam, thank you for bringing this business opportunity to our attention."

Liam smile back at them. "Of course."

Clothes rustled as the five gentlemen turned after bidding us farewell and retreated up the harbor. I listened to the wind snap in the sails behind me until the final colorful suit had been swallowed up by the warehouses. Narrowing my eyes, I turned to Liam.

"How much did you tell them?"

He scratched his mop of curly brown hair. "They know that the wares don't exactly come through the normal import route so they have guessed that it's some form of smuggling happening."

"But do they know that the actual merchandise is counterfeit?"

An innocent smile spread across his face as his sparkling eyes locked on me. "I may have forgotten to mention that particular detail."

After lifting my arm to signal to Samuel that he could retrieve the crate, I let out a long laugh and shook my head at Liam.

He gave me a light shrug. "We're not exactly friends. To be honest, I think they're kind of pompous. Just because they run the most high-end jewelry stores in the city, they think they're better than the rest of us." His mouth broke into a mischievous grin. "So I didn't really feel the need to tell them that they'd now be selling forgeries in their fancy-pancy shops."

While wiggling my eyebrows, I bumped his shoulder with mine. "So, you can take the boy out of the Underworld but you can't take the Underworld out of the boy, huh?"

He beamed at me. "Maybe."

Still grinning, he motioned for us to start back towards the city as well. I lifted a hand in thanks to Samuel before falling in beside my friend.

So, remember how I said that I needed two things to start my own smuggling empire? A supplier and a runner. Well, technically, I needed three things. A supplier. A runner. And a distributor. I glanced at the young man with twinkling blue eyes next to me. Thankfully, I also happened to know an influential hat merchant who could introduce me to his business acquaintances.

Who in the world would ever have believed that someone as rude and socially incompetent as I would end up having that many connections? I for one would never have guessed it. But I did. And now I had everything I needed to run a successful smuggling operation that could one day push the Rat King off his throne.

The city wall cast dark shadows over us as we drew near. Breaking his smuggling monopoly was a long-term goal, and also a way to increase my fortune so that I could really go up against him without having to worry about money, but it wasn't the only thing I had up my sleeve. I was also going to completely ruin the other part of his business so that he lost his other revenue stream.

Flicking my gaze over the shops Liam and I passed on our way to the Lemon Tree Café, I let a malicious smirk spread across my mouth. I was also going to drag his name through the dirt. Yes. The name *the Rat King* would mean nothing once I was through. I chuckled. And I would let him live just long enough to realize it.

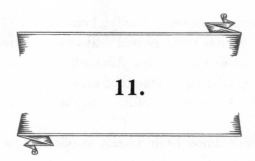

11.

"**O**kay, you know what to do."

After I'd seen the other thieves nod in acknowledgement, I scrambled up the side of the nearest building and took off across the rooftops.

Every day, more people arrived at the Black Emerald and requested to join my gang. Among my now rather impressive crew, I had discovered several others who had chosen thieving as their trade of choice. For this mission, I had picked the best of the bunch. I grinned at the dark shapes disappearing into the shadows around me. It was so nice to run with thieves again.

My target rose in the distance. I slowed to a trot as I reached the roof of an expensive shoe store. No light peeked out from the wooden shutters below. Swinging myself over the edge, I started down the side of the building.

The windowsill was silent underneath my feet as I stopped briefly at the topmost window and peered inside. Two figures lay sleeping in a double bed in the darkened room. I watched them for a couple of minutes to make sure they were really sleeping before I continued down to the bottom floor. The muscles in my arms tensed as I lowered myself the final bit to the next windowsill.

Crouching on the wooden ledge, I reached for a lockpick to lift the latch open but then paused halfway to it. A thick shadow was visible across the shutters. After adjusting my position, I looked through the gaps and studied the inside.

"Really?" I muttered softly. "They've barred the damn windows?"

Instead of a simple latch, a heavy wooden bar lay across the shutters to prevent them from being opened from the outside. Still peering through the gaps, I swept my gaze across the rest of the room. Similar contraptions were present on all other windows I could see. And on the door too.

"Why would anyone need this much security for shoes?" I breathed into the silent night. "*Shoes.*"

Since there was no way in through either the door or the windows on street level, I reached for a crack in the wall and started back up the building. Despite the annoyance building in my chest, I couldn't help being impressed. The sleeping couple in the room I now once again stared into at least had a solid taste in shop security. Pulling out a lockpick, I stuck it through the gap in the shutters and lifted the latch. Not so much in bedroom security, though.

The obliging piece of wood swung open on soundless hinges. After sending a quick prayer to Nemanan, I climbed through. The God of Thieves appeared to have heard me because the spotless planks stayed silent too as I dropped down on the floor inside the window.

On the bed, the man rolled over on his side and draped an arm over his wife's body. She let out a contented sigh as she nuzzled against his body in her sleep. I shook my head at them. How did people sleep this soundly?

After closing the shutters behind me, I snuck across the room. A slight gap had been left in the bedroom door so I just slunk through it without touching it. There was another door further down the hallway outside but I ignored it and headed for the stairs on the other side. Staying as close to the wall as I could, I made my way down the wooden steps.

Colorful shoes with frills and gleaming buckles stood artfully placed on shelves and podiums throughout the shop downstairs. Flowers and other greenery decorated the spaces between them. I frowned at the cacophony of bright hues. Not a practical leather boot in sight. Did people actually pay money for this kind of inconvenient footwear?

Shrugging, I pulled out a large sack and got to work. One impractical pair of shoes after the other hit the bottom of bag with soft thuds as I move throughout the shop. While I reached for a particularly strange pair of pink heels, I wondered who actually decided what was fashionable and what was not. Whoever had decided that it was *this* had to be a bloody lunatic.

A shrill shriek sounded. My heart leaped into my throat as I snatched my hand back from the shelf and whirled around. Thudding footsteps sounded from upstairs. I dove towards the nearest bench and rolled under it. The flower arrangements on top of it wobbled as the hulking sack I was carrying slammed into it. Throwing up my free hand, I managed to stop a white vase filled with blue flowers from tipping over the edge. My heart thumped in my chest as I pushed it back on the bench before yanking my hand out of sight again.

Blood rushed in my ears while I waited for the owners of the shop to come thundering down the stairs to discover that almost their whole stock was missing.

"There, there," a woman's voice cooed from somewhere upstairs. "It was just a nightmare, darling. It wasn't real."

A child's voice mumbled and sobbed in reply.

Oh. So the scream hadn't been for me. I shook my head. Well, of course it hadn't been. What had I been thinking? As if I would ever be so careless as to get caught when breaking into someone's house. How ridiculous.

Two pairs of feet moved across the hallway upstairs. Wood creaked and covers rustled as the couple no doubt climbed back into bed having comforted their child. I kept myself pressed against the floor under the canopy of flowers until I was certain that they had fallen asleep again.

Moving on silent feet, I swept through the rest of the store and gathered up all the remaining shoes. Once my sack was so full that I could barely close it, I tiptoed towards the window I had planned on using as my entry point. Briefly setting my loot down, I reached for the heavy wooden bar. It let out a muffled groan as I lifted it from its fastenings. I froze.

When no one came down to see what had caused the sound, I carefully placed the slab of wood on the floor and edged open the shutters. Night winds blew gusts of fragrant air into the now thoroughly empty shoe store. Picking up the stack, I cast a look back over my shoulder.

I almost felt a bit bad for the couple sleeping upstairs but then I remembered that I didn't really have a conscience so I just shrugged and climbed out the window and into the waiting night.

Sitting atop the roof of the building, I watched dark shadows slink in and out of buildings down the street. Our plan had been a simple one. Word had reached us that all the stores on this street paid the Rat King for protection. In exchange for the money they gave him, he would make sure that no one touched these businesses and his reputation was of course based on his ability to keep that promise. So naturally, we had decided to rob these stores blind.

Well, not all of them. There were more stores on this street than there were skilled thieves in my gang so we had just picked some random ones in the middle. All of them were located next to one another though, so that people would understand that this wasn't just a random occurrence. I glanced at the sack of shoes next to me. Trying to fence shoes was more trouble than it was worth so I would probably just dump them somewhere in the poorer parts of town. After all, we weren't robbing them to make money. We were doing it to send a message.

Standing up, I gazed down the street. The others seemed to still be working on their targets. Flicking my gaze to the building behind me, I considered. The shoe store was where our little burglary outbreak ended on this side of the road but... A wicked grin spread across my mouth. Maybe just one more shop. To really make a statement, you know.

After stashing the sack of colorful shoes on the roof for now, I scuttled down the side of the adjacent building. Heavy bars locked the windows on street level in this store as well so I aimed for another upstairs entry point. Peeking through the shutters, I studied the room inside.

This did not appear to be a bedroom. Bookshelves and desks littered with scrolls, tools, and glass beakers filled the darkened room. *Huh. Strange.* I stuck a lockpick through the gap and lifted up the latch. After pulling open one of the shutters, I climbed inside.

Sneaking on soundless feet, I studied the contents of the room. Powders and ingredients were arranged in neat containers along the wall while papers full of scribbled formulas lay scattered on the tables. A soft groan sounded from the floorboards. I stopped. My pulse smattered in my ears while I waited for any potential footsteps to arrive.

When nothing happened for a few minutes, I went back to searching the room. Maybe these ingredients were valuable? I still needed to search the main shop, which I assumed was located downstairs, but as I studied a bookshelf next to the window, I considered whether I could grab some stuff from this room as well. Just as I decided that it wouldn't be worth it, the floor creaked from somewhere by the door behind me. My breath hitched as a man's voice cut through the darkness.

"If I throw this glass vial in my hand, the whole room you're standing in will fill with poison."

Oh shit.

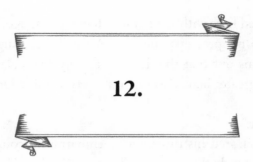

12.

Since I'd been inspecting the shelves, I was standing with my back to the door. If whoever the voice belonged to was actually holding a vial of poison, they could throw it before I could turn around. Based on the contents of this room, it was highly likely that he was telling the truth. I couldn't risk it.

Very slowly, I raised my hands so that he could see that I wasn't holding any weapons. Still keeping my palms out, I edged around to face the poison-wielding man.

"The Oncoming Storm?"

I jerked back at the sound of my name and squinted against the darkness. A man with a short mustache and glasses stared at me from across the room. Surprise was written all over his face. My mouth dropped open.

"Haber?" I blinked at the chemical genius from Keutunan who made the blackout powder and exploding orbs I often used. "What are you doing here?"

Apothecary Haber lowered the glass vial in his hand. "I was just about to ask you the same thing."

Letting out a surprised laugh, he walked over to the table between us and lit one of the candles. Flames sputtered to life and flickered over our equally stunned faces.

"I moved here with my family a few months ago," he said in response to my previous question. A small smile tugged at his lips. "It turns out that the demand for my particular products was much greater here. Pernula has a very sizeable Underworld, you see."

"I know."

Haber cleared his throat in an embarrassed cough as if he had just realized who he was talking to. "Right. Of course you do." Cocking his head, he watched me with curious eyes. "But I haven't seen you here before. Did you just arrive?"

"Got back, is more like it, but yeah I've been..." How was I even supposed to summarize what I'd been doing since I left Keutunan two years ago? I lifted my shoulders in a light shrug. "...away. Yeah, I've been away for a while."

"I see." Paper rustled as the brilliant inventor straightened a stack of scrolls on the desk before glancing up at me again. "Why were you breaking into my shop?"

"Uhm..."

Was I supposed to tell him that I'd been about to rob him blind? Probably not. An apologetic grin flashed over my lips as I waved a hand in front of my face.

"Never mind. Just pretend that you didn't see me."

For a moment, it looked like he was about to press the matter but then he seemed to come to the conclusion that he was better off pretending that this never happened. He gave me a nod.

"I do have a huge order for you, though," I said.

The previous minutes' worry melted off his face and a satisfied smile spread across his mouth. "I'm glad to have my best customer back."

"I'm glad you're here too, Haber."

Now that my powers were temporarily out of commission, I had to stock up on some more blackout powder and exploding orbs. Both for me and my gang. Having Haber set up shop on this side of the ocean was the best piece of news I'd had for weeks. It would make it so much easier to get my hands on his amazing inventions. And if I was to take control of the Pernulan Underworld, I was definitely going to need them.

Once Apothecary Haber had finished writing down my rather considerable order on a spare piece of paper, he looked up at me. "I'll have it ready for you in about a week. Come by whenever you're ready after that."

While nodding in acknowledgement, I removed a small pouch from my belt and threw it towards the table. The pearls inside rattled as it thudded down on the tabletop before skidding to a halt next to Haber's paper with my order.

I flashed him a quick smile. "For your discretion."

"Which you will always have regardless." His fingers closed around the pouch while a satisfied smile played over his lips. "But the gesture is very much appreciated anyway."

Letting out a soft chuckle, I strode back to the window. While bracing myself on the window frame, I threw a look over my shoulder. "I'll put out word to my people that your shop is off limits."

"Much obliged."

I climbed up on the windowsill. "It's good to see you again, Haber."

The chemical genius gave me a sincere smile in return. "Likewise, the Oncoming Storm."

After swinging myself out on the other side, I disappeared towards the roof again. *Huh.* This night had taken an interesting turn. But with Haber setting up shop in Pernula, maybe the gods were finally on my side?

MORNING LIGHT BATHED the road in a soft orange shimmer. I jerked my head up as a group of people approached the mob that had gathered in the middle of the cobbled street. *Showtime.*

"What is the meaning of this?" a tall man demanded from the front of the mob, and stabbed a hand towards the shop behind him. "When I woke up this morning, everything was gone. Everything!"

"He's right," the woman next to him joined in. "Our whole stock is gone too. Every single dress. Gone."

"Isn't this exactly what we pay you protection money for? So that we won't get robbed?"

When the Rat King held up his hands in a placating gesture and started weaving excuses, I had to suppress a very strong urge to cackle.

After I'd left Apothecary Haber last night, I'd taken a quick detour to dump the shoes I'd stolen and also to make sure that all my other thieves had succeeded in cleaning out their targets. They all had. Then I'd snuck back and waited on the roof just to see this. I mean, what could be sweeter than to revel in the misery of your enemies?

"This is unacceptable!" the shoe store owners said in unison.

"Yes," a woman with red hair joined in. "If you can't hold up your end of the bargain, then why should we pay you?"

With a wide smirk on my face, I absentmindedly traced circles on the warm roof tiles while the Rat King promised to find those responsible, get their goods back, and that something like this would never happen again. As if he would actually be able to keep those promises.

His words were reassuring and placating but I could see the fuming anger dancing behind the calm mask on his face. He did not like having people disrespect him in this way but he couldn't very well kill these upstanding citizens either because that would send a bad message to his other clients. In our world, something like that would work. But not in the Upperworld.

At last, the merchants seemed somewhat satisfied. When the skinny king whirled around and stalked back up the street, he let the mask slip from his face. Blazing fury burned in his beady eyes. Oh he was going to kill someone for this. Probably me. Or he would try to, anyway.

Discontent still lingered over the whole street after the Rat King and his goons had left. I watched the merchants argue with each other for a few minutes more before they all went back to their respective shops. Time for phase two.

After pushing to my feet, I gave my stiff body a quick stretch before I climbed down the side of the building again. A small bell tinkled as I opened the door and sauntered into the expensive shoe store.

"We're closed," the man muttered from behind the counter.

"Oh, by all the gods," I said and swept surprised eyes over the gaping shelves as if I wasn't the one who had emptied them a few hours ago. "Is it all gone?"

"Yes." The brown-haired man glared at me. "What do you want?"

"It's just, I've heard that the Rat King has trouble keeping his contracts. A lot of other stores under his protection have been robbed too." With an innocent look on my face, I shrugged. "If you're ever interested in switching to someone else, I'd suggest sending word to the Black Emerald."

"Honey?" A blond woman descended the stairs with graceful steps. "Maybe we should consider going to someone else. We can't have this happen again."

"I know," her husband muttered.

Turning in a lazy circle, I waved a hand in the air. "Just think about it."

Before either of them could question who I was or why I had just happened to be in the area right now, I strolled out the door and set course for the next shop in order to give them the exact same suggestion. A wicked smile graced my lips. Soon, the Rat King's empire would be cracking at the seams.

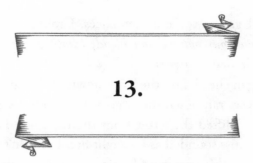

13.

My heart rate sped up. I recognized this handwriting. Morgora had finally replied to my letter about my missing powers. Letting out a deep breath to steady my nerves, I shot a stiletto blade from my sleeve and used it to open the envelope. I flicked my eyes over the words scrawled in black ink.

"It's not possible to complete the ritual without consent," I breathed as I stared at her words.

So they weren't gone forever as they would be if I gave them up to Aldeor the White. Tipping my head back against the wooden wall of the booth, I stared up at the ceiling and let out a long sigh of relief. My magic wasn't permanently gone. I could still get it back.

All around me people chatted, laughed, and drank as if a large stone hadn't just lifted from my chest. I sat there for a moment, just letting the relief flow through me, before tilting my head back down to read the rest of the letter.

It was possible to block magic powers with a curse? I frowned at the paper in my hand. Was that what the Rat King's crew had done? Cursed me? But how? My eyes scanned the rest of the letter. She told me to find someone who specialized in curses. Alright, I would put the word out and see if anyone knew someone like that.

When I got to the final sentences, I rolled my eyes. *How could you lose your powers, you bloody idiot? Go get them back. Right now.* Signed, *Morgora.*

Shaking my head, I set the letter down. "Old bat."

White wax ran down the edge of the candle as I yanked it towards me. I lifted the letter from the table and held it over the flame. A hiss sounded as it caught fire. I couldn't have other people reading this letter and finding out that I didn't have my powers anymore. It had to stay a secret until I could get them back.

Turning the paper in my hand, I made sure the whole thing burned before dropping the last piece on my plate. Flakes of black ash swirled in the air as it landed. Once the final corner had been consumed, I dusted off my hands and took a swig of ale.

Find someone who specialized in curses. Right. As if I would know what kind of person that was. Who even specialized in curses? It wasn't as if they just hung up a sign in their window saying *curse specialist.* But no, just find someone who specialized in curses, Morgora had said. I blew out an exasperated breath. Sure. Piece of cake.

Metal clanked as weapons were drawn across the whole tavern. I shot to my feet. From my booth in the back, I could see all the way to the door so I quickly realized what—or rather who—had triggered this armed response. A woman with copper hair and green eyes stared straight at me from across the crowd. Two men with dark brown hair flanked her.

"Storm," Vania said with a sharp note in her voice as she elbowed her way towards me. "It's Red Demon Rowan."

"Yeah, it is." With a slight smile drifting over my lips, I raised my voice to carry across the tavern. "Stand down."

Chairs scraped and swords clanked as the room sheathed their weapons and sat back down. Rowan, who had been the leader of the second largest gang in Pernula when Shade won the election, motioned at her bodyguards to get a drink before she strode towards me. Vania tensed.

"Are you sure about this?" she asked quietly. "She could be here on the Rat King's orders."

"I'm sure. Thanks, Vania."

The blond warrior shifted her eyes between me and the approaching gang leader before finally giving me a reluctant nod and moving a respectful distance away. She took up position by the stairs and remained standing there with a hand on her sword, though.

Still standing, I held out my arm as Rowan stopped on the other side of the table.

"Rowan."

A smile flashed over the copper-haired woman's lips as she clasped my forearm. "Storm."

It wasn't until both of us were seated comfortably that the usual chatter in the tavern started back up again. Helena came by and placed a mug of ale in front of Rowan before hurrying back to the bar again.

The fierce gang leader held my gaze with that smile still playing over her lips. "When I said to let me know if you ever decided to *set up shop* in this city, I never thought you'd interpret that as challenging the Rat King for control of the Underworld."

"Me neither." I tilted my head to the side. "But it turns out that I don't like it when someone tries to force me to kneel to them."

"Yeah, I caught that." She chuckled. "I think everyone heard about the storm you threw at him that first night. Is it really true that your final words to him were: *you'd better run*?"

A sly smile spread across my lips. "Maybe."

"Ha!" She let out another laugh and shook her head. "Blowing up his rum warehouse. Sacking those shops he was protecting. That was you too, wasn't it?"

Not bothering to deny it, I just lifted one shoulder in a lopsided shrug.

"Of course it was. You should've seen his face after he found out you robbed those stores."

"I did. I was watching from the rooftops when he arrived."

Rowan let out a breathy chuckle and gave me an approving nod. "I like your style." Raising her chin, she locked eyes with me. "Consider my crew allies."

"If the Rat King finds out that you've sided with me, he's gonna come after you too."

Green eyes glinted dangerously as Red Demon Rowan spread her hands. "Let him try."

"You know what, I like your style too." With a grin on my face, I held out a hand across the table. "Allies."

Reaching out, she shook it. "Allies."

Pots clanked from the kitchen. Vania, who still stood alert by the stairs, flicked her eyes towards the sound before shifting her attention back to us. I took a swig of ale.

"My thieves and I are gonna keep hitting his stores." I ran a thumb over the mug's sturdy handle before locking eyes with Rowan again. "How would you feel about taking over the protection contracts on those stores?"

"You've gotten them to ditch the Rat King because of your break-ins?"

"Not all of them, but most, yeah."

She narrowed her eyes at me. "Your cut?"

I brushed a few stray crumbs off the table and shrugged. "No cut. You're a gang leader too so you don't answer to me. Just make sure the Rat King doesn't get the money for those contracts."

Rowan let out a wicked chuckle. "I *really* like your style. Deal."

Raising my mug, I grinned at her. "Alright, my crew will keep robbing the stores he's supposed to be protecting and then we'll send them your way for a new contract."

She lifted her mug as well and pushed it into mine. "To a new business, new allies, and knocking the Rat King off this throne."

"Indeed."

After downing her drink, she pushed back her copper hair and stood up. "I'm glad you decided to set up shop here." Turning, she threw me a grin over her shoulder. "I'll see you around, Storm."

"Yeah, see you."

Her two brown-haired bodyguards fell in behind her as she strode through the crowded room. I watched her confident posture. Not once had she seemed worried about walking into a tavern full of armed people loyal to me. Red Demon Rowan. What an ally to have.

Now I could hand over the protection contracts to someone I trusted so that I could focus my own gang's attention on wiping the Rat King from existence without having to spread my people too thin. As Rowan disappeared out the door again, I glanced down at the black ashes still on my plate.

And I had received a clue about how to get my magic back. Now that the Rat King's doom was firmly on track, maybe I could divert some time to that particular problem too. I had to be careful who I told, though. I wouldn't want the rest of the Underworld to find out that I was looking for a curse specialist and then put two and two together.

But Elaran and the other elves would be arriving soon, and since they had magic in their own city, maybe they would have ideas on how to find someone who knew about curses. I pushed off from the table and blew out a sigh. No rest for the wicked.

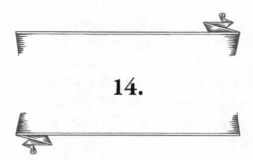

14.

Boots echoed between the buildings as ranks upon ranks of soldiers moved in tight formations across the city. Hoisted flags snapped in the wind. Elves in green and brown led the procession while men in gleaming armor of silver and midnight blue marched behind them. At the head of the force prowled an elf with auburn hair and a huge black bow across his back. Staying low, I followed the army from atop the rooftops. My gang members did the same.

That would probably never stop being weird. My gang. I still couldn't quite believe that I actually ran a gang now. I now had people who watched my back and obeyed my orders. Granted, the ones stalking the rooftops with me were there because they wanted to see the armies of Keutunan and Tkeideru arrive in Pernula and not because I had ordered them. But still.

Aiming for a lower building, I broke into a run. Tiles thudded softly as I slid down the slanting roof and jumped straight out. Sharp intakes of breath echoed from the citizens lining the street and watching from the windows as I landed in the middle of the road and rolled to my feet. Not a single elf went for their weapons, as if they'd seen me coming. Which they probably had. Damn elves. Adopting a carefree swagger, I fell in beside Elaran.

Behind us, Haela chuckled. "I was wondering if you'd actually do it. You never disappoint, do you?"

Twisting around, I found the black-haired twin grinning at me. Her brother seemed undecided whether he should be greeting me or admonishing me so I sent them both a satisfied smile and a playful salute before he could decide. Next to me, Elaran cut me a glare.

"You're ruining our procession," he muttered.

"Hi, Storm," I said in an overly cheerful voice. "How have you been all these months we haven't seen each other? Fine, thanks. And you?"

"If you hadn't just strolled up to me in the middle of our formal army parade, I might've said that."

Glancing up at him, I snorted. "No, you wouldn't. You would've said something like..." I crossed my arms, drew my eyebrows down, and imitated his grumpy voice. "*So, you haven't blown yourself up yet.*"

A laugh burst from Haela before she slapped a hand over her mouth. I flashed her a grin before turning back to the eternal grump next to me. The corners of Elaran's lips twitched slightly. Still staring straight ahead, he ran a hand through his hair to wipe the almost-smile off his face. Auburn hair shimmered in the sunlight as a soft wind caught the strands and sent them billowing behind him.

"I don't sound like that."

"Uh-huh."

Boots echoed between the buildings as we made our way up the wide street. I flicked my gaze around the area. People were crowded together in open windows and on balconies that were covered in colorful flowers and dark green vines. Two young boys leaned over a windowsill to see past the yellow awning beneath. Their eyes practically sparkled as they watched the ranks of soldiers. In fact, most of the onlookers' faces were filled with awe as they beheld the smart ranks of the two armies marching past.

"I'm assuming you're not just here to say hello," Elaran said. "So what do you want?"

"I just wanted to ask you something."

"And why couldn't that have waited until after we'd finished this ceremony?"

Glancing up at him again, I lifted my shoulders in a light shrug. "For the same reason I don't knock."

Elaran huffed but then broke his straight ahead stare and flicked his gaze to me for a second. "Ask."

"You have magic too," I began. "Do you know if there's any way to make someone lose their magic? Like, with a curse or something." Shrugging again, I sent him a cautious look. "And how to get it back in that case?"

When his yellow eyes met mine again, I was pretty sure he had already figured out the reason I was asking. He held my gaze. "I don't know. But I'll look into it." Returning his attention to the street ahead, he flicked a hand at me in a shooing motion. "Now scram. You're ruining the formality of this."

I chuckled. "It's good to see you again, Elaran."

While the grumpy elf huffed, I turned to the twins. "The Lemon Tree Café later?"

"For sure." Haela beamed at me.

"Sounds good," Haemir filled in. "You have a lot to tell us."

"I know." Branching off from the ranks of soldiers, I set course for a barrel next to the wall and broke into a run.

Wood groaned as I jumped into the air and used the sturdy lid as a springboard. With a swift push, I launched myself towards the roof. My muscles tensed as I pulled myself the final bit onto the sun-warmed roof tiles. Rolling over the edge, I climbed to my feet.

"You're friends with the elven commander?"

I looked up at Yua, a slim dark-eyed thief, who stared at me from across the roof. "Yeah."

"Wow."

What did she mean by *wow*? It was just Elaran. Throwing a quick look over my shoulder, I once again took in the army of elves prowling the streets with lethal grace. Huh. Well, I guess someone who didn't know them might find them cool. I gave Yua a light shrug before following the moving soldiers again. The rest of my thieves started out as well.

Yngvild, Vania, and the rest of my gang wasn't very comfortable running across rooftops so they most likely watched the procession from somewhere below. The thieves in my gang, on the other hand, had no problem traipsing about the city in this fashion. As expected.

They fell in beside me as we reached the final building before the houses flattened out in the huge square that surrounded Blackspire. Forming a line at the edge of the roof, we took in the scene. I let out a low whistle.

A sea of black and red was spread out in orderly lines before the obsidian palace. At the front stood High King Shade and Senior Advisor Malor in spotless attire in those same colors. None of the gathered spectators dared speak as the armies from the Lost Island filed into the open space and came to a halt before the soldiers of Pernula. Shade detached himself from the waiting ranks and strode across the stones. On the other side, Elaran did the same.

A soft summer wind was the only one who disturbed the stillness as Shade and Elaran approached each other. Authority seemed to drip from both of them as they drew up in front of each other. Shade held out his arm.

"Commander."

Elaran clasped it. "High King."

While Shade launched into a ceremonial speech about the joining of the three armies and Elaran's appointment as Commander, I couldn't stop the smile tugging at my lips. The first time those two had arrived in Pernula, they'd hated each other. They'd wanted to shove a sword through each other's throat every time the other so much as drew breath and now... Now they clasped forearms with brotherly love and trusted each other with their armies. I shook my head as the crowd cheered at the end of the speech. Who'd seen that coming?

"Now we'll be safe, right?" a woman said from the window below me. "With the armies from the Lost Island and our city, the star elves will never be able to conquer us. Will they?"

"That's right," a man replied. "Now they'll never breach the walls."

With a tight knot forming in my stomach, I glanced towards the huge city walls in the distance. I hoped they were right. But the problem was that I knew the star elves a lot better than those two confident citizens. I knew that a large army wasn't the only trick that Queen Nimlithil had up her sleeve. Not by a long shot. If we were going to win, we'd need to be smarter. I flicked my eyes towards the harbor and the warehouse full of smuggled jewelry

I'd set up there. And for us to even stand a chance, I had to end my war with the Rat King.

Jerking my chin, I motioned for my thieves that it was time to go. The upperworlders might be satisfied now that the three armies had joined under a capable commander. After all, the battle wasn't here yet. Not for them, at least. But for us underworlders, circumstances were a bit harsher. As they always had been. While we ran back across the rooftops, plans for smuggling, burglaries, and business-wrecking swirled through my mind. Yes. For us, the war was already here.

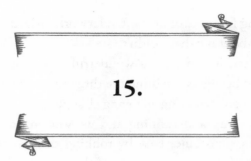

15.

The stack of papers flapped in distress as I heaved a deep sigh. Leaning back against the dark wooden panel of my booth, I rested my feet on the chair tucked under the table on the other side and shook my head. Who knew that being in charge required so much paperwork? Or maybe it wasn't *being in charge* that required it but rather *juggling multiple different plots and schemes to take down the current King of the Underworld while also trying to get my powers back before anyone finds out they're gone* that had brought on the mounds of letters, notes, and ledgers.

I was still glaring at the huge stack of paper that refused to sort itself out no matter how much I threatened to stab it when Helena came by to give me a refill. Swapping my empty mug for one brimming with ale, she gave me a sympathetic smile before retreating to the bar again. I picked up the topmost paper. An account detailing the stock at one of our warehouses. Oh joy.

In the weeks since Elaran and the twins arrived, I'd been so busy I'd barely seen them. And so had they, for that matter. Well, at least after the long evening we'd spent at the Lemon Tree Café, eating, drinking, and catching each other up on everything that had happened since we last saw each other. To my surprise, they hadn't been at all shocked that I had decided to challenge the Rat King for control of the Underworld. Maybe they knew something about me that I didn't.

Regardless, it had been a wonderful night. But after that, the elves had been busy training the three armies to become one and I had been... running my gang, I suppose. The smuggling operation was up and running and we were making dents in the Rat King's customer base by robbing the stores under his protection and then sending some of them over to Red Demon Rowan and her crew.

More people had joined my gang too. The big surge of new recruits that happened when I'd saved Yngvild and Vania hadn't happened again but there was still a small trickle who wanted to join every day. I glanced around the tavern of dark wood and emerald cloth. It was packed. And far from everyone in my gang was even here tonight. I shook my head. All these people obeyed me and they would fight and die for me if I asked them to. It still took my breath away.

"You haven't stabbed the stack of paper yet." Wood vibrated as Yngvild's enormous form sauntered down the steps to my left. "I'm impressed."

Snorting, I swung my feet off the chair and sat up straight as he approached my booth. "No. But it's been very close a couple of times."

Vania descended the stairs after the muscled axe-wielder and wandered over as well. A smile played at the corner of her lips as she looked over my table. "I have no doubt." After plucking the paper from my hand, she flicked her intelligent eyes over it. "This is an old report. Kildor should have an updated count by now."

Not only had I been stuck in this booth all evening reading reports, but I'd also been reading outdated reports? It took tremendous effort not to throw a knife at something. Man, I really hated paperwork.

Sharp intakes of breath echoed through the tavern, followed by clanking metal and scraping wood as the whole room shot to their feet. I jerked my head up to see what had caused it.

A man in tight-fitting black clothes stood just inside the door. Amusement flickered in his dark eyes as he swept them over the room full of underworlders. Shade. Almost every single person in the tavern had pulled a weapon and was pointing it in his direction but the Master Assassin didn't even bother reaching for the twin swords sticking up behind his shoulders as he took a step forward. The line of people before him tightened and raised their weapons higher, even as apprehension blew across their faces.

I was impressed. By all the gods, I was damn impressed. There wasn't a single person in this city who didn't know who Shade was. High King of Pernula *and* Master of the Assassins' Guild. Deadly, ruthless, and able to kill anyone with a wave of his hand – or with his own wicked blades if he chose to. Everyone in my gang knew it. And yet they all pulled weapons on him and blocked his way to me without hesitation. What in Nemanan's name had I done to deserve such loyalty?

Meeting my gaze from across the crowd, Shade raised his eyebrows. When I found a slight smirk lurking on his lips, I decided that it was high time to settle some old scores. Inside, I was cackling. High time indeed.

"Let him through," I said.

My gang members stepped aside to let him pass but didn't lower their weapons because technically, I had only told them to let him through, not to stand down. Lifting a lazy hand,

I twitched two fingers at the assassin. His eyebrows rose even further. For a moment he remained standing there by the door, but when I made no move to approach him, he shook his head and strode across the floor. His well-honed muscles shifted with lethal grace as he moved.

Yngvild and Vania flicked their gaze to me. I gave them a nod. Still gripping their respective weapons—a huge battle axe and a long sword—they withdrew to the staircase again. Locking eyes with Shade, I jerked my chin at the empty table next to me.

"Blades on the table," I said.

He came to a halt in front of my booth and, with calculated slowness, turned to look at the indicated table before shifting his gaze back to me and narrowing his eyes. "You do remember that I am the High King of Pernula, right? I have an *army* at my command."

A challenging smirk spread across my face as I lifted my arms in a cocky gesture to motion at the room full of armed underworlders. "Where's your army now?"

Staring wide-eyed at me, he let out a surprised laugh. I jerked my chin at the table again.

"Blades on the table."

Shade held my gaze for another few seconds before reaching for his swords. The whole tavern tensed up. I understood the feeling because even I wasn't entirely sure whether he did it to actually put his swords on the table or to run me through with them. Something incredibly dangerous glinted in his eyes as he placed them carefully on the empty tabletop next to us. Oh I was going to pay dearly for this later. But it was so worth it. And I wasn't even done yet.

Once he had deposited his blades in the indicated spot, he turned back to me. I kicked out the chair from under the table. It scraped against the floor before wobbling to a halt. I nodded at it.

"Sit."

His mouth dropped open just a tiny bit. It was the worst placed seat in the whole room because he would have to sit with his back completely unprotected and a whole gang of armed underworlders behind. Exactly what he had forced me to do in the Black Hand tavern back in Keutunan all those years ago. My challenging smirk deepened.

Shade dropped into the chair and locked eyes with me. "Been waiting a long time to do this, have we?"

"Just returning the favor."

His black eyes glittered dangerously. "There will be hell to pay for this later."

With that wicked grin still on my face, I raised my chin. "Come try it."

A dark laugh slipped from his lips. I matched it with an evil smile before motioning for my gang to stand down. Clothes rustled and furniture scraped as the room sat back down. Bracing my forearms on the table, I leaned forward and met the Shade's gaze.

"So, what do you want, High King of Pernula?"

"I heard you got into smuggling."

"I did."

"How about branching out from jewelry to guns?" The arrogant smirk that had lingered on his lips disappeared and was replaced by a grim expression. "We'll need guns in the war to come."

Straightening, I raked my fingers through my hair and released a long sigh. "Yeah, we will. How's it going? With Elaran and the armies, I mean."

"All three of them have very different fighting methods so getting them all to move and work together without getting in each other's way will take a bit of work." Shade shrugged. "But Elaran is good. He already has the respect of all the soldiers."

"I'm not surprised."

A lopsided smile spread across Shade's lips. "Did you know he even turned down my offer for him to stay in Blackspire? He insisted on staying in the barracks by the west wall with the rest of the wood elves so that it would be easier to get to the training field he's set up outside the walls."

I chuckled. "Of course he did."

Pots clanked from the kitchen. Yngvild and Vania tensed up where they still stood by the stairwell but relaxed again when they saw Helena pop out of the door with arms full of plates. I straightened the stack of papers next to me.

"So, how about becoming a gun smuggler?" Shade said.

"Sure."

"Good." He nodded at me. "I'll set you up with my contacts back in Keutunan."

To be honest, this was a pretty fantastic opportunity. Guns were very lucrative and it would also serve to break the Rat King's monopoly even more. But the fact that it was Shade suggesting it and that he had come to me for it made me more than a little suspicious. He always had fifteen different schemes up his sleeve and it was impossible to tell what his endgame was.

"I don't mind running guns but..." I narrowed my eyes at him. "If they're your contacts, why aren't you just doing it yourself?"

Amusement glittered in his eyes. "Suspicious, are we?"

I shot him a glare.

He chuckled but then straightened and folded his hands on the table. "The reason I decided that you would be the best person for this is because I don't think the upstanding citizens of Pernula are quite ready for a smuggler king just yet."

"Ah." I huffed a short laugh. "So if the smuggling is discovered, I take the heat."

"Correct."

"I see." While tracing circles on the table with my finger, I looked up at him with a lazy smile. "So, what's in it for me?"

He raised his eyebrows. "Apart from helping us win the war against the star elves?"

Of course I had planned on running his guns regardless because we had to win the war against Queen Nimlithil. But the High King of Pernula and Master of the Assassins' Guild had come to *me* with a request. There was no way I'd let this opportunity slip through my fingers. I shrugged.

"Yeah, apart from that, of course."

Shade locked those intense black eyes on me. "I'll actually buy the guns from you instead of seizing them as illegal property."

I met his stare. "How generous."

For a moment, neither of us spoke. We just continued watching each other from across the table full of paper, candles, and mugs. Then, he loosed a breath. Amusement, and something I could've sworn looked a lot like approval, swirled in his eyes.

"And I'll owe you a favor."

The grin on my face widened. "Done."

Pushing aside a half empty mug of ale, I reached a hand across the table. Shade took it. His warm calloused hand held mine in a firm grip for a few seconds before he withdrew again. Outside, a wagon rattled down the road.

I slumped back on the dark green cushions again. "You know, it's so—"

"This is what happens to anyone who deserts and joins the Oncoming Storm!" a man's voice bellowed from outside the tavern. "Courtesy of the Rat King!"

A heavy thud sounded. Followed by wheels rattling quickly over stone. I shot to my feet. The rest of the tavern was already moving and the table closest to the door had darted outside to see what the thud had been. Yngvild and Vania fell in behind me as I swept through the room. I was only halfway to the door when the table who had gone outside returned. My heart stopped.

Red Demon Rowan hung limply between their arms. Her eyes fluttered open and closed like erratic butterflies. Blood coated her whole body. I sprang across the room as my gang members gently laid her on the floor just inside the door. Running quick eyes over her, I took in the state of her body. Dread welled up my throat.

Not caring who obeyed the order, I stabbed a hand towards the front door. "Don't let them get away! I want at least one of them alive!"

As Vania, Yngvild, and a dozen others sprinted out the door, I snapped my eyes to Shade who had just skidded to a halt next to me.

"And you, I'm cashing in that favor right now! I want a doctor for my gang. Someone I can call on at any time. Starting *right now*!"

"Done." A sleek black streak shot through the crowd as he disappeared out the door.

A strained wet cough racked Rowan's body. I had no idea what was happening in the rest of the tavern. All I could see was the copper-haired woman before me. Blood leaked from shallow gashes across both her arms but the worst two wounds were elsewhere. A long slash across her abdomen was quickly turning her shirt crimson and I could barely see her face behind the red mask of blood. Someone had cut a long line from her forehead, through her eyebrow and then down her cheek.

"Don't you dare die on me," I said.

Rowan's eyes went in and out of focus. I slammed a fist into the floorboards, making the wood vibrate from the force.

"Hey! Do you hear me?" I growled. "I didn't drag your ass through a burning building just so you could die on me two years later." Slamming my fist into the planks again, I locked eyes with her. "Do you hear me? You are not dying."

"You really are..." Another wet cough racked her body as she smiled up at me through the blood. "...a violent one."

Despite the awful situation, I laughed. It was a desperate pleading sound. When I'd rescued her from that burning warehouse two years ago, I had slapped her. Twice. It had been to keep her conscious. She had informed me that I was a violent one, which I of course already knew. My anxious gaze flicked over her body again. A slap wouldn't solve the problem this time. We needed a skilled doctor otherwise she was going to die.

This is what happens to anyone who joins the Oncoming Storm, they'd said. Fury spread like blue flames through my body. If I'd had my powers, I could've razed a whole street to the ground with the intense rage that burned inside me. Someone was going to die for this. I glanced down at Red Demon Rowan bleeding out on my floor. But it would not be her. I swore to the God of Death I would send a whole host of souls to him as an offering if he did not claim her tonight. Because, by all the gods and the demons in hell, someone was going to die for this.

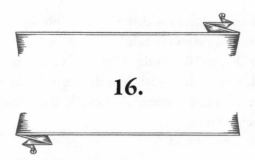

16.

Blood coated my forearms like red gloves. With rage and insanity dancing in my eyes, I fixed them on the man tied to the chair before me. I slashed another cut across his arm.

"I am running out of patience," I growled. "Where is your gang's headquarters?"

"P-please," he stuttered.

"You are going to die." I flung out an arm and pointed at the two dead bodies next to us in the darkened alley outside the Black Emerald. Blood dripped from the edge of my knife. "Just like your friends. The only question is how much you will suffer before I finally let you die." My voice lowered to a deadly whisper. "Where is the Blue Sword's headquarters?"

"Down by the d-docks. At the–"

"Liar!" I snapped. Placing my hands over his arms, I leaned down until I was close enough to feel his erratic breaths on my face. "Don't you think I can tell when people are lying to me?" A promise of violence shone in my eyes. "You have one more chance. Or this is going to be a very long night for you."

He sucked in a shuddering breath but then slumped back in his chair. "In the Outer Ring. West side. The freestanding house next to the tannery with the crooked roof."

"Thank you." Madness dripped from my lips as I smiled down at him. "I'll see you in hell."

I slit his throat. He was dead before I'd even turned around on the dark stones slick with blood. Yngvild, Vania, and the dozen others who had captured the now dead men had formed a half circle behind me.

"Get everyone," I said.

Vania tied her blond hair behind her before whirling around to carry out my orders.

"What do we do now?" Yngvild asked.

The row of underworlders parted before me as I stalked out of the darkened alley. Blood dripped from the blades in my hands.

"Now, we get revenge."

THE MOONLIT STREET lay silent and still as we passed a tannery with a crooked roof. I turned to the army of underworlders that had amassed behind me and motioned for them to wait. They obeyed without question.

A freestanding house rose from the shadows as I snuck forward. Its wooden walls had been painted a dark blue color. Before I came into view of the guards who no doubt watched the front door, I slunk into a side alley and skirted around the building until I approached it from the side. Two figures became visible on the slightly raised porch. I sprinted towards the nearest wall. Pressing myself against the rough wood, I waited for an alarm to sound. Nothing. They hadn't seen me. I started up the wall and climbed halfway to the roof before changing direction and moving towards the front of the building.

"–at first but now..." a soft voice cut through the darkness as I moved closer to the guards. "This'll for sure move our gang up the ladder."

"If they managed to deliver the message," another voice muttered. "Just dumping the body on her doorstep doesn't take this long. They should've been back by now."

Moving silent like a wraith, I positioned myself right above them. The two unsuspecting guards continued discussing how pleased the Rat King would be with their gang for carrying out his orders, all while death stalked them from above. I let go of the wall.

A soft thud sounded as I landed between them. Whipping my arms up, I shot the stilettos from my sleeves and rammed them into the side of their necks. They didn't even have time to look surprised before their bodies collapsed on the planks. While the light dimmed from their eyes, I wiped my blades and retracted them again before letting out a long whistle. My gang crept out of the shadows but the rage boiling in my blood didn't want to wait. I kicked open the door.

The two men closest to the entrance dropped to the floor with throwing knives sticking out of the back of their heads before the door had even banged against the wall inside. Shouts rang out. Blue curtains and pillows were flung away as the people seated in the expensively furnished living room scrambled to their feet to meet the demon who had barged through their front door. Steel sang as swords were drawn. I yanked two more throwing knives from my shoulder holsters.

Men shoved cushioned chairs aside while forming a semi-circle before me. Upstairs, feet thudded against wooden planks. With insanity dancing over my feral smile, I crouched into an attack position and spun the blades in my hands.

"Come on then," I growled.

They attacked. Roars vibrated off the painted walls as the row of armed men descended on me. I hurled the knives towards the two in the middle. Their heads snapped back as the blades buried themselves in their eyes but I didn't stop to study my handiwork. Instead, I snatched up two more and flung them as well. Another pair of attackers went down just as the remaining ones reached me.

A huge battle axe cleaved the face of the closest man. Yngvild loosed a battle cry and swung his heavy weapon into the charging men again. Behind him Vania and the rest of my gang poured through the open door and flooded the room. I yanked the hunting knives from their sheaths right as another wave of the Blue Sword gang sprinted down the stairs to swell the ranks of their companions on the bottom floor.

Ducking under the strike of a long sword, I twisted inside the man's guard and rammed a knife into his heart. A squelching came from his chest as I pulled out the blade before shoving his body aside. The battle spread out as the rest of my gang members barreled through the door and engaged the swarm of attackers. I jumped the nearest blue sofa to get at the ones in the back. Wood groaned in distress as I landed on the low table on the other side and ran across it before pushing myself into a flying attack. Terrified shrieks vibrated off the delicate paintings as I flew towards the three men hiding in the corner.

My knees connected with the man in front and the impact sent him tumbling back into the other two. All four of us went down in a tangle of limbs and steel. I threw out my arms and stabbed at the two men to my sides. One of my knives went wide and buried itself in the planks but the other one struck home. A sharp thud, a loud crack, and a wet squish sounded. I yanked the blade from the right-hand man's throat and drew it across that of the one whose ribcage I had broken when he slammed into the floor with me on top of him.

The man on the left screamed and scrambled away while swinging his sword at me. Since my other hunting knife was still stuck in the floorboards, I was forced to let go of it in order to evade his strike. Rolling over the corpses of the other gang members, I got clear before the sword struck. The remaining man stared in horror as his weapon hit his dead friends. I jumped to my feet before he could recover and slashed my knife across his throat. He crumpled to the ground on top of the other two.

My corner of the room was clear for a moment so I used the time to heave a few deep breaths and to yank my other hunting knife from the floorboards. On the other side of the room, Yngvild and Vania fought with such synchronization that I just gaped at them for a second. Vania, sleek as a snow leopard, darting in and out of her attackers' guards while Yngvild kept her protected with blows powerful enough to rattle the very walls.

It was such an impressive display of fighting skills that I almost missed the ambusher sneaking up behind me. Almost.

Twisting down and around, I evaded his swing and rammed my knife into his exposed wrist as it went wide over my head. He bellowed in pain and the sword clattered to the ground beside me. His screaming came to an abrupt end as I slit his throat with my other blade. Blood coated my hands and knives. I wiped them on the dark blue curtain next to me so that I would have a better grip before I advanced on the stairs.

All the gang members who had thundered down them to provide backup had already reached the bottom floor and were locked in battle with my people so I managed to slip onto the staircase unchallenged. Clanking steel, screams, and grunts echoed between the painted walls downstairs but the second floor was quiet. Suspiciously quiet. Staying close to the wall, I slunk up the steps on silent feet.

Another living room waited at the top of the landing. Keeping my head low, I scanned the room. Candles flickered on desks made of pale wood and chairs stood crisscrossed across the space as if the occupants had left them in a hurry. Which they probably had. Since I'd showed up with my gang to kill them all.

A few more couches in dark blue fabric stood pushed against the wall on the other side and curtains of the same color hung limp around the windows. Empty. I glanced at the corridor leading further into the building. There were probably bedrooms that way. Tilting my head up, I tried to see up through the ceiling to the top floor. I should probably have swept this floor before heading up there but I had a feeling that it would be empty and my final target would be hiding upstairs.

Still staying low, I snuck into the living room and then towards the second flight of stairs. No groaning wood betrayed me as I climbed them. With a quarter of the way to go, I paused and pressed myself into the wall. Straining my ears, I listened.

Nothing. Not a single sound came from whatever rooms lay at the top. Only moonlight fell across the planks and illuminated the floor above me. I waited another few seconds and then...

There! Leather creaked softly. It was a mere whisper in the night air but with the battle still contained to the bottom floor, I'd been able to hear it. So, there were people waiting for me upstairs. I crept forward.

Since I had no idea what the layout was up here, I would have to risk a quick glance before I left the safety of the stairs. Reaching the final few steps, I peeked onto the landing.

A crossbow bolt whizzed past me. I yanked my head back just as the bolt struck the wood behind me with a sharp thud. *Shit.* If they had ranged weapons, I would never make it up there without getting skewered. But at least my quick peek had revealed the enemies that waited for me.

In the hallway beyond the stairs, there had been six men standing guard before a plain wooden door. If I'd had my powers, I could've created dark clouds to obscure their vision or thrown a blast at them from here. I shook my head. Thinking about that right now was pointless. I would just have to work around the problem. Sticking my fingers into my belt pouch, I pulled out a smooth round object. And I had just the thing.

I threw the orb in my hand. Glass shattered against wood while I flattened myself against the stairs. A deafening explosion reverberated throughout the hallway. I grinned as men screamed and stomped above. It was so nice to once again have easy access to Haber and his bloody brilliant inventions.

Yanking out my hunting knives again, I darted from the stairwell. The three closest men had been killed by the exploding orb and the remaining three were so busy staring at their injuries and trying to put out the fire licking the floor before them that they didn't see me until it was too late. Leaping across the flames, I spun midair and slashed my blades through the throats of the two injured men in front. The third one jerked up from trying to stop the fire from devouring his pant leg just in time to see me ram a dagger into his heart. A surprised moan slid from his lips before he collapsed on the floor.

Flames still licked the wood behind me so I paused long enough to stomp them out. If I needed to get back out this way, it would be really inconvenient if the corridor was on fire. Once I was satisfied that I wouldn't have to wade through a sea of flames on my way out, I turned towards the door. After drawing a deep breath, I threw it open and darted into the room.

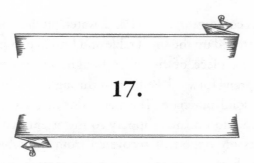

17.

The Blue Sword's gang leader stood in the middle of a lavish bedroom. I flicked my gaze across the room. Dark blue curtains fluttered in the breeze from the open window behind him while candles burned atop a nightstand next to a large four-poster bed. Apart from the man before me, there was no one else here. The middle-aged gang leader crouched into an attack position and spun his weapon in his hand. It was a sword made of something that gave it a pale blue color. I suppressed a sudden urge to laugh. Could he have been any more literal when picking a name for his gang?

He shot across the floor. I darted to the side and kicked a chair in his direction. Moving with fluid grace, he sidestepped it and swung his sword towards my head. It cleaved the air with a whoosh. I rolled to my feet after the dive I had executed to evade the strike and swiped at his ribs. Metal clashed as he brought his blade up to stop it. Yanking my other hand up, I stabbed at his side but he was already moving.

Steel glinted in the flickering candlelight as the Blue Sword's gang leader whirled around and drew his blade in a swift circle. I had to throw myself backwards to avoid having my gut split open. Ceramic shattered on the floor as I accidentally stumbled into a table containing a bowl and water pitcher. Shifting my knives, I snatched up the small table and hurled it at him.

The flying piece of furniture bought me a few precious seconds. I sprang forward. Panic shot through me as my left boot didn't find solid purchase. The water sloshing across the floor had made the floorboards slippery so my attempted attack fell short just as my opponent recovered from the table that had crashed into him. Praying that I was fast enough, I twisted out of reach when he swung again. Pain flashed through my body. Blood welled out of a shallow cut across my collarbone and ran down my chest. I barely had time to register it before he swiped at me again.

While trying to push out the rising panic, I retreated towards the bed. This wasn't going to work. He was way too skilled with that damn blue sword for me to win this in a straight-up fight. Ducking another strike, I flicked my gaze across the room. *There.* Since my mind had been preoccupied with schemes, I reacted a fraction of a second too late.

The sword-wielder before me slammed his blade towards my head. I threw up both hunting knives to block it but they failed to push it off completely. A hiss ripped from my throat as the sharp edge sliced along my left forearm on its way down. I stuck my knives back in their sheaths and threw myself across the bed right before his next blow struck.

Dark blue fabric rumpled as I rolled over the sheets and dropped into a crouch on the other side. Wood vibrated. My opponent roared as he yanked his sword from the bedpost it had struck instead his true target. Blood ran down my left arm and dripped from my fingers but I snatched up a burning candle from the nightstand and threw it at him.

White wax splattered across his chest. He loosed another furious roar as the still burning candle thudded to the floor between his boots. I hurled the vial I had pulled from my belt pouch while yanking a throwing knife from its holster. Glass shattered and a whoosh sounded. As dark smoke filled the room, I threw the blade. And then another. And another.

Three soft thuds sounded, followed by a much louder one. I slumped down on the rumpled bed and waited for the darkness around me to dissipate. Since I couldn't see through Haber's blackout powder either, it would've been impossible to hit my opponent once I'd thrown the vial. I glanced at the flickering flame cast by the candle on the floor. If not for *that*. With the light marking his location, I had a target to aim for. And besides, I'd thrown three knives. I figured at least one of them must've hit.

Once the black smoke had finally cleared, I heaved a deep sigh and pushed myself off the dark blue sheets. On the floor in front of the bed lay the Blue Sword's gang leader. One blade sticking out of his throat and two in his chest. Huh. Pretty decent aim, all things considered. I strode towards him and bent down.

"You know, you would've won in a fair fight," I said as I yanked the knife from his throat. "But see, here's the thing. I don't fight fair."

The dead man of course couldn't answer. Blowing out a deep sigh, I scrubbed my hands over my face in a weary gesture but then frowned when something wet smeared all over it. I lowered my hands again. Right. The wound. I shook my head but didn't bother wiping off the red streaks my bloody hands had painted across my face. I was already covered in blood anyway.

After retrieving my other knives, I stalked back towards the door. Heavy footsteps thundered up the stairs across the corridor. I pulled out my hunting knives but put them back when a muscled man with dark brown hair tied back in a bun appeared on the landing. The battle axe in his hands was slick with blood.

Wild blue eyes met mine. "Clear?"

I nodded. "Yeah, they're all dead. Downstairs?"

"All clear. Though we kept a few alive in case you had questions."

"No questions." I started down the stairs, fury still blazing in my eyes. "Only a message."

A couple of bodies littered the halls of the second floor. So, there had been people hiding there after all. Good thing they hadn't gone upstairs to help out the friends that I'd blown up. Or maybe that was why they hadn't come.

Wood vibrated underneath my feet as I stalked down the final steps to the bottom floor with Yngvild close behind. The living room was a mess. Overturned chairs and couches joined broken tables and bits of shattered pottery on the floor. Well, that and bodies. Lots of bodies. Splatters of red clung to everything that had once been blue.

While I went about finding the throwing knives I'd used early in the fight, I swept my gaze across the dead men. Relief and satisfaction coursed through me when I realized that none of them were mine. The element of surprise had been on our side, as had vastly superior numbers. Good.

"Get everyone outside," I said.

The battered and bloodied members of my gang who'd lingered inside nodded and started towards the door. I shifted my gaze to Yngvild. The battle frenzy in his eyes had died down and he now watched the room with an air of steady calm around him.

"The survivors," I began, "I want them conscious and outside."

"Got it."

While the rest of my gang made their way out the door, I turned and took the stairs two at a time. Eerie calm hung like a soundless void over the now empty house. Once I'd reached the top floor again, I strode straight to the gang leader's room. He was still lying dead on the floor. Moving to the side table I'd knocked over, I broke off one of its thin legs before stalking to the curtains. I ripped the blue fabric from its fastenings and twined a scrap around the table leg.

The candle I'd thrown to mark my target still spluttered on the floor. I picked it up and put the flame to the cloth. Fire spread across it with a faint crackling. With a steady hand, I set fire to the bedding. And then the remaining curtains. The crackling in the room grew louder. I started towards the door.

Making a split-second decision, I snatched up the long blue sword as I passed its dead owner. I drew the burning torch along the wall as I made my way towards the stairs. Only some parts of it caught fire but I knew that it would spread soon enough.

After setting the curtains by the landing aflame, I made my way downstairs. The dark blue cushions in the sofa were next. I made a slight detour and darted into two of the closest bedrooms to start a fire with their sheets as well before I finally stalked down to the bottom floor. Here, I took my time.

Beginning in the back of the living room, I put everything that would burn to the torch. Paper, curtains, and cushions. It all went up in flames. The whole room around me hissed and crackled as orange flames licked the walls and the expensive furniture. I threw the torch on the table. Lifting the blue sword, I rested it over my shoulder as I strode out of the building.

Outside, my gang was waiting a safe distance away. Three bloodied men knelt in front of them but they weren't the only people watching who weren't mine. Faces peeked out of every window of the buildings surrounding us. Ordinary citizens who'd been awoken by the screams, and now the light dancing between the walls, and who wanted to see what it was all about.

"You tell everyone you meet," I bellowed into the night, "that the Oncoming Storm does not forgive."

Locking eyes with the three survivors on their knees, I flipped over the blue sword in my hand and drove it straight into the porch. It vibrated as it sank into the wood. A grave marker. A threat. And a promise.

"You tell everyone you meet," I repeated. Striding forward, I threw out my arms to indicate the burning building behind me. "*This* is what happens to anyone who dares touch any of my people!"

The sound of popping wood echoed into the night as flames burst from the windows and reached for the darkened heavens. Yanking out my hunting knives, I stabbed one of them in the direction of the Blue Sword survivors. They shrank back against the stones.

"You *hurt* one of mine, I will kill ten of yours." Rage and insanity twisted on my blood-smeared face as I threw my blades out and turned in a slow circle. "You *kill* one of mine and I will burn down your fucking building with you in it!"

A boom rang out as part of the house collapsed. Orange embers sailed into the dark sky when the flaming timbers crashed to the stones.

"No one touches my people." My voice was a feral growl drawing out each syllable. "No one."

True terror marred their faces as I prowled towards the three kneeling survivors. My hand shot out and yanked the middle one to his feet. Even though he was taller than me and I had to crane my neck to meet his eyes, he stared at me as if I was a fire-breathing demon from hell. Still keeping my grip on his shirt, I drew his face closer to mine.

"You tell everyone that," I said in a voice dripping with lethal calm, "and maybe, *maybe*, I won't hunt you down."

Not daring to look away, he nodded with quick jerky motions. I let go of his collar and flicked a hand.

"Get out."

He didn't even wait for his friends to climb to their feet before he sprinted away. The other two weren't far behind.

Vania and Yngvild, followed by the rest of my gang, fell in behind me as I strode away from the burning building. A plume of black smoke rose towards the star-speckled sky. If you wanted to send a message, you had to make sure people heard it. Another boom echoed between the walls as more of the house collapsed. And after this, I was pretty sure that everyone would've understood my message. No one messed with my people.

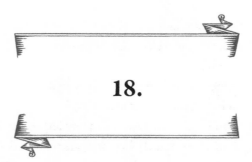

18.

"You look like hell."

I snorted. "You're one to talk."

After closing the door behind me, I strode across the floor and dropped into the chair that had been left by the bed. I had gotten my wounds dressed last night and I'd managed to clean off some of the blood but after that, I'd collapsed on the couch and fallen asleep in my battle torn clothes. Dried blood, dust, and ash still coated me when I finally woke up about half a day later.

"How are you feeling?"

Red Demon Rowan cast me an amused look. "I've been better."

"Right. Stupid question." Worry creased my forehead as I motioned at the bandage covering half her face. "How's your eye? Can you still see?"

She reached up to touch it but then winced in pain when the motion disturbed the wound across her abdomen so she let it drop again. "Yeah, I can still see. I'm gonna have a wicked scar down over it though."

The tightness in my chest loosened slightly. I met her one visible eye while an afternoon breeze filled the room with air smelling of warm spices.

"I'm sorry."

"Why are you sorry?'"

Still holding her gaze, I waved a hand over her bandaged body. "Because this happened because you sided with me."

"No." She shook her head. "This happened because the Rat King is an insecure piece of shit. You have no idea what I've done to piss him off before you got back. Trust me, it was only a matter of time before something like this happened."

I didn't agree with her at all but I decided it was best not to argue with gravely wounded women currently stuck in a house that wasn't theirs so I just blew out a soft sigh.

A grin tugged at Rowan's lips. "And besides, I think this scar across my eye will make me look rather badass, don't you?"

My mouth drew into a smile as well. "It'll enhance the Red Demon vibe for sure."

She laughed but it quickly turned into a coughing fit. I reached for the mug of water that had been left on the bedside table. Once her coughs had died down, I held it to her lips while she drank. The mug produced a soft thud as I put it back on the table.

Rowan cleared her throat. "Thanks."

"Anytime."

"Not just for the water. Or for letting me stay at the Black Emerald."

I threw her a mischievous grin. "Well, the doctor said we can't move you yet so I didn't really have much of a choice, did I?"

She huffed another laugh and shook her head but then leveled a green eye full of seriousness on me. "Thank you. For burning your favor from the High King on me. That can't have come cheap. And for that brutal retaliation on my behalf. I hear it was pretty epic."

My grin turned evil. "Yeah, I think they got the message."

"Is it true, then? That you obliterated the whole Blue Sword gang and burned their headquarters to the ground?"

"I left three of them alive to spread the word, but yeah." I ran a hand over the dried blood on my forearm. "When I have something to say, I make sure that people hear it."

Another huff of laughter made it past her lips, followed by some more coughing. When it stopped, she turned her head on the pillow to study me again. "It sucks, doesn't it? Being a leader. Being responsible for people."

Now it was my turn to let out an exasperated chuckle. "Yeah, it really does."

Voices of chatting people drifted in through the open window from the street below while furniture scraped against the floor in the tavern underneath us. I leaned back in the chair and released a long exhale. For a moment, the two of us just listened to the sounds of other people going about their lives. When Rowan finally broke the silence, her voice was softer than I'd ever heard before.

"I owe you," she said. "More than I can repay. Me, my crew, if you ever need anything, we've got your back."

A small smile drifted over my lips as I reached out and placed a hand over hers. After squeezing it lightly, I stood up.

"Well, you can start repaying me by not dying on me." I threw her a wicked grin over my shoulder as I strode towards the door. "So hurry up and get better."

Her chest shook with a few puffs of laughter. "Yeah, I'll get right on that."

Once I'd closed the door behind me, I leaned back against the dark wooden wall and closed my eyes while letting out a long breath. Rowan had survived. I don't know what I would've done if she hadn't. People I cared about couldn't die because of me. They couldn't. That was why I'd gone so overboard with my vengeance last night. To make sure that no one ever dared go after my friends again.

Opening my eyes, I pushed off from the wall and made my way down the stairs. I hated this feeling. Hated caring about people. It was so damn stressful. And for every year that passed, I just seemed to pick up more and more people to care about. Liam, Bones and the Thieves' Guild back in Keutunan, Shade, the elves, Zaina and Norah, King Edward, Yngvild and Vania, Marcus, Red Demon Rowan.... The damn list kept growing all the time. And now I had the Black Emerald gang to worry about and keep safe too. Feelings. Such an inconvenience.

"How is she?" Yngvild asked as I joined them on the floor of the tavern.

"She's gonna pull through," I said.

Vania looked me up and down with observant blue eyes. "How are *you*?"

"I'll live." Weaving through the sea of table and chairs, I shrugged. "But after this, there'll be a lot less people who'll want to join us."

The two tall warriors flanking me exchanged a glance. Frowning, I flicked my gaze between them.

"What?"

"Actually, boss," Yngvild began as he led me towards the front door.

With suspicion rolling over me, I followed him. After placing his hand on the handle, he pushed it down and flung open the door. Golden light streamed inside. I raised a hand to my brow to shield my eyes before sticking my head through the opening and peering out the door.

The road was packed. I stared at the waiting people with wide eyes as a ripple went through the crowd and they all turned towards me.

"They're all here to join," Vania supplied.

"Yeah." Yngvild clapped a large hand on my shoulder. "Looks like people like how you run things. How you protect your own."

By all the gods, a whole street full of people who wanted to join my gang. Both gratitude and dread swirled inside me while a wry smile tugged at my lips. Yep. Being a leader definitely sucked.

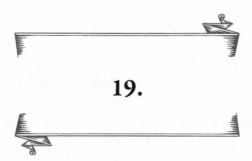

19.

Swords whizzed through the air as the two guards by the door whipped them towards the intruders. By the bar, I jerked my head up. Elaran threw a disinterested stare at the men pointing swords at him while Haela looked like she would've taken them up on that challenge if Haemir hadn't placed a hand on her arm. After discarding the sword-wielding humans as a non-threat, Elaran leveled his grumpy glare on me.

Rolling my eyes, I motioned for the two men currently guarding the entrance to the Black Emerald to stand down. The auburn-haired ranger didn't spare another glance at them before prowling across the floor but Haela sent a wide grin in their direction as they lowered their weapons. While the three elves approached, I passed my empty mug to Helena and twisted in their direction.

Elaran, drawing himself up to his full height as he came to a halt before me, crossed his arms and drew his eyebrows down. "I should never have taught you how to make a fire."

"Fire?" I let an innocent smile spread across my lips. "I have no idea what you're taking about."

"Storm." Haemir shot me a pointed look. "The barracks we're staying at are also located on by the wall on the west side."

"Ah." The innocent smile shifted into a grin. "So you saw that, huh?"

"Saw it?" Elaran huffed.

"We were on our way there to help put out the fire," Haemir explained.

The grumpy elf narrowed his eyes at me. "And we would have. If Shade hadn't stopped us."

Shade. So he *had* been there. After he'd returned to the Black Emerald with the doctor for Rowan, I'd told him to let me handle this on my own. Actually, that wasn't quite true. I had *ordered* him to stay out of my retaliation hit. To my complete and utter surprise, he'd actually obeyed. But apparently, he had followed me to watch the show.

"I thought I told you not to burn anything down," Elaran pressed on.

"Screw that." An expression of mock hurt descended on Haela's face as she turned to me. "I thought I told you not to get into any fun mischief without me."

Haemir heaved a sigh and shook his head at his sister. "I wouldn't exactly call that mischief."

She gave his arm a shove. "Technicalities."

"Yes, and *technically*," I shifted my gaze to Elaran and raised a finger in the air, "I didn't start any fires. I just made a small flame that was already burning a bit bigger."

A wide grin flashed over Haela's face as she elbowed her brother in the ribs while Elaran just muttered under his breath about troublesome underworlders. To my right, a large group of people thumped their palms on the tabletop in anticipation of a pair of rolled dice. I watched half of them straighten and pump their fists in the air in celebration before turning my attention back to the three elves.

"Do you wanna grab a drink or...?" I trailed off. Elaran wasn't the kind of person who would just come here to grab a drink when he had an army to train. I narrowed my eyes at him. "You're here on business."

"The..." He swept a suspicious gaze across the room and lowered his voice slightly. "The thing you asked me to look into, I've looked into it. I've found someone you should meet."

Hope sent a pulse through my body. Elaran had found someone who specialized in curses and who might know how to get my powers back. While trying not to let the giddiness I felt shine through, I approached Vania to let her know that I'd be out tonight and then darted to my room to get ready. After what I'd done to the Blue Sword, there was no such thing as being too careful so I strapped on all my blades and tools before heading back downstairs.

A short while later, the three elves and I were strolling through the darkened streets. Elaran was doing his best to look grumpy but I also found him assessing the wounds on my arm and collarbone with critical eyes. I pretended not to notice as I turned to Haela.

"So, how's the training exercises going?"

The constantly cheerful elf threw her black ponytail back behind her shoulder and fired off a beaming grin. "I love it! *This* is my kind of mission. Not sitting around tables discussing boring trade agreements or other tedious things that would put an insomniac to sleep."

"Those missions are important too," Haemir pointed out.

Haela slapped his chest with the back of her hand. "They're boring. But now we get to shoot and spar and do all the fun things!"

"We're training so that we won't be conquered by the star elves," Elaran grumbled.

Throwing her arms in the air, Haela blew out an exasperated breath. "Always with the gloom and doom, you two. Seriously. Do you hate fun or something?"

I chuckled, as did Haemir, and even Elaran's lips twitched upwards in a smile. While Haela continued to regale me with her escapades among the human soldiers, we drew closer to the east side of the city walls.

"Hand it over!" a woman suddenly growled from a darkened alley on our right.

Casting a glance in the direction of the voice, I found a mixed group of men and women pointing raised weapons at two other underworlders. The outnumbered pair looked like they were about to fight back but then they just threw the brown bag they'd been clutching on the ground. It jingled as it landed in the dust before the ambushers' feet. Moonlight fell across the opening and made the precious contents glitter.

The elves looked to me questioningly but I just shook my head. This happened almost every time I went outside. Underworlders stealing from other underworlders, or screwing each other over in some other way, so that they could claw a little further ahead of the pack. It made me gag. A world that worked like that was not at all the kind of world I wanted to live in. Releasing a long sigh, I turned my attention back to the road ahead. Someone definitely had to do something about that once the Rat King was gone.

Silence fell while we continued our trudge towards our mysterious destination. I frowned at Elaran as he led us out through the gate to the docks and then steered us towards the far side of the harbor instead of continuing towards it.

Salt and seaweed filled the evening air as we made our way towards a large warehouse that sat apart from the rest of the area. No light flickered in the windows of the wooden structure.

I cast a glance between the wide sliding door and Elaran. "You sure this is the right place?"

"I'm the tracker, remember?"

Biting back the snarky reply on my tongue, I settled for a glare.

"The elf who lives here is said to be a bit... eccentric," Elaran continued as he grabbed the long handle and got ready to slide open the door. "But they say that if anyone knows about curses, it'll be her."

Wood groaned as he pulled open the entrance to the warehouse. Moist air filled with earthen aromas drifted out. The four of us exchanged a glance but then Haela just shrugged and strode across the threshold. We followed her.

Once we were all inside, the door groaned again. Twisting back around to see who of us had closed it, I instead found... nothing. I jerked back as panic flickered through my mind. The door was gone.

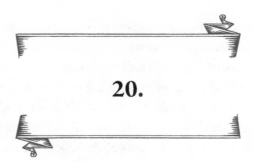

20.

A thick forest enclosed us on all sides. Every wall was covered in ivy and its dark green tendrils seemed to have swallowed the door. I tried to locate the way out again by pulling on the clingy plants but my efforts were useless. Only another layer of green appeared underneath the one I'd tried to peer through.

"Well then, tracker," I said and shifted my gaze to Elaran. "Now what?"

The grumpy elf was busy scowling at the inconvenient greenery around us so Haela answered for him. She stabbed an arm straight ahead.

"Now we go forward and see where this adventure takes us," she chirped.

"Why yes, let's walk straight into this magical forest that's been planted in a warehouse and apparently likes to eat doors." I let out a huff. "Because none of this is suspicious at all."

"Exactly," was all Haela said before she charged right into the bushes.

"Wait!" Haemir called as the rest of us scrambled to keep up with her.

Thick green leaves pressed in on all sides but the stubborn twin elbowed past them without hesitation. I flicked my gaze between the elves in front of me and the strange forest that grew inside this building as we followed the trail Haela made. Haemir kept urging his sister to be careful until he stopped dead in his tracks. I bumped into Elaran's muscled back as he screeched to a halt in order to avoid him.

"Haela," Haemir said. There was a sharp note of panic in his voice. "Haela! This isn't funny."

"What's going on?" I asked, trying to peer over Elaran's shoulder.

"She's gone," Haemir breathed.

The auburn-haired archer in front of me drew himself up and raised his voice. "Haela! Get back here. Now."

Only silence answered his command. The tall plants around us seemed to grow even larger. I pushed down the dread building in my chest.

"She's probably just up ahead and can't hear us because of the thick bushes," I said, but even I wasn't convinced by that flimsy explanation.

"Yeah." Haemir took off with hurried steps. "That's probably it."

"Hey, wait," Elaran protested but the black-haired twin was already moving.

I pushed myself to keep up with their long legs as Elaran strode after him. Leaves rustled around us as we shoved them out of the way but other than that, the whole warehouse was dead silent.

A violent string of curses broke the stillness. I slammed into Elaran's back again as he stopped abruptly midstride.

"He's gone too," the elf said.

"What?"

Elaran whirled around and grabbed me by the collar. "Stay close. Step exactly where I step and don't fall behind."

I would've slapped his hand away if it hadn't been for the panic that flared behind his eyes. So in the end, I just nodded. He let go of my shirt and turned back around again. Moving slowly, he took a step forward. I mirrored it.

We continued further into the warehouse. My heart thumped in my chest as the dense forest around us seemed to suck all the light out of the room. Where the hell were the twins?

A branch snapped behind me. I whipped my head around while continuing my path forward. Nothing. Only more green leaves filled the space behind my back. I turned around again.

"Elaran, I..."

I stopped. The elf was nowhere to be seen. When I'd jerked my head around, I had been so close behind him that I could almost feel the heat radiating off his body *and* I had continued walking while I looked behind. How was it even possible that I'd lost sight of him?

"Shit," I breathed.

Only a dead silent forest of dark green stared down at me as I turned in a helpless circle. My pulse sped up. What the hell was I supposed to do now?

Pale blue light shimmered to my right. I squinted at it. The light came from a flickering orb that floated in the air over a wide green leaf. I jerked back as another pale blue orb bloomed a few steps away from the first one. And then a third one lit up the darkness even further in. They were lighting a path. I took a step towards it.

"What the hell am I doing?" I slapped my forehead. "Yes, Storm, do follow the mysterious glowing orbs that just sprung to life out of bloody nowhere. They surely won't lead to some kind of trap. Idiot."

The forest around me stayed dark and still as I consider where to go instead. To my right, the floating lights taunted me with their illuminated path. I glanced at them.

"Oh what the hell." I threw my arms in the air and stalked towards the blue orbs.

I had absolutely no idea how else to get out of this warehouse so I might as well see where my stupidity took me next.

More glowing orbs flickered to life and guided me towards whatever fate this damn forest had in store for me. I stomped through the underbrush until the thick plants gave way to a small flat clearing. A large blue light burned over a pond in the middle.

"This has gotta be the stupidest thing I've ever done," I said as I made my way towards it.

The glowing orb moved up and down slightly over the clear blue water. I arched an eyebrow at it and waved a hand at the pond.

"Yeah, I'm not getting in that so whatever you need to do, you might as well get on with it."

When the blue light didn't respond, I clicked my tongue and scowled at it before edging closer to the water. Very carefully, I bent forward and squinted at it. The pond went black. I jerked back but vines had slithered up my legs and kept me trapped in place.

"Your only way out is to show me that you are pure of heart," a melodious voice came from the glowing blue orb above the pond.

Before I could reply, the watery surface transformed into a moving scene. It was in another forest and there were men in dark blue and silver uniforms fleeing in terror through the trees. And then a wraith. A girl wreathed in black smoke darting between them. Flashing steel and sprays of red blood. A memory.

"Is this you?"

I watched myself kill King Adrian's guards in the forest outside Keutunan after we had assassinated the king. "Yeah, it is."

The scene changed. Lord Makar stood tied to a tree across a clearing. I watched myself stalk across the grass, hurl ten knives into the trunk around his face, and then finally slit his throat. Blood ran down and soaked his shirt as I returned to Liam and the elves on the other side.

"Is this you?" the voice repeated.

"It is."

Once again, the old memory fizzled out and another took its place. This time, I was striding through columns of dead trees with my arms held out. Fire flickered beside me as I put the dry trunks to the torch and burned the Salt Woods to the ground.

"Is this you?" it said once more.

Right. A sentient bush was asking me if I was the one who'd burned down what was probably one of its forest friends. This would probably end well.

I blew out a sigh. "Yeah, that's me."

"Killing and burning are not evidence of a pure heart. Do you deny that you have done these things?"

The pond flickered between the three scenes while I studied it. "No."

"You're a murderer of plants and people. Actions that will doom you to hell. How will you prove to me that you are pure of heart?"

Letting out a soft chuckle, I tore my eyes from the pond and trained them on the glowing orb. "I don't know what your deal is, but I've known for a very long time that I'm going to hell. If you want someone with a pure heart, you're talking to the wrong person. Mine is as cold and black as they come." I shrugged. "I'm a villain. And I'm fine with that. So if you're not gonna show me the way out of here then stop wasting my time."

Silence fell over the small clearing. I studied the vines around my legs, trying to estimate their thickness and if I would be able to cut through them fast enough to run before new ones sprouted. Just as I was about to pull out my hunting knives, the greenery around me shifted.

The vines unfurled from my legs and snapped back into the ground while the bushes to my left leaned aside to reveal a wide path. I glanced at the blue orb but it had winked out of existence.

"Uhm, thanks?" I said.

Not sure what to make of all this, I just shrugged and started down the path. Firelight, normal orange firelight, flickered in the distance. Maybe it led out. Maybe it led straight to hell. Who knew? But I had no other options so all I could do was follow it.

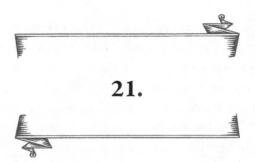

21.

The path emptied out in another, much larger, clearing. Colorful fabric hung from the branches of thick trunks, a hammock made of vines swung between a couple of them as well, and logs created a square seating arrangement around an open fire. I gaped at it. What in Nemanan's name was going on here?

But before the God of Thieves could enlighten me, three more people stumbled out of the woodwork. Elaran, the twins, and I blinked at each other.

"Did you also...?" Haela began.

Haemir waved a hand in front of his face. "I do *not* want to talk about it."

Given the rather unflattering memories the pond had shown me, I was very curious about what the twins and Elaran had seen. But before I could ask them, that melodious voice drifted through the warehouse.

"I do apologize for the rather unfriendly welcome."

I whipped my head around in search of another glowing blue orb but found something else entirely. A wood elf wearing a long green dress that looked to be made of actual vines and flowers glided out of the bushes at the back of the clearing. Her long blond hair was infused with leaves and flowers and her face... Gods, her face. She had one of those extraordinarily beautiful faces that could make people kill each other, or themselves, just for the chance to look at her.

Haemir was actively gaping at her with his jaw halfway to his chest, as was Haela, but Elaran just scowled at her as if he'd seen better. A small smile tugged at my lips. In his heart, there was probably no one who could compare to Illeasia.

"But I had to see what kind of people you were," the gorgeous elf finished.

If that test had been to see what kind of people we were, then I was pretty sure I hadn't passed it. As if she had heard me, she turned her sparkling yellow eyes to me.

"You all passed the test."

I blinked at her.

"Yes, even you," she said. "The test wasn't to see if you were pure of heart. It was to see if you were true of soul. True to who you are. Regardless of who that might be. If any of you had lied and tried to deny the things I showed you, you would not have been allowed in here." She cocked her head. "You see, I have had quite enough of people who pretend to be one thing only to reveal their true colors later. I would much rather see the color up front." Her knowing eyes flicked to me. "Even if it is black. Though it might not be quite as black as you think."

While she approached the line we'd formed at the edge of the clearing, Elaran crossed his arms.

"I don't approve of mind games," he said.

"I know. And I am sorry." She stopped before us and plucked four leaves from her hair before holding them out to us. "Here. A gift for you as compensation."

Exchanging a glance, we all took the offered gifts. I frowned down at the large green blob in my hand for a few seconds and then shifted my gaze back to the beautiful wood elf.

"It's a leaf," I stated.

"Yes," she confirmed.

Haela was turning hers over in her hands. "What does it do?"

"If there is ever anything in the air that you do not want to breathe in, you can breathe through that." She smiled. "But use it wisely. It only works once."

Breathe through a leaf? What was I, a toad?

"Cool!" Haela said and fired off a beaming grin at the wood elf.

Shaking my head, I rolled up the leaf and stuffed it into one of my belt pouches. Eyes that seemed far too old to belong to someone who looked so young drifted over all our faces as the stunning elf studied us. I had a sudden urge to retreat into the greenery again but stood my ground as she finished her examination.

"Who are you?" Haemir asked, mirroring my own thoughts.

"Me?" She tilted her head again. "I am no one. And everyone. I am a relic from a time long gone. Waiting for the time to come again." Orange flames from the fire cast dancing shadows over her breathtaking face. "You can call me Vilya."

"We're here because we need your help, Vilya," Elaran said.

"I know. That is usually why people seek me out." Her brilliant white teeth glittered in the light as she smiled. "But it does not come for free. One truth in exchange for one question."

I frowned at her. "A truth?"

"Yes. You will share one truth, one important truth, that you have never told anyone and then you get to ask one question."

My three elven friends turned to look at me. I waved a hand in the air to tell them to wait. I needed to think. First, I had to figure out a truth that was important, that I hadn't told anyone, and that I would be willing to share with Elaran and the twins. Then, I also had to decide how to phrase the question.

If I just asked, is there a curse blocking my powers? Then, she could just reply that there was and I would be no closer to finding out how to break it. I had to really make the question count.

Tapping my foot on the grass, I massaged my brow while running through options in my head. Leather creaked as Elaran shifted his position next to me. At last, I straightened and gave Vilya a nod.

"Alright. One truth." I let out a long calming breath as my heart pattered against my ribs. "I hide it behind arrogance and snarky words but I'm actually terrified that I'm not enough... that I won't be enough to keep everyone I love safe when the war comes."

Next to me, Elaran and the twins turned slightly. I could feel their eyes on me but I didn't want to meet them so I kept my gaze on the gorgeous elf in front of me. She smiled sweetly.

"I accept your truth. Ask your question."

"How do I break the curse that is blocking my powers?"

This was the best possible phrasing I could come up with because she would have to both confirm that there was a curse blocking my powers and tell me how to break it. So, two answers for the price of one.

Her gaze turned pensive as she studied me. For a moment, only the popping of the logs in the fire and the slight rustle of leaves filled the silence. Vilya remained staring at me. Then, she closed the distance between us. Her soft hands were warm as she placed them against my forehead, my neck, and then over my heart.

"Yes, Ashaana, there is something blocking your powers," Vilya said, her delicate eyebrows creasing. "But it is not a curse. I do not know what it is so I cannot tell you how to break it. The source feels too..." She drew her elegant fingers down my cheek. "Modern. I cannot tell you how to break it but I can tell you with absolute certainty that you have not been cursed."

Not cursed? What in Nemanan's name was causing it then?

Vilya let her hand drop from my face and turned to the others. The vines and flowers covering her swayed slightly as she moved. "And you? Do you want to ask me anything? One truth for one question."

Haela looked uncharacteristically anxious as she shook her head with quick jerky motions. Her brother shook his head as well. The silence stretched for another few seconds and just when I was sure that none of the others were going to ask a question, a voice full of worry and exasperation cut through the air.

"Can I ask the question first to know if you can even answer it before I share the truth?" Elaran asked.

"No," Vilya said. "The truth first and then the question."

"And if you can't answer it?"

"That is a risk you will have to take. Your friend wasted her truth on a question I could not answer." Vilya gave him a sympathetic look. "It is a gamble. But if the question you want to ask is important enough for you, then you will have to risk it."

Elaran ran a hand over his tight side braid while uncertainty flickered in his eyes. Then, he let his hand drop and blew out a sigh.

"If it came down to a choice between Illeasia and Tkeideru, I don't know for certain what I would choose."

The twins and I stared at him. For Elaran, *Elaran* for Nemanan's sake, to admit something like that... He didn't meet our gazes and just kept his chin raised as he watched Vilya. I knew he wouldn't want my pity so I kept my face neutral but inside, my heart was breaking. The weight of those feelings he carried around in silence every day must be crushing. To even think about having to choose between his people and the one he loved... I prayed to any god who would listen that he would never have to make that choice.

"I accept your truth," Vilya said. "Ask your question."

"Will we win this war against Queen Nimlithil?"

More sympathy filled her face as she looked at him. "I cannot answer that because I do not know."

For a single second, regret and devastation washed over Elaran's face but then the tactical commander was back again as he gave her a tense nod. He had risked *that* truth for *that* question? By all the gods. I wanted to pull him into a hug and tell him that it would all be alright in the end, but I had a very strong feeling that he would put an arrow through my eye if I did that, so I kept quiet.

"But I will tell you this," Vilya said. "And listen carefully so that you remember it when the time comes." She locked eyes with Elaran. "There is a third way."

"A third way?" He frowned back at her. "To where? For what?"

"Remember that," was all she said before turning to the twins. "Are you sure you do not wish to ask any questions?"

"Yep." Haela held up her hands in front of her while Haemir nodded vigorously. "Completely sure."

Vilya nodded and swept her arms to the side. The thick foliage behind us creaked and rustled as it parted down the middle. A wooden sliding door waited on the other side of the wide path that now lay waiting for us.

"Thank you for your visit." A genuine smile spread across Vilya's gorgeous face. "And for your truths."

The four of us nodded in unison before turning around and starting back towards the door. Glaring at the dark green leaves and snaking vines, I waited for them to attack us and swallow us whole during the entire walk to the entrance but they only rustled slightly in a wind I couldn't feel.

When Elaran had finally slid the door closed behind us again and an actual breeze caressed my face, I found myself drawing a deep breath of relief.

"Uhm, guys," Haela said.

I turned from the warehouse to look at whatever it was that Haela wanted us to see. Blinking, I drew back.

Sunlight glittered across the water and painted the whole harbor in warm orange light. Fishermen were braving the waves and workers went about their daily chores while wealthy nobles strolled along the piers. It was morning.

"Were we inside that warehouse all night?" Haemir blurted out.

Not being able to take my eyes off the bright dawn we had walked into, I nodded. "Looks like it."

"By Nature's grace, we're going to be late to training." Elaran looked like he was about to sprint off but then he screeched to a halt and flicked his gaze between the three of us and the wooden building behind us. A flicker of uncertainty crept into his eyes. "What we saw and said inside that warehouse...?"

"Never happened," I finished.

"Agreed," all three elves confirmed with force.

A look of understanding passed between us. Elaran gave me a final nod before he took off towards the gate with Haemir close behind. Haela lingered for another moment.

"Interesting things always happen when you're around." She fired off a beaming smile and a mock salute before breaking into a trot as well. "Let me know if you've got any more mischief up your sleeve!"

The bright morning sun warmed my face as I watched the three elves disappear from view. This had definitely turned into an interesting night. Night. Gods, I still couldn't believe we'd been in there for hours. Whoever that wood elf in the warehouse was, she was a strange one. And she hadn't been able to tell me how to get my powers back but at least now I knew that I hadn't been cursed.

By all the gods, when did things like this become normal to me? I shook my head and started my trek down to the harbor as well. The days when I was just a random thief roaming the streets of Keutunan suddenly felt very far away.

Chatter hung over the docks as I reached the busy area and wove my way through the warehouses. The ordinary citizens of Pernula went about their morning business as usual while all the shady creatures of the night had probably scurried back into their holes again. Speaking of, when I got back to my gang I would need to–

"Storm!" a voice cut through the salt-tasting winds and pulled me from my scheming.

Whipping my head around, I found a blond warrior hurrying towards me. "Vania?"

"There you are. We've been trying to track you down for hours."

Suspicion crept into my mind and I flicked my gaze over the warehouses around us. "What's going on?"

Her face was grim as she jerked her head in the other direction. "You'd better come and see."

I followed the warrior in silence as we strode around the large wooden structure and towards a building on the other side. The storage we approached was a nondescript wooden thing but it was very familiar. Namely, because it was mine.

"Kildor discovered it this morning," Vania said as she led me towards the front door that had been left gaping.

Once we were inside the empty room, I turned to her. "Where are all the crates?"

"Gone."

"What do you mean *gone*?"

"Stolen. Every single piece of jewelry we stored here."

Irritation flashed through me like lightning. Stolen? People didn't steal from me. I was the thief. I was the one who did the stealing.

"The Rat King?" I asked.

Vania shrugged, but there were tight lines around her mouth. "We think so. Probably as payback for all the shops we've been robbing."

My boots echoed off the empty walls as I stalked back and forth across the room. "How did he even know about this place?"

"We don't know. But all our other storage sheds are intact."

Seagulls sent mocking squawks into the open doorway as they shot past in a cloud of white feathers. Tipping my head back, I closed my eyes and blew out an annoyed sigh. *Just because I take one night off. One night where I'm doing something other than trying to win my war against the Rat King and then something like this happens? That's it. I'm not going to focus on my missing powers until all this is settled. I have to focus on one mission at a time. I can't spread my efforts thin or I will fail both missions.* I tilted my head back down.

"Alright, the Rat King thinks he can steal from me?" A malicious smile spread across my lips. "I have just the thing."

Vania matched my wicked grin as we left the empty building behind and set course for the Black Emerald. Oh, the Rat King had no idea what he had just started. Schemes swirled in my mind as I strode towards the gate. But he was going to learn, in no uncertain terms, that you do not steal from thieves.

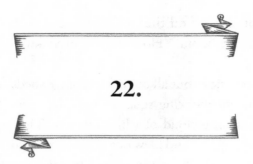

22.

Leather creaked as I shifted my weight on the beam. Next to me, the rest of the thieves with me did the same. Getting Yngvild, Vania, and the other warrior types to climb up here had been impossible so I'd had to adjust my plan slightly. While they lurked in the shadows further away, we sneaky types had been sitting atop the rafters in this large warehouse for hours while waiting for our prey. Metal clanked faintly as someone touched the chain across the door. They were here.

We all tensed up. I raised a hand to motion at them to wait but stuck the other into my belt pouch. While my fingers closed around a smooth object, the intruders finished picking the lock and removing the chain from the door. Wood groaned as they pulled it open.

"Remember," someone whispered down on the floor, "this is supposed to be her first gun shipment so take them all. I want her humiliated and in debt to her suppliers."

The rest of the people breaking into my warehouse murmured in acknowledgement as they slunk through the door and went straight for the crates stacked at the back of the room.

"And if any of her guards show up," the first voice continued, "kill them on sight."

Yua, the black-haired thief on the beam next to me, arched an eyebrow in my direction. I motioned for her to get ready. While she repeated the command to the others, I kept a close eye on the burglars below who had now made it all the way to the far wall. Creaking, followed by a sharp snap, echoed through the room as a thick lid was pried open.

"Uhm, boss?" The man who had forced open the box swung his head between it and his leader. "You sure this is the right place?"

"Of course it is. Several of our sources have gotten wind that this is where the Oncoming Storm stores her smuggled guns."

"But... it's empty."

More creaking and groaning of wood sounded as others pried open their crates. The leader finally left his place by the entrance and stalked across the straw-covered floor.

"Don't be ridiculous, they're probably just hidden. Have you–"

I gave the signal. Faint hissing sounds drifted through the room as six objects fell through the air. I threw myself down on the sturdy beam and pressed my body flat against its rough wooden surface while Yua and the rest of my thieves did the same. Glass shattered.

Six deafening explosions roared through the room. Covering my head and ears with my arms, I didn't dare look up as the exploding orbs we'd dropped flung fire across the warehouse. Searing hot air wafted towards us where we hid in the rafters and rolled over my body in thick waves. Once the screams that had been cut off by the loud booms had transformed into soft moaning accompanied by crackling flames, I lifted my head.

Bodies lay scattered across the floor below and fire licked the walls and empty decoy crates. Next to me, Yua stared at the scene with wide eyes. All my thieves seemed slightly terrified but none of them appeared to be hurt so I took it as a win. While the sound of stamping feet drew closer from outside, I motioned for us to climb back down.

My boots hit the floor right as Yngvild barreled through the door. He whipped his head around in search of potential enemies but lowered his battle axe slightly when none popped up.

"All dead?" he asked.

I waved a hand towards one corner. "I think there are some who are not quite dead yet over there."

Yngvild motioned at two sword-wielders to take care of it while the rest of the warriors lugged buckets of water inside to put out the fire. Vania joined us by the entrance and lifted a pale eyebrow at the flames and carnage before her.

"Very efficient."

"Right?" An evil smile flashed across my lips.

We had taken out an entire room of enemies without exposing ourselves to a single injury. I repeat: it was so nice to once again have easy access to Apothecary Haber and his brilliant inventions.

"All clear." The two sword-wielders at the back had woven their way through the room and made sure that everyone was dead before stopping next to us. "No one's breathing anymore. And the fire's out."

"Good." I strode to the closest body and yanked a small knife from his belt. "Then let's get out of here."

After all my thieves and warriors had exited the building again, I turned back towards the entrance. Leaving the door open so that people would see what lay inside, I instead stalked to the wall next to it. Paper rustled as I pulled out a short note from inside my vest. I twirled the dead man's knife in my hand before flipping it over and using it to nail the piece of paper to the wall.

Yngvild appeared behind me and read it over my shoulder. "*This is what happens to anyone who tries to steal from the Oncoming Storm.*" A laugh rumbled in his chest. "Short and to the point."

"Yep." I grinned. "Figured the bodies would do the rest."

Soft summer rain fell from the dark night sky as we started back towards the Black Emerald. The Rat King's minions were so gullible. A few whispers to some strategic people and suddenly their sources were all telling them that my first gun shipment would be stored here tonight. Honestly, fools like these give thieves everywhere a bad name. I shook my head as we passed through the harbor gate. *Amateurs.*

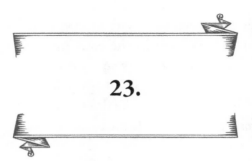

23.

"This is most likely a trap."

Twisting slightly, I turned to Vania. "I know."

The blond warrior was walking beside me with confident steps but her face held a grim expression and her hand rested on her sword. She was worried. On my other side, Yngvild lumbered steadily while his watchful blue eyes constantly flicked back and forth across the street ahead, scanning for hidden threats. A large portion of my gang trailed behind us. Uneasiness hung like storm clouds over our whole party. They were *all* worried.

"I still think you should've turned it down," Vania said.

"I couldn't." Turning my attention back to the darkened cobbled street ahead, I shrugged. "Not without looking like I was scared."

She gave me a tense nod. Vania and the rest of my gang might not like my decision, but they understood it.

The day after we'd dropped explosive orbs on top of the people trying to steal from me, the Rat King had sent a message. In it, he had claimed to want a meeting to find a way to put an end to these hostilities but we all knew that there was more to it than that. The Rat King would never give up the iron grip he had on the Underworld and he would not stop until I knelt at his feet and offered him my submission. Which we both knew would never happen. So whatever this meeting was about, it was most likely a trap of some form or other. That didn't change the fact that I still had to attend it, though.

The smell of rain on warm stones filled the air after the light summer rain that had blanketed Pernula last night and most of today. In the bright moonlight beaming down from the clear night sky, puddles shone like silver mirrors on the darkened streets. An anxious stillness hung over the area. Only the soft creaking of leather and rustle of weapons broke it as we made our way towards the huge square where the Rat King had tried to corner me two years ago. It had not ended well for him then, and it would not end well for him now.

Striding out of the alley mouth, I continued until I was sure that all my warriors had room to move into the square as well. They spread out like an armored wall behind me while I took in the area. Torches flickered along all four sides of the open space and another wall of people had gathered on the other side. A thin man at the front raised his arm.

All over the roofs on our side of the square, people popped up and leveled crossbows at us. I could almost feel the Rat King's smirk from all the way on the other side as he lowered his arm but no one in my gang panicked or so much as shifted nervously. I let out a long whistle.

Figures materialized atop the buildings on the Rat King's side as Yua and other stealthy people from my gang rose from the shadows like ghosts. Firelight flickered over their own raised crossbows. A nervous ripple went through the army on the other side as they whipped their heads around to take this surprise threat into account.

Seconds ticked by. Then, the Rat King broke from the group and made his way towards the middle of the square. After a quick nod to Yngvild and Vania, I strode forward as well.

No one spoke, and I was pretty sure that some of the spectators barely dared breathe, because the silence was so thick that the thudding from the Rat King's boots bounced between the walls of the building around us. My feet were silent as I advanced. Stopping in the middle of the empty square, the King of the Underworld waited for me to come to a halt as well before he raised his voice.

"The Oncoming Storm," he said. "I didn't think you would come."

His voice carried across the stones and echoed over the armies of underworlders we both had brought to this meeting.

"Why wouldn't I?" A challenging smirk spread across my face. "You've tried to ambush me... is it five times now? Seven times? You know, I've quite lost count. But none of them ever succeed so what in Nemanan's name would I have to worry about?"

On the other side of the square, the Rat King's crew stirred and shifted as if unsure what to do about the insult I'd just thrown in their leader's face for all to hear. The insulted king was seething but when he spoke, his voice was calm.

"Are you always this insolent?"

"Yes."

Surprise flickered in his beady eyes and for a moment, he couldn't figure out how to reply so I pressed the advantage.

"What? You think I'd try to deny that?" I lifted my shoulders in a nonchalant shrug. "Being insolent is like one of the cornerstones of my personality so it's not really a secret. Now, you're the one who called this meeting. What do you want?"

"You're interfering with my business." This time, there was an undercurrent of rage in his voice. "The people who pay me for protection get robbed all the time."

Cocking my head, I shot him a wolfish grin. "Do they?"

"And you're expanding into the smuggling trade," he continued as if I hadn't interrupted. "You also kill my subordinates. You wiped out practically the whole Blue Sword gang and yesterday you blew up half of another gang, including the leader."

"Correct."

"What you're doing is hurting the Underworld." He fixed me with a confident stare and raised his voice. "When you rob my stores, you're ruining the reputation of all underworlders. It makes the upperworlders think we're weak and can't protect them."

"It makes them think *you're* weak."

"No." The Rat King shook his head. "To them, we're all the same so you're hurting everyone's reputation. Same with the smuggling. This internal fight is weakening the Underworld's hold on the market. And lastly, and most importantly, you are killing other underworlders. You are killing *your own people*. Everything you do only hurts the Underworld."

It took considerable self-control to prevent myself from blowing out an irritated sigh. Now I understood what the trap was. Gods damn him. And I had played right into his hands.

He'd wanted me to think that this meeting was a trap so that I would bring the bulk of my people. That, in combination with the mass of underworlders he had brought himself, would ensure that every word being said tonight would have reached every shady corner of the Underworld before the night was over. Everyone would know that *I* was the villain in this fight, the bad guy who killed our people and ruined our reputation, while he tried to put a stop to it. It was brilliant. Who would support me after hearing this?

"Please stop this now before you rip our world apart." Malice shone in his eyes as he locked them on me because he knew that I had just figured it out. Because he knew that he had won. "Is your pride really worth more than our people? Stop this now and bow to me before the damage you do is irreparable."

Uncertain murmuring drifted through the clear night air and leather creaked as people shifted in discomfort. I didn't let myself consider whether any of it had come from my side of the square. By all the demons in hell, I had to salvage this. And fast.

Adopting a casual stance, I flicked my braid back behind my shoulder. "Sounds to me like you're scared."

"I am scared." Only I was close enough to see that it wasn't fear but a smirk full of superiority and victory that decorated his face. "I'm scared for the Underworld and the damage you do to it because of your childish fight with me."

Shit. What could I do to turn this back on him? Winds whistled through the buildings and filled the stretching silence. If I didn't say something soon, it would be too late. But what? My heart thumped in my chest. *Think.*

"I will take your silence to mean—"

"You will take my silence to mean no such thing," I snapped before he could finish because I knew what he had been about to say. "The only thing my silence means is that I'm still trying to process the sheer stupidity that you've vomited these last few minutes." An idea, a brilliant fucking idea, struck my mind like a lightning bolt. "I'm the one damaging the Underworld? How ridiculous. If you really don't want to drag the rest of the Underworld into this then how about settling it with a one-on-one?"

The Rat King's dark eyes widened and he took an almost imperceptible step back.

"If you win, I bow to you. And if I win, you bow to me." A malicious grin flashed across my lips. "No harm done to the Underworld. Just a test of strength between you and me."

"That's–"

"I won't even use my Storm Caster powers," I interrupted. "Just a normal fight with weapons. Completely fair."

I had no idea if the Rat King already knew, or suspected, that my powers were blocked but I didn't want to confirm it so offering to fight without them was the best course of action. Like I said, I was a knife-fighter long before I knew I was Ashaana so I had no doubt that I would win regardless.

"That's..." I could almost see him running scenarios in his head as he trailed off.

"Yes?"

Hatred and fury blazed in his eyes as he locked them on me because he knew that as soon as I had suggested the one-on-one duel, I had won. Strength was everything in our world and there was no way he could refuse the fight now. Not without both looking like a scared weakling and like he was going back on his word about stopping the damage to the Underworld. If he really wanted to bring an end to the collateral damage, he would agree to it. Unless he feared for his life enough to refuse. Either way, he would lose.

"I accept," the Rat King ground out between gritted teeth.

"Splendid." I grinned at him. "Tomorrow. Same place. Midnight."

"Agreed."

"So glad we could find a way to work this out without anyone else getting hurt." Spinning on my heel, I sauntered back towards my people. "See you tomorrow."

There was a quite strong possibility that he would stab me in the back as soon as I had turned around but it was a risk I was willing to take. A move like that would be as good as admitting that he was scared of fighting me. Still, the spot between my shoulder blades itched as I strolled away so when I reached Vania and Yngvild without having a sharp point shoved into my back, I let out a soft breath.

"Quick thinking," Vania said.

"And bold," Yngvild added.

The noise of the retreating people on the other side of the square prevented their words from being heard by anyone from the Rat King's crew. I let out a short chuckle and raked my fingers through my hair.

"Yeah, well, I had to do something to stop him from dragging my name through the dirt." I motioned for everyone to start back to the Black Emerald before turning back to the two tall warriors beside me. "Now, I just need a breakdown of his fighting style and then we're all set."

Yngvild and Vania exchanged a glance as we started out as well.

"What?" I asked.

"We don't know what his fighting style is." Worry crept into Vania's perceptive blue eyes. "I don't think anyone does. As far as I know, no one has ever seen him fight."

"Seriously?"

"Yeah."

Footsteps echoed between the buildings as our thick wall of people turned the corner and started down another street. I furrowed my brows.

"How in Nemanan's name has he managed to become King of the Underworld without being in a fight?"

The large battle axe across his back shifted as Yngvild shrugged. "He's always got other people to fight for him."

"How courageous."

"No. But smart."

Tipping my head back, I blew out another sigh. "Yeah. Well, I guess I'll just find out tomorrow then."

Warm summer winds caressed my face as we continued towards the Black Emerald in silence. If he never fought himself, then odds were that he was terrible at it. So I really had nothing to worry about. I was definitely going to win. Right? I swept my gaze over the puddles glowing silver in the moonlight. Unless he had some secret technique and was so ridiculously good at it that fighting others was beneath him. Panic tried to claw its way up my throat. Shaking my head, I forced it down. I had to win this. I had to. Otherwise, I would have to bow to the Rat King. Man, I was so screwed.

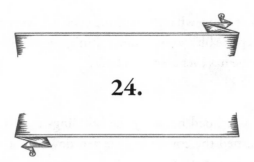

24.

Anticipation bubbled through the waiting crowd. The roofs around the deserted square had started filling with people long before midnight and now every single vantage point, both on and off the ground, was crammed with spectators. Apparently, this was a fight no one wanted to miss.

I let out a chuckle. "So, you found out about this too, huh?"

After giving my arm one final stretch, I turned around and raised my eyebrows at the dark figure that had materialized in the shadows of the alley I used for some privacy while getting ready. Shade lounged against the wall of a wooden building. His arms were crossed over his chest and he studied me with calculating black eyes.

"This is my city. Did you really think you could keep an event like this secret?"

"No." I strode towards him and only stopped when I was close enough to stab him, if the mood took me. "But I thought you'd have more important things to do than watch me fight the Rat King."

"You staked your whole claim on this." It was a statement and not a question so I didn't bother nodding. When I said nothing, Shade continued. "What will you do if you lose?"

My mouth drew into a confident smirk. "I don't lose."

At the use of his own words from last year, a small smile tugged at his lips as well. "Arrogant, cocky, and not a shred of humility. You don't ever change, do you?"

"*We* don't ever change."

Shade let out a chuckle. "No, I guess we don't."

In the square behind me, excited chatter was spreading as the time drew closer to midnight. Yngvild and Vania stood guarding the entrance so that no one could sneak in and stab me before the fight even began. Well, no one except the Master of the Assassins' Guild, apparently.

"You have a plan?" Shade asked.

I lifted my shoulders in a light shrug. "Stab him with the pointy end?"

Exhaling deeply, the assassin peeled his shoulder off the wooden wall and straightened before taking a step closer to me. I didn't want to give him the satisfaction of making me retreat a step so I stood my ground even if it forced me to crane my neck to meet his eyes.

"This is serious."

"I know," I muttered.

Shade placed a hand on my jaw while his black eyes bored into me. "I meant what I said. I would kill them all for you." He released a soft sigh. "If it weren't for the war with Queen Nimlithil that's drawing closer every day. We need a united Underworld."

"I know," I repeated.

"If you lose this—"

"I already told you," I interrupted. "I don't lose."

"If you lose this," he pressed again, "you will have to bow to him. Because if you lose, the respect the underworlders have for you will be gone. And without that, there is nothing I can do to give you the crown. You *will* have to bow."

I slapped his hand away. "I don't need you to *give* me the crown. I will take it on my own." Steel crept into my emerald eyes. "And I don't bow to anyone."

"That's what I wanted to hear." A smirk spread across his lips as he turned and sauntered back into the darkness. "Now, go win this. I'll be watching."

"Bastard," I grumbled into the shadows.

That damn obnoxious, arrogant assassin. I shook my head and stalked towards the other end of the alley. But as much as I hated to admit it, his baiting and teasing had been just what I needed. Before he showed up with his rude remarks, I'd been nervous. Nervous because I had no idea what to expect from this fight with the Rat King. But now, the irritation and the fire-breathing demon that was my stubborn pride had shoved out the anxious worry and replaced it with raging fury.

"You ready?" Yngvild asked as I passed him and Vania.

"Yeah."

They fell in behind me as I stalked towards the square. The crowd parted before me. Once I reached the edge of the wall that the audience had formed around the square, Yngvild and Vania stopped while I continued forwards alone. On the other side, the Rat King did the same.

In the middle of the stone square, a tall man with long brown hair waited. I had never seen him before but I assumed he was to act as some sort of referee. He was probably in the Rat King's pocket but it mattered little. As long as the gathered underworlders saw me clearly beat the pompous king, then there would be no need for anyone else to officially declare me the winner. Everyone would know it and that would be enough.

Silence fell across the packed space as both of us reached the brown-haired man. He raised his voice.

"This is a one-on-one fight," he said. "That means that no one else is allowed to intervene. No one. If you involve other people in this fight, you will forfeit the fight. Do you understand?"

"Yes," the Rat King said.

"Yeah," I replied as well.

"Good." The tall referee nodded. "But that is the only rule. This is not an Upperworld duel where you have to declare your weapons and fight fair. This is the Underworld. Everything is permitted. The fight is over when one of you is dead or submits. Understood?"

The Rat King and I nodded our understanding.

"Good," the tall man said again. "I will retreat to the sidelines now. When the clock strikes midnight, you will begin."

Without waiting for an answer, he turned and strode towards the wall of people on my left. A hushed silence had fallen over the square. The Rat King and I stood facing each other a few strides apart but neither of us went for our weapons. It appeared as though both of us were unwilling to show our hand until the bell tolled. My weapon of choice was more or less obvious since I was covered in knives, and the Rat King had the handle of a thin sword peeking up over his shoulder, but first looks could be deceiving. After all, this was an Underworld fight. Everything was permitted.

Neither of us would go as far as to actually kill each other, though, because we each needed the other to publicly submit in order to solidify our power. Trying to win a fight without being able to go all in was tricky. My heart pattered against my ribs as the seconds dragged on. I resisted the urge to wipe my palms on my pants and instead forced my arms to remain casually positioned by my sides. No darkness, no clue as to his fighting style, and no killing intent. This was going to be tough. But I had no choice. I had to win.

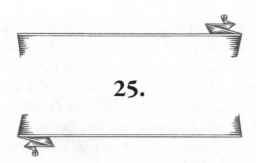

25.

The bells tolled midnight. I yanked a throwing knife from my shoulder holster and hurled it at the Rat King while darting to the side. A sharp *snap* reverberated through the air. Steel clattered against stone as my knife hit the ground and bounced away. My mouth dropped open slightly as I trailed to a halt and stared at my opponent.

A malicious smile stretched across his lips. The Rat King's skinny body was locked in a straight-backed pose, as one bony hand held the thin sword, and the other gripped the handle of a whip. I stared at the coil of black rope that slithered across the ground like a snake as the Rat King moved his hand. A whip. Who the hell fought with a whip?

He snapped his wrist. I had to throw myself backwards to avoid the black cord as it cracked in the space I'd occupied only seconds before. Twisting around, I flung another throwing knife at him. He deflected it with the whip before swinging it back around and launching another attack. I danced out of reach. The air vibrated next to me as it narrowly missed my ribs.

Spinning with the motion, I shot forwards. Boots thudded against the ground as I closed the distance between us while the Rat King was still pulling his arm back from his strike. Almost there. Black flashed in the corner of my eye. *Shit*. I skidded to a halt and threw myself down in a roll to the other side.

Pain shot through my body. I gasped in a breath as the whip cracked over my back before I rolled out of reach again. A collective hiss went through the audience. Pushing the pain to the back of my mind, I got to my feet but the Rat King was already advancing again. Another snap split the air as he swung. I jumped back. Wicked satisfaction shone in my opponent's eyes as I retreated across the stones.

How the hell was I supposed to win this? I had been in a lot of fights in my life, and I mean *a lot*, but never during any of those countless battles had I ever had to fight someone who used a whip. Ranged attacks were out because he could just deflect them before they struck. That left a close-range fight. I was pretty confident that I could win one of those but the problem was that I couldn't get close enough to try. As soon as I moved into range, he could just hit me with that whip. I had to find some way around that.

"Backing away like a frightened animal," the Rat King said. "Don't tell me you suddenly lost your nerve."

"You wish. I just figured I'd give these people a show before I beat you."

He kept advancing on me, that black cord slithering across the stones as he rolled his wrist, while I continued backing away.

"You have a big mouth, but I can see it in your eyes. I've trained enough rats with this whip to know..." He flicked his wrist and the whip cracked right in front of my face, making me flinch. "...when they fear it."

Dread spread through my body like cold poison. By all the gods, he was right. And if I didn't stop retreating soon, the other underworlders would see it too. Once they realized that the Rat King had me on the run, they'd lose all respect for me. I couldn't let that happen. Gritting my teeth, I yanked my hunting knives from the small of my back. This was going to hurt.

I sprang forward. The Rat King had been so distracted by his own little speech that I'd managed to catch him off guard. When he raised his arm to strike, I was already halfway across the stones. Blinding pain flashed through me as the whip struck the side of my ribs but the speed behind my movements carried me the final bit towards him. I jabbed my knives forward.

Quicker than I had expected, the Rat King flung his sword up and ducked to the side. He parried my left-hand blade and redirected the strike but my other knife grazed his cheek even despite his evasive maneuver. Sucking in a sharp breath, he continued his sideway twist while I tried to recover my balance from the missed blows. Black rope whizzed through the night but he was slightly out of position so it only cleaved the air.

"You were saying?" I taunted as both of us straightened again.

The Rat King lifted a hand and wiped away the blood trickling down from the thin cut in his cheek. He looked from the red smudge on his hand to me with hatred burning in his eyes. "You will pay for that."

"Come try it."

It was fake confidence that dripped from my lips because I still had no idea how to win this fight. I flicked my gaze across the square. A mass of people boxed in the wide space and they watched us with exhilaration on their faces. But at least that last attack had bought me some time because it looked like I hadn't lost the audience yet.

Inside the human walls, the square was empty. Nothing to use as leverage. Gripping my knives tightly, I made one final sweep. Come on, there had to be something I could use.

Air vibrated next to my arm as the whip fell just short of striking me. I jumped back again.

Damn. Other than me and the Rat King, there was nothing else here. The only things I could use to beat him were the things I was wearing. The whip cracked in front of me again and I twisted away. *Think!*

The Rat King knew that I wouldn't try to kill him because I needed him to kneel to me. The fact that he knew this wasn't actually a fight to the death had to provide him with some calm and certainty, which appeared to be vital to his fighting style. An idea flared to life in my mind. That was it. I had to rattle him enough for him to start making mistakes. Good thing crazy was my natural state.

A grin tinted with madness flashed over my lips as I darted forwards. The Rat King blinked in surprise but recovered quickly and flicked his wrist. Searing pain shot through me as the whip cracked against my ribs again. I continued my rush. A feral howl ripped from my throat as I lunged.

The Rat King brought his sword up and parried the first strike while the other one narrowly missed his throat. Surprise bloomed in his eyes. I grinned back at him with insanity dancing over my face as I stabbed towards his throat again. He drove the blade off course by slamming his fist down on my forearm. Staggering a step to the side, I got ready for another launch. The whip snapped through the air again.

For a moment, I hesitated because I couldn't for the life of me figure out why he had used it now. I should be way too close for it to do any damage. So what had he aimed for?

Black rope snaked around my ankle. I sucked in a breath between my teeth right as the Rat King yanked the cord towards him. The world tipped backwards as I was pulled off balance and crashed back first into the stones. Air rushed out of my lungs.

While I was busy blinking black spots from my vision and refilling my lungs, the Rat King tugged on the rope again. Stones scraped against my back as I slid over the rough surface and towards my opponent. He raised the sword over my chest.

Sheer panic flared up my spine. I had bet everything on this fight. Staked my whole claim on it. If I lost now, I would have no other choice than to submit to his rule, and the freedom I so desperately wanted would be out of reach. I would once again be forced to bow to someone else's authority and let them decide what my life would be like. By all the gods, I'd sworn never to do that again and I'd sworn that when I finally put down roots somewhere, I would make sure that no one ever looked at me like I was their property again. I couldn't lose! The Rat King brought down his blade.

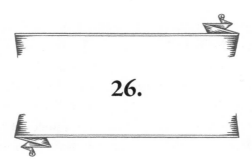

26.

Kicking out my free leg, I slammed it into the side of his knee while I rolled with the motion in order to evade the sword coming for my chest. Metal dinged faintly as the tip connected with the stones just behind my back instead. While the Rat King recovered from my kick, I swept my hunting knife across the black rope binding my ankle.

With the cord severed, I rolled away before shooting to my feet again. My opponent glared at me and the fraying end of his whip for a few seconds. I yanked the remaining rope off my ankle before retreating another step. A rustling sound echoed through the night as the Rat King threw the broken whip on the stones beside him and pulled out a new one from somewhere behind his back.

Of course he had another one. Gods damn it. He shifted his hand and let the black cord slither over the dust-covered stones. Then he struck. But I had already formed a plan so I stepped into range and brought up my forearm in front of me. The whip twisted around my arm but the bracers I wore absorbed most of the impact.

The Rat King yanked me forward. I stumbled a step at the sudden pull but didn't try to fight it. Instead, I turned my arm in circles, winding the rope even more around it as I closed the distance between us.

"What are you...?" the Rat King began.

I slashed the knife in my free hand across the black cord. It severed it clean in the middle. A wicked grin spread across my mouth as the other half of the whip fell uselessly towards the ground. Shock flickered in his eyes as I darted towards him.

He dropped the damaged whip and snatched out another one. I changed direction and dove for cover but it cracked over my back anyway. Pain thrummed through my body as I rolled to my feet just out of reach again. How many damn whips did he have?

And now he wouldn't fall for that same trick again so I had to change my strategy. Narrowing my eyes, I stuck the hunting knives back in their sheaths and pulled out two throwing knives instead. He was unbelievably fast, both with the whip and the sword, so could he probably dodge two of them but I had to try. I hurled them at him.

He knocked both of them aside. A confident smile filled with certain victory stretched his lips as the blades bounced across the ground. Just as I'd predicted. Now I only had six throwing knives left. My next move would require all of them. If this didn't work, I would lose. My heart slammed against my ribs as I reached up and pulled out two more blades.

The whip coiled and uncoiled on the stones beside him while his smile turned patronizing. I threw the knives. They sailed wildly off course. As soon as they'd left my hands, I'd reached up for two more and hurled them as well. These barreled straight for him. I flung the final two knives in the next breath and watched them spin wide.

Whips cracked and metal dinged. A triumphant smirk decorated the Rat King's face as the only two blades that had flown straight at him clattered to the ground. Two sharp thuds sounded.

All around us, the whole square held its breath as the Rat King slowly tipped his head down to find two knives sticking out of his shoulders.

He had never seen me use that move before so I'd been fairly confident that he would just assume that I'd missed because I was in a hurry to throw all of them. Little did he know that I had learned how to redirect blades in the air. The first two had been thrown wide on purpose, the second two had been the decoy, and the final two had pushed the real attack back on course. And he had never seen it coming.

Stealing the victorious smirk right off his face, I yanked my hunting knives from the small of my back again and shot towards him. He lifted his arm to strike me with the whip. Nothing happened. His left arm didn't move at all.

Panic flared in his eyes and he tried to bring his sword up to meet my attack. He managed to lift his right arm but the effort made him cry out in pain and I slapped the sword away easily. While he'd been busy with his futile attempts to defend himself, I'd closed the final distance between us. Zigzagging across the stones, I delivered a kick to the side of his knee that he was powerless to block again. He crashed to the ground while I flashed back in front of him and planted a boot in his chest.

With one arm currently out of commission and the other causing severe pain, he barely managed to break his fall as I shoved him backwards. His back hit the stones with a heavy thud. I kicked the sword from his grip and then crouched over his chest. My lips drew into a malicious smile as I rested both hunting knives against his throat.

"Submit," I said in a voice that carried across the otherwise dead silent square.

Hate, defiance, and a slight hint of fear swirled in his eyes as he stared back at me but he made no move to speak. I pressed the blades harder against his skin.

"Submit," I growled. "Or die."

The Rat King only continued glaring at me. Boots thudded against stone somewhere to my left. I cast a quick glance in the direction of the sound and found the tall brown-haired man from before striding towards us. No one spoke. Only the wind dared whistle through the buildings while the referee crossed the square. Flames from the torches danced over his grim face.

"The rules were clear." He came to a halt next to us and drew the long sword at his hip.

Ringing steel filled the air as it cleared the scabbard. I shifted my gaze back to the Rat King and poured every smidgen of evil inside me into the smile I gave him. It was time for him to bow.

Cold metal appeared under my chin. I narrowly prevented myself from jerking back in surprise, which would only have served to slit my throat open on the sharp edge. Very carefully, I shifted my gaze to the tall brown-haired man who now held a sword to my throat.

"The rules were clear," he repeated. "No one else was allowed to help in this fight. During that final move, you obviously had someone else redirect the knives."

Incredulity filled my eyes but disappeared quickly as let out a long laugh. "So, you were on his payroll after all."

He pushed the sword higher up under my chin. "Remove the knives and back away."

Relaxing my grip on the handles, I slowly took my blades from the Rat King's throat and stuck them back in their holsters. The edge of the sword pressed further in. I shot the tall man a glare but followed his instructions and rose from my crouch. Silence hung like a heavy wet blanket over the whole area as I backed away from the Rat King.

Everyone knew that the accusations had been false because they'd all seen with their own eyes what I'd done, but no one dared say anything. Metal clattered faintly as the corrupt referee removed my throwing knives from the Rat King's shoulders and dropped them on the ground. While he helped the injured king to his feet, I made a split-second decision.

Yanking out my hunting knives again, I raised my arms and turned in a slow circle to address the gathered crowd. "You know it. I know it. He knows it."

I didn't need to specify because everyone already understood what I was talking about. I stabbed my right-hand blade in the direction of the Rat King and raised my voice to a furious shout.

"Is this what you want in a leader? A pathetic coward who can't keep his promises? He can't protect his own shops." My teeth glinted in a malicious smile. "From me. And he can't keep his word to kill people who desert because you know that I will slaughter you all and burn down the building around your heads if you touch any of my people."

Firelight flickered over worried faces all around me. I jabbed the knife in the air again to indicate where the Rat King and his pet referee were standing.

"And now, he runs from a fight like a coward and gets this pitiful fool to say that *someone else* threw my knives for me." I rolled my shoulders and flicked my arm in a nonchalant gesture. "Seriously, what kind of ridiculous excuse is that even? Like, what kind of underworlder doesn't even know how to cheat better than that?"

Scattered laughter broke out across the audience. The Rat King opened his mouth to say something but the tall man supporting him beat him to it.

"You forfeit the fight," he called across the square. "Leave now while we still allow you to leave."

I leveled hard eyes on them both as I advanced on them with my knives out. "No, *you* leave now while *I* still allow you to leave."

Clothes rustled and feet slapped against stone as a large group broke off from the audience and ran towards us. They swarmed around me and blocked off my route to the Rat King and his subordinate. Wood creaked as they all raised loaded crossbows at me.

Madness danced over my face as I let out a crazed laugh. "Coward!" I raised my chin and spread my arms to the waiting warriors. "Do it. Do it!"

The metal tips gleamed in the flickering firelight but no bolts were fired. Behind the ring surrounding me, the Rat King was limping away. I kept my eyes locked on his back until he was swallowed up by the wall of people on the other side. Once they were gone, the crossbow-wielders backed away as well.

I let out a snort and shook my head before stalking away in search of my missing throwing knives. What an idiot. I had won the fight but apparently not the war. Not yet, anyway. The stunt he pulled here tonight would spread like wildfire through the Underworld and it would eat away his support from the inside. I stuck another blade back in my shoulder holster. The Rat King would soon be ready to fall.

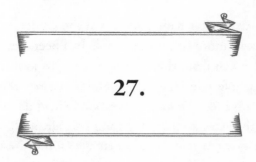

27.

"Where is everyone?"

Looking up from my stack of papers, I found a hulking man with brown hair striding through my unusually empty tavern. Lind. At first, I'd always just assumed that he was one of Rowan's bodyguards but I'd since learned that he was actually her Second. He came by the Black Emerald every day to check on his gang leader, who had finally healed and would be moving back home tomorrow.

"Word is that the Rat King's retaliation for me beating him in that fight a few weeks ago is coming tonight." I shrugged and closed the ledger I'd been skimming. "His crew is apparently gonna hit all my warehouses all at once so I sent out everyone I could spare to discourage them from that."

"Makes sense." Lind had reached the staircase but paused for a second and looked back at me in my booth. "Let us know if you need help."

"Thanks."

Boots thudded against wood as he disappeared up the stairs. I hooked a foot around the leg of the chair opposite me and pulled it closer before swinging my feet up on it and leaning back against the dark green cushions. Closing my eyes, I let out a long sigh.

Ever since the Rat King had shown the Underworld what a coward he was, more and more people had been deserting him. Some had broken from their previous gang to join mine but it was mostly whole gangs that left and instead threw their support behind me. Like Red Demon Rowan's crew had done earlier. To be honest, that was a relief. My gang had already grown quite large and I wasn't sure if I could manage an infinite number of people. It was much better when gang leaders managed their own crew but still pledged support to me. Because, you know, being responsible for people still sucked.

"Napping again?"

I opened my eyes to find a grinning Yngvild and a frowning Vania standing on the other side of the table. "No. I was actually visualizing where to stab the Rat King next time I saw him."

"Course you were," Yngvild said.

Vania smacked his arm with the back of her hand and shook her head. "Don't tease her about that. She sleeps less than anyone I've ever met. She could most certainly use some rest."

"I can sleep when I'm dead." Swinging my feet off the chair, I straightened again. "What've you got?"

"None of our warehouses have been hit yet," Vania said. "But we think that–"

Glass shattered. I shot to my feet right as a boom shook the walls of the Black Emerald. Vania and Yngvild whirled around and ducked but the explosion had been contained to the front of the tavern. The two tables closest to the entrance had taken the worst hit and fire licked the broken furniture that lay scattered there. I sprang forward but only made it a couple of steps before the door banged open.

"This is for the Blue Sword!" someone screamed.

Three men poured through the doorway with weapons raised. I yanked a throwing knife from my shoulder but Yngvild was already barreling towards the attackers so I couldn't throw it without risk hitting him. A whoosh reverberated through the air as he swung his huge battle axe at the first man. Ringing steel accompanied it as Vania drew her blade as well and flashed forward. I stabbed a finger at Helena who was peeking up from behind the bar.

"Put out the fire!" I called.

Not waiting to see if she nodded, I turned back to the battle ahead and switched from a throwing knife to a hunting knife. But the fight was already over. Two men lay in a bloody heap in front of Yngvild and the third one toppled backwards as Vania slashed her sword through his gut.

"Wait!" I blurted out as she raised her blade to deliver the final blow.

Wet coughing mixed with sounds of moaning as the dying man on the floor clutched his stomach. The coppery tang of blood filled the air. I stalked towards him before dropping into a crouch and grabbing the front of his shirt. With a firm grip, I yanked him up into a sitting position.

"I remember you," I growled in his pain-twisted face. "You are the three members of the Blue Sword that I let live. Is this how you repay my generosity?"

His eyes went in and out of focus so I gave his body a forceful shake. He sucked in a breath. Once his eyes were focused on me again, I leaned closer to him.

"The Rat King sent you, I presume?"

"No." A violent cough shook his frame. "We just wanted to be here to see your face when you heard about the attack on your friends."

"What?" I snapped. "What attack?"

"You're too late. When you get there, the attack will already have started. Your friends are going to die."

Panic and dread sent a pulse through my body that was so strong I almost choked. His eyes were starting to glaze over but I jerked him back and forth anyway.

"Who is going to die?" I spat. "Who? Answer!"

But he was already gone. I let go of his shirt and shot to my feet. His corpse thudded back onto the planks at the same time as heavy footsteps thundered down the stairs. Lind jumped the final steps and landed on the floor with his sword out. His eyes darted around the room and he opened his mouth to speak but I cut him off.

"Please," I croaked, fear clawing its way up my throat. "Send everyone you can. The school for poor kids in the Middle Ring. The teacher and the hatmaker. And the barracks on the west side of town. Where the elves are staying. The commander, the one with auburn hair, and the two black-haired twins. And to Blackspire. They're being attacked."

Lind didn't even bother sheathing his sword as he nodded and sprinted out through the open front door. I turned wild eyes to Yngvild and Vania.

"I don't know how long before they can..." I began but the two warriors already understood what I wanted to say.

"I'll take the barracks," Vania confirmed.

"Blackspire," Yngvild said.

Without another word, the three of us darted out of the Black Emerald and raced into the night. My heart slammed into my ribs as I ran across the rooftops at breakneck speed. Wind ripped through my hair and clothes. I couldn't be too late. *Please don't let me be too late.*

When Norah's school finally became visible in the distance, my legs were screaming with exertion but I didn't dare stop for even a second. I didn't even bother climbing the whole way down from the final building and instead just dropped from halfway down. Pain jarred through my bones as I connected with the ground but I pushed it out as I sprinted towards the school.

No one was outside but if it was true that the attack would've already started when I got there, they could already be inside. There was no time to navigate through the whole building so I just jumped up on the nearest windowsill and scrambled up the wall towards where I knew Liam and Norah's bedroom to be.

Soft grunts and moans drifted out through the closed shutters. Alarms blared inside my head. Either they were fighting or they were already hurt and... dying. My thoughts stumbled over the last word. With worry and panic banging furiously against my skull, I pulled myself up on the final windowsill and smashed through the shutters. Splinters of wood flew through the air as I barreled into the room.

A shrill shriek rang out. With two hunting knives gripped tightly in my hands, I whipped my head from side to side in search of the attackers. Confusion drifted through my mind as I took in the room.

There were no armed men attacking my friends. In fact, apart from me, the only people in the room were Liam and Norah. The gorgeous teacher was curled up against the headboard of their double bed with the sheets pulled up over her chest while Liam was frozen halfway out of the bed. Candlelight flickered over his bare chest and hips before the rest of his body was covered by the edge of the sheet. I blinked at them.

"Storm!" Liam called. "What the hell are you doing?"

"There was supposed to be an attack... I thought you were under attack."

"We're not under attack." Liam shot me a look filled with both exasperation and slight amusement. "Except by you, apparently."

"But the grunts and the moans, I thought..." I trailed off as my clueless mind finally put two and two together. The noise, Liam's lack of clothes, the mortification of Norah's face as she clutched the sheets to her chest. "Oh."

Heat flushed my entire face. *Ohh*. Had I really just walked in on them...? And not just walked in, I had burst through the bloody window. By Nemanan. Well, better embarrassed than dead.

Norah let out a self-conscious laugh. "Would you mind leaving?"

"Right. Yes." I cleared my throat. "There'll be some underworlders keeping watch outside tonight. If nothing's happened by now, nothing probably will but... uhm... just in case."

"Okay." Amusement played over Liam's face. "Thanks."

"Right," I said again and then strode to the door. With one hand on the handle, I paused and looked back at the couple in the bed. "Could you... uhm... like, not tell Zaina about this? She's gonna kick my ass."

Norah lobbed a fluffy pillow at me. "Get out!"

Laughter followed me as I disappeared into the hallway. No matter how embarrassing that had been, I was beyond relieved that I had checked on them and that Liam and Norah hadn't been the target for the attack. They were the ones least capable of defending themselves. Out of all my friends, they should've been the most obvious target. I frowned. So why hadn't they been?

Don't get me wrong, I was incredibly grateful that Liam and Norah hadn't been attacked but it also didn't make sense. Why leave them alone and go for more difficult targets? If the Rat King tried to attack the elves at their barracks, they would most likely be cut down by lethal arrows before they even got close. Same with Shade. One did not exactly attack Blackspire and expect to succeed.

Worry gnawed at my chest as I swept the rest of the building just to be sure before hurrying out the front door. A mass of people met me as I exited the school's stone courtyard. I recognized several of them. Rowan's gang.

"There's no attack happening right now," I said to the leader of the group. "But could you stay for a while and make sure that nothing happens?"

"Yeah," he replied.

"Thank you." I gave him a nod before sprinting towards the closest building.

Once I was back on the rooftops, I set course for the barracks and broke into a run. If Liam and Norah hadn't been the target, it would most likely be the elves. As I mentioned, they were more than capable of taking care of themselves but the horrible tightness in my chest wouldn't let up until I saw with my own eyes that they were okay.

A wide training area eventually opened up before me. I slowed to a trot as I reached the final building that separated the barracks from the rest of the city. The open space in front of the long buildings was full of people. Some of them standing, and a lot of them lying dead on the ground. My heart thumped in my chest as I climbed down to street level and hurried towards the standing ones.

Rowan's crew parted before me as rushed towards the taller figures standing further in. Relief flooded my chest. Elaran, flanked by the twins, was talking to Vania while keeping his huge black bow in a loose grip. Behind them, other wood elves were retrieving arrows from now dead attackers.

"You okay?" I said as I skidded to a halt in front of them.

Elaran shifted his gaze to me. "Yeah."

"Anyone hurt?"

"No. No one got close enough to try."

Haemir nodded at Vania. "And then she and all these other humans showed up and cut them down from behind."

"Yeah," Haela added and frowned at the dead bodies before them. "I don't know what these people were thinking. Like, they know we're elves, right? This wasn't even a fair fight." She shrugged. "Good ambush practice, though."

That knot in my chest loosened slightly and I let out a soft chuckle. "Yeah, the Rat King didn't think this through at all." Seriousness crept back onto my face as I met each of their gazes. "This is all on me. Again. I'm sorry I keep dragging you into shit like this."

I didn't apologize often, so on those rare occasions when I did, Elaran never seemed to know how to handle it. This time, he cleared his throat and motioned with his bow at Haela.

"Yes, well, like she said. It was a good opportunity to practice dealing with an ambush."

A grateful smile drifted over my face before I turned solemn eyes on them all. "This will never happen again. I swear it. You will never be in danger because of me again." Shifting my gaze to Vania, I clapped a hand on her shoulder. "Thank you."

"Of course." She gave me a nod. "What do you want to do about all these dead bodies?"

"Load them all up on carts. I have a message to send." I flicked my gaze between all four of them again. "I've gotta check on Shade."

Elaran nodded. Before any of them could say anything else, I whirled around and jogged across the crowded training area. Based on the number of bodies I passed on my way out, though, odds were that this was the only attack. But I still had to make sure. If something had happened to Shade... I didn't want to finish the thought.

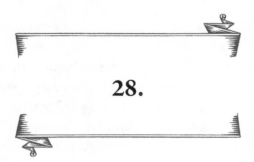

28.

My legs were throbbing after the third nonstop sprint this night but I kept pushing. Warm night winds lent speed to my tired feet as the obsidian spikes grew larger. When I reached the final building before the city emptied out into a large square surrounding the black palace, I was well and truly exhausted. Both from the run and from the worry. My chest heaved as I surveyed the area before me. It was completely empty.

"Wanna tell me why a horde of underworlders led by Yngvild suddenly showed up and formed a protective ring around Blackspire?"

I whipped around. Behind me, Shade was striding out of the darkness on the roof with a sly smile tugging at the corner of his lips. The final bit of tension evaporated from my chest and I sucked in a deep breath. He was okay. They were *all* okay. Weariness washed over me like a tidal wave. Man, I really hated caring about people.

Letting out a tired chuckle, I turned back towards Blackspire and sank down on the roof. My legs dangled over the edge while I braced my elbows on my thighs and rested my forehead in my palms. The air shifted slightly as Shade sat down next to me.

Once the tiredness and the awful worry had receded to a dull throbbing, I inhaled deeply and let my arms drop again. Bracing my hands on the edge of the roof, I turned to face the assassin next to me.

"They came because I sent them," I finally replied to his question. "The Rat King ordered an attack on my friends as retaliation for the fight."

"Elaran and the elves?" Shade asked. "Liam and Norah?"

"All safe. No one attacked the school and the ones who went after the elves died before they even got close."

The assassin's mouth drew into a wicked smile. "Yeah, Elaran is good like that."

"That he is." I searched his face for signs of injury. "No one attacked you?"

"No."

"Good." A chuckle slipped from my lips. "Apparently not even the Rat King is stupid enough to attack the High King of Pernula." I motioned at the empty square. "Where are my people?"

"I sent them back." Amusement glittered in his black eyes as he looked at me. "I'm more than capable of defending my own palace, you know."

Pushing back a few loose strands of dark brown hair that the wind had ripped from my braid, I let out a huff. "I know. But I wanted to make sure."

"Aw." His smile widened. "You were worried about me."

I gave his arm a shove. "Shut up."

His rippling laugh drifted into the night air. For a while, we just sat there on the edge of the roof and watched the silver light from the moon play across the smooth obsidian walls of Blackspire. Somewhere below us, wooden signs creaked as they swung in the breeze.

"I've been meaning to ask..." Shade began but didn't take his eyes off the black palace before us. "What happened with Marcus?"

"What do you mean?"

When he finally turned and met my gaze head on, he just looked at me expectantly because we both already knew that I understood what he meant. I blew out a sigh and drew my fingers through my hair.

"Nothing happened with Marcus. There never was anything like that about to happen." Letting my arms drop again, I gave him a light shrug. "I mean, he's nice and good-looking and, like, a super powerful Storm Caster and all, but he's not y–" I cleared my throat. "He's not... We're just friends."

Shade's penetrating gaze was locked on me. Before he could say something about that half-started word that I hadn't finished, I let a teasing grin flash over my face.

"What about you?" I tipped my head in a quick nod towards Blackspire. "What happened to all of your strategically important daughters?"

A breathy chuckle escaped his lips. "I flirted with them all so they would convince their fathers that I was the best thing that ever happened to Pernula until they believed it enough to make me High King."

"And now?"

"And now they're back to flirting with other lords." He lifted his toned shoulders in a nonchalant shrug. "I never had any intension of actually marrying one of them."

I let out a dark chuckle and flicked my eyes to his chest, right where his heart was. "Still cold and black, huh?"

He answered with a sly smile.

Stars glittered like silver dust in the darkened heavens above as we fell silent again. Below us, the vines clinging to the balcony rustled faintly in the wind. Shade turned his gaze towards the horizon.

"You're running out of time," he said softly. "My spies are telling me that the star elves are up to something."

"How soon?" I asked.

"Not sure. But if you do end up winning and there is a change of leadership in the Underworld, then it will require an adjustment period before everything settles down again. That window is closing fast. So if you're going to do something, you have to do it now."

Leaning back on my hands, I tipped my head back and let out a sigh. "I know."

"If you don't win this power struggle soon, you'll have to wait to challenge him again until after we've survived the war against Queen Nimlithil."

I twisted my head to meet his eyes. "*If* we survive the war against Queen Nimlithil."

"Yeah." He blew out a long breath and then turned to face me again. "So, what's your plan? How is he still in power after that fiasco of a fight?"

"You stayed and watched, huh?"

"Of course." He shot me an approving smile. "You handled that really well."

I snorted and rolled my eyes but couldn't stop my lips from quirking upwards as well. "As far as I can tell," I said in response to his first question, "the only reason that not everyone has abandoned him is because he buys their loyalty. He's apparently filthy rich."

"Hmm. So, what are you going to do about it?"

The wind whistled through the buildings. I drummed my fingers against the warm tiles underneath me as I considered. Shade was right, time was running out. If the star elves really were getting ready to move then I had to finish this quickly. But more than that, I had meant what I'd said to Elaran. What happened tonight could never happen again. We'd been lucky tonight but I had to end this before the Rat King tried to hurt my friends again. Grand schemes formed in my mind as I finally turned back to the Master Assassin next to me.

"I'm gonna do what I always do." A wide grin spread across my face. "I'm gonna steal it."

He chuckled. "Of course you are. My little thief."

Jumping up from the roof, I gave my body a quick stretch while an evil grin spread across my lips. "But first, I have a message to send."

While climbing to his feet as well, Shade raised his eyebrows at me but I just threw another wicked smile in his direction before strolling away.

"You'll hear about it soon enough," I called over my shoulder before breaking into a trot.

I could feel him shaking his head at me but I just continued into the darkness. Indeed, I had a message to send. An important message. And as always, when I have something to say, I make sure that people hear it.

SOFT THUDS SOUNDED as Yngvild and I positioned yet another body in front of the wall. Moving them all without the guards spotting us had taken much longer than I would've preferred and it had used up a lot of my very limited patience. But it would be worth it.

I dipped two fingers into the sticky liquid before drawing them down the wall. Once I reached the bottom, I dipped them again. A curving line. Another dip. And then a diagonal one. And like that I continued until my message was at last finished.

Sneaking back, I joined Yngvild, Vania, and the rest of my gang in the shadows of a building further down. They watched the scene before them with grim expressions.

"If that message isn't crystal clear, I don't know what is," Yngvild rumbled.

Across the open square in front of the Rat King's headquarters, dark shapes were visible. It was the bodies of the men who had tried to kill my friends tonight. Their corpses formed a long line in front of the walls surrounding the building and as if that wasn't enough, I'd added one final touch. Written in blood across the stone walls was one word. *Run.*

29.

Candlelight flickered over several layers of paper. I squinted at one of the hand-drawn maps at the top while reaching for my mug. When I tipped it towards my lips, I realized that it was empty. Which I already knew because I'd done the exact same thing only a minute ago. After placing the disappointing mug back on the table, I let out a long sigh and massaged my eyebrows.

"This is not encouraging," I said.

Vania leaned forward in her chair and shot me a sympathetic look. "Well, his whole fortune is located in that vault so I wouldn't expect it to be easy."

I once again frowned at the map before me. In the days since I'd advised the Rat King to run, I had been putting together a plan. The scrawled notes and maps on the table in front of me were the product of that. No one in my gang knew everything about the vault that lay in the basement of the Rat King's headquarters but by piecing together bits of information from everyone, I had managed to get a mostly complete map of the building all the way down to the vault.

"I know," I grumbled in reply. "But it didn't have to be this hard."

Wood creaked as Yngvild shifted his considerable weight in the chair. "You can't do it?"

A sly smile spread across my lips. "I didn't say *that*. But I'll need some help."

Emerald cushions rumpled as I slid out of the booth and stood up. I raised my mug to drain it but then remembered that it was empty. Giving myself an internal facepalm, I put it down again and started forward. Chairs scraped against the floorboards as Yngvild and Vania got to their feet as well.

"Where are you going now?" Vania asked and made as if to follow.

Twisting around, I waved them back in their chairs. "To call in some favors."

"Do you even have any more favors to call in?"

"Uhm... no."

Yngvild flashed me a wide grin. "So you'll be begging for favors, not calling them in?"

Vania slapped his chest with the back of her hand in reprimand but both of them laughed at the affronted expression on my face. I shook my head at them.

"Just make sure that everything is ready in two days," I called and swung around again.

On my way to the door, I passed Helena with a tray full of mugs. I was half tempted to swipe one of them and drain it before I got to the door just to make up for all the times I'd lifted the empty one but I managed to resist the urge. And besides, I needed a clear head if I was to face a certain someone. Especially if that someone had been informed of my recent actions. I drew a bracing breath as I slipped into the night. This would probably end well.

HEAVENLY SCENTS OF spices and cooking meat drifted through the hallway. I snuck forward on silent feet and followed the faint sound of voices. Apparently, two of the four people I needed to ask for favors were in the same place. That would've been convenient but, as I made my way through the candlelit corridor with my heart pattering in my chest, I really wished they hadn't been.

Lingering in the shadows, I peered into the kitchen. Candles burned brightly around the room and the table was overlain with dishes. Three people were seated at the sturdy wooden table. Liam. Norah. And Zaina. They were chatting and laughing like they hadn't a care in the world while eating the delicious meal that Norah had no doubt prepared. I hesitated. They were just living a normal happy life and here I was, bringing trouble to their door again. A flash of conscience that I didn't know I had made me turn around again.

"Aren't you going to come in?" Liam called.

I froze. Slowing turning back again, I found him looking straight at me. "You heard me, huh?"

"I used to be a thief too, remember?"

A teasing grin spread across my face as I moved away from the shadows and into the brightly lit kitchen. "A very noisy thief, if I recall correctly."

Liam sent me a beaming smile and waved me towards the table but I lingered by the doorway.

"I can't stay." I shuffled my feet and flicked my gaze between Liam and Zaina. "I need a favor. From both of you, actually."

"Of course," Liam said. "Whatever you need."

Once I'd explained what I needed from them, they exchanged a look and then nodded.

"Sure, shouldn't be a problem," Zaina said. "When?"

"Day after tomorrow."

"Yeah, I can swing that," she replied while Liam backed her up with a nod.

I smiled at them both. "Thanks." After a nod at their table, I started to turn around. "Well, I'll leave you to your dinner before it gets cold."

Relief flowed through me. I had managed to get through the whole conversation without anyone bringing that up. Something sizzled in a frying pan to my right as I took a step back towards the door.

"Oh, and Storm?" Norah said.

My heart sank and I briefly closed my eyes. Gods damn it.

"Yes?" I said in as innocent a voice as I could produce.

"You didn't knock on the door this time either." A teasing smile tugged at her beautiful face. "Maybe you should try to develop a habit of knocking so that... certain situations can be avoided."

Zaina's black eyes glinted in the firelight as she cracked her knuckles. "Yes, I heard that you walked in on my sister in a very private setting."

Crap. I shifted my gaze to Norah.

"You promised you wouldn't say anything."

She giggled and winked at me. "I promised no such thing. After all, that story was too funny not to share."

"Uhm..." I flicked my eyes around the room.

The black-haired smuggler was still watching me intently with one hand wrapped around her fist. Aw, shit. Zaina was going to kill me.

"But..." she began and lowered her hands to the table again. "You also sent like half an army to keep Norah and Liam safe." She flashed me a grin that held no malice whatsoever but instead boatloads of amusement. "So, I guess we're even."

I stifled the sigh of relief and instead shot her a wicked grin. "Good. That way I won't be forced to tell Lady Smythe what an overprotective mama bear you really are."

Utensils clattered and chairs scraped as Zaina lunged but I was already moving.

"*Now* we're even," I called over my shoulder as I disappeared down the hall again.

Boisterous laughter bounced off the wooden walls behind me as the three of them let me slip into the night without further admonishment. I chuckled as I climbed the nearest building and took off towards my next target.

That had gone surprisingly well. Not only had I managed to enlist their help but I had also escaped unscathed despite Zaina finding out that I had burst into her sister's bedroom unannounced and seen things I shouldn't have seen. Though, after my last remark, I had a feeling that an ass-kicking was coming my way soon regardless. I grinned. Oh well, one problem at a time.

When my next target appeared before me, I had already figured out the best way to get inside so I just slunk through the maze of buildings until I found the right one. Getting inside was as easy as scaling the side of the building, prying open the shutters with a lockpick, and sneaking inside.

The mattress creaked as I plopped down on the bed and waited. I shook my head. Man, I really needed to teach these people how to better protect themselves from thieves.

Before long, soft footsteps sounded in the corridor outside. I simply remained on top of the neat covers when the owner of the room pushed down the handle and stepped inside.

"Gah!" Elaran yelped and jerked back.

"Now you know how I feel when you sneak up on me in the woods," I said.

The athletic elf appeared to have just returned from taking a bath. A large towel was wrapped around his hips and his auburn hair was damp and fell freely down his bare back. I cocked my head. This was probably the first time I'd seen him without that tight side braid that otherwise always gathered up the hair on the right side of his head.

Elaran readjusted his towel and glared at me. "Where did you even come from?"

"The window."

"Of course you did." He shook his head. "Why is it always the bloody window?" Huffing, he shut the door and then stalked towards the dresser. "You ever heard of knocking on the door?"

"Why does everyone keep telling me that tonight?"

"Maybe because you don't knock."

"Exactly." I gave him a short shake of my head. "I would've thought you all knew that already."

Elaran muttered something under his breath while pulling open a drawer. His lean muscles flexed as he picked up a tight-fitting green shirt and pulled it over his head. Once it was on, he lifted a pair of brown pants. Frowning, he paused for a second and then looked between me and the garment in his hands as if he had just realized that he would need to take off the towel to put on the pants. He blew out a forceful breath and dropped the pants back in the drawer before shoving it shut and leaning back against it with his arms crossed.

"What do you want?"

The mattress groaned again as I shifted my weight self-consciously and averted my eyes. "I need a favor."

Elaran chuckled. "And you thought breaking into my room was the best way to go?"

"Well, thieves, you know," I said lightly. But when I shifted my gaze back to him, my tone was serious. "Please."

He blew out a sigh. "Alright. What is it?" After I'd explained what I would need his help with, he nodded without hesitation. "Yeah, no problem."

"Thank you."

"Yeah." He mumbled something incoherent and then made a shooing motion. "Now get out so I can put some pants on."

Laughter bubbled from my chest. Unfurling my legs, I stood up and strode back to the window. After placing my hands on the window frame, I looked back at him and nodded at the candle on his desk.

"Oh, and you really should blow out the candle before you go and take a bath." I jumped up on the windowsill and swung myself out. Facing Elaran again, I sent him a wicked grin. "It might start a fire."

I only had time to see surprise flash over his face before I dropped out of sight.

"You *do not* get to lecture me about starting fires!" followed me into the night.

Cackling, I disappeared into the dark shadows below the building and sprinted away. Alright. Three out of four favors secured. Now, the only one left was the one I dreaded most. Shade.

All my other friends were reasonable and had agreed to help me without question but there was no telling what that damn assassin would make me do in exchange for one simple favor. I blew out a sigh as I jumped the gap between two buildings. Well, only one way to find out. I set course for Blackspire.

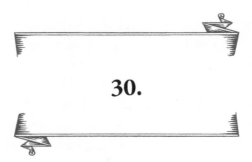

30.

Well, hadn't that been anticlimactic? I frowned as I stalked up the stairs at the Black Emerald and headed for my room. After bracing myself and sneaking into the castle, I hadn't actually been able to find Shade. And his assassins didn't seem to know where he was either. Shaking my head, I unlocked the door to my room and stepped inside before pushing it shut behind me again.

"Damn assassin," I muttered.

Metal clattered against wood as I removed all the knives strapped to my body. My custom-made vest followed. I looked down at the tight-fitting black shirt I wore underneath. Could I really be bothered to change clothes before I crammed in some sleep? Nope. I kicked off my boots and headed for bed.

The air shifted behind me. I ducked and threw out an elbow just as a black-clad arm sailed past in the space where my head had been. My elbow cut the air harmlessly as Shade jumped back. He flashed me a smile from a few strides away.

The very first time I met him, I had come to the conclusion that I wouldn't win a hand-to-hand against him. I was pretty sure that was still true. My knives waited in a neat pile on top of the drawers to my right. Shifting my gaze, I threw a quick glance at them while considering.

That proved to be my downfall. I let out a yelp as Shade darted towards me during that second of inattention and swiped my legs from underneath me. Managing to break my fall slightly, I tried to roll away right as two knees connected with the floorboards on either side of me.

Something cold clamped around my wrist. With my movements abruptly halted, I stared in disbelief from the assassin straddling my chest to the contraption locking my left wrist to the leg of the bed.

"Seriously?" Metal rattled as I yanked my arm. "Again with the handcuffs?"

A wicked smirk played over Shade's lips as he forced my other arm down on the floor and leaned so close that his breath danced over my skin. "Admit it. Admit that I won."

"Yeah, I don't think so." I yanked at the manacles again but with my other hand pinned above my head on the other side, I couldn't pick the lock on them.

"Then we'll be here all night."

I narrowed my eyes at the arrogant assassin leaning over me. "You're a bastard, you know that?"

His eyes glittered dangerously as the smirk on his face deepened. "I told you there would be hell to pay for that little power trip you went on down there in the tavern."

Oh. That. Every time I'd seen him since I forced him to strip off his swords and sit in that chair, I'd been waiting for his payback. But after I while, I'd realized that he enjoyed seeing me flinch and worry about when and how he would exact his revenge so I'd stopped thinking about it. Apparently, *that* was what he'd been waiting for. A moment when I wasn't on high alert anymore.

I pulled against his strong grip and tried to wiggle out from under him but his muscled body kept me mercilessly pinned to the floor.

Shade leaned down until his lips almost touched mine. "Say it. Admit that you lost to me."

"Not gonna happen."

"I was hoping you'd say that." His breath danced over my skin as he released a dark chuckle. "Because every time you refuse, I will make this harder for you. *Now*, if you want to ever get up from this floor, you'll have to admit that you lost *and* say 'please allow me to get up.'"

A baffled laugh shook my chest while I raised my eyebrows at him. His dark eyes were full of wicked mischief as he kept them locked on me. I met his gaze head on.

"In your dreams," I whispered against his mouth.

The evil smile on his lips widened. "Oh, please do keep going. *Now*, you will have to admit that you lost and say 'please allow me to get up, *Master Shade*.'"

Small splinters from the floorboards caught in my hair as I shook my head with an incredulous look on my face. "I've told you you're a bastard, right?"

"Yes. And I've told you there would be hell to pay." His lips brushed against my jaw for a second before he tilted his head to level those glittering eyes on me again. A smirk curled his lips. "I hope you enjoyed the power trip."

Narrowing my eyes, I glared at him. Gods damn it. He *was* petty enough to keep me trapped on the floor until I admitted defeat. Arching my back, I tried to heave him off me but my hips rose barely a breath before meeting a wall of hard muscle as he pulled back from my face and settled more firmly on top of me.

"Now say it." That wicked smile still played over his lips. "Or do you want me to make you beg for it?"

Damn assassin. Gods fucking damn assassin. Make me beg for it? I would make *him* beg for it. Metal rattled as I yanked against the manacles again. If I could just get out of this.

Heavy footsteps sounded on the stairs outside the door. Satisfaction coursed through me as I let out a chuckle.

"Oh you're in so much trouble now," I said.

Shade's dark eyebrows creased slightly but he didn't take his eyes off me.

"That's Yngvild coming to give me the reports I asked for," I explained. "What do you think he'll do when he opens the door and sees you straddling me while I'm handcuffed to the bed?"

Shade shot a panicked glance at the door. The footsteps drew closer. I gave the suddenly nervous assassin a wicked smile.

"Oh I can't wait to see this."

Spitting out a curse, he tossed me the key to the handcuffs and jumped back. I unlocked them and shot to my feet just as the heavy footsteps reached the door.

And then continued down the hall.

An evil smirk descended on my face as I locked eyes with the Master Assassin on the other side of the room. His eyes widened.

"You did *not* just..." He trailed off when he saw the grin spreading across my lips.

With black eyes glittering, Shade advanced on me. I stood my ground as he came to a halt before me and placed a hand on my jaw. Still grinning, I let him tilt my head up to meet his eyes.

"My scheming little liar." He let out a dark chuckle. "What am I to do with you?"

I stared into his intense eyes. "You could admit that *I* won."

Leaning down, Shade placed his lips right below my ear. His hot breath sent a shudder coursing through my body.

"Never," he breathed against my skin.

And then he withdrew and stepped back. I sucked in a deep breath and instinctively ran my fingers over the place where his hand had been. Shaking my head, I pushed out the ridiculous images that had flashed through my mind. It was more difficult that I had expected so I cleared my throat and took a step back to put even more distance between our bodies.

"So," I shot him a teasing grin, "did you just come here to fail at getting revenge on me or did you want something else?"

A lopsided smile tugged at his lips. "I need a favor."

I blinked at him. Well, wasn't that a surprise? And a stroke of luck. If I had gone to Shade to ask him for a favor, he would've most likely tried to make me beg for it. Again. But now that he wanted something from me, I could just demand whatever I wanted in return. How about that? I sent a quick prayer of thanks to Cadentia, Goddess of Luck, for actually having my back for once.

"What kind of favor?" I asked.

"There's a cooperative of traders who is making the wrong kind of noise, but I can't just have them killed."

"That must really suck for you."

Shade leveled an exasperated glare at me before shaking his head. "I don't care how you do it but I want you to make them look dirty. I need them to lose their positions so that I can swoop in and save them."

I arched an eyebrow at him. "And then they'll be indebted to you."

A sly smile spread across his lips. "Correct."

"That could be arranged."

"What do you want in return?"

Matching his smirk, I spread my hands. "I want a favor too."

"Name it." Once I'd explained what I wanted, he nodded. "Done."

Summer winds blew air smelling of fragrant spices into my room. In the tavern far below, people laughed and talked in loud voices while someone stalked down the stairs again. Shade tilted his head to the right and for a moment, we just remained standing there, staring at each other. Then, he broke my gaze and strode towards the open window. Pausing on the windowsill, he turned back to me.

When I met his eyes, all the amused teasing was gone and had been replaced by seriousness. "It's a dangerous plan."

"I know."

Shade shifted his gaze to the night outside again. "You'd better make it out of there alive."

I opened my mouth to respond but the assassin was already gone. Shaking my head, I let out a long sigh. Yes, it was a dangerous plan. But it was all I had.

Now, all favors had been called in and final preparations were underway. In two days, I would be breaking into the Rat King's highly secure vault where he kept his entire fortune. If this didn't work, I didn't know what else to do. Though, if it didn't work, I probably wouldn't be alive to worry about it so there was that. I flopped down on the bed and draped an arm over my eyes. At least I would die the way I lived. As a thief.

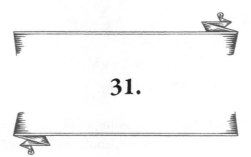

31.

"**N**ot another step."

Steel rang and leather creaked as swords were drawn. I kept very still as the guards outside the Rat King's mansion approached the wagon that had stopped right outside their walls.

"Is that really any way to greet an old business partner, Tedan?" Zaina replied.

"Zaina?" the guard called Tedan said. When he spoke again, his voice held a note of authority. "Stand down. I know her."

I shifted my weight on the metal bars secured under the wagon where I currently hid. My vision was pretty restricted below the wooden vehicle but I could make out two pairs of boots coming to join the six pairs that already surrounded my transportation.

"Haven't seen you in ages," Tedan continued.

"Yeah, I know," Zaina said. "I tried my hand at pirating."

"How did that work out?"

"Not nearly as well as my smuggling."

"That why you're here?"

"Yeah."

Fabric rustled as Zaina threw back the cloth covering the boxes on the wagon bed above me. I suppressed the urge to flinch because I knew they couldn't see me through the wood. In front of me, dust swirled over the stones in the golden light of the setting sun.

"I heard you're engaged in some kind of smuggling war, which is good for me, not gonna lie." Wood groaned faintly as Zaina lifted the lid of a box. "So I came to see what you'd be willing to give me for these?"

The wagon creaked and shifted to the side as Tedan leaned against it to no doubt peer into the box. The movement made me slide a little to the left on the metal bars below but I didn't dare wiggle back to my original spot in case it would give away my position.

"Hats?" Tedan asked, a hint of surprise in his voice.

"And gloves, scarves, stuff like that."

"That's unusual wares from you."

Of course it was. But when one is friends with a hatmaker, one takes what one can get. I hadn't wanted to use any of my real smuggled goods for this deception so instead, I'd had Liam help me out. He'd convinced his merchant friends to let me buy their surplus of low-quality items. After all, the wares didn't have to actually pass inspection, they just needed to distract them long enough for part two of my plan to be set in motion.

"I know, right? But upperworlders are crazy about this kind of stuff so if you can steal–" Zaina chuckled. "I mean, *obtain* the right ones, you can make a lot of money."

"True. But you know the Rat King's gotta sign off on this before..."

Tedan trailed off as running footsteps echoed between the buildings. The metal bar was digging into my chest so I used the sudden noise to shift into a slightly more comfortable position.

Twisting my head, I could just about make out a pair of boots sprinting towards us from behind. Another cloud of dust swirled in the golden light as the man skidded to a halt a few steps from Tedan.

"The High King..." He sucked in a deep breath. "...is coming."

"What?" Zaina and Tedan snapped in unison.

"He's got soldiers and assassins with him," the scout panted.

"Get the Rat King!" Tedan stalked back towards the mansion. "And get everyone ready to defend against an attack."

Above me, Zaina slammed the lid back on the box. "I'm *not* getting busted for smuggling. You either help me hide this inside or I'll leave you to deal with this mess too."

His boots ground to a halt a few strides way. Then, he spit out a curse and snapped his fingers at someone further away.

"Park this wagon inside the walls," he said. "And then show Zaina and her people out the back."

The wagon lurched forward as Zaina and her gang members steered it towards the gate. Wooden spokes groaned in protest as the wheels rattled hurriedly against the stone street until it was finally inside the wall surrounding the Rat King's mansion. Noise filled the afternoon air.

People rushed in and out of the front door while yelling instructions. Steel rang and crossbow strings creaked as weapons were readied. In the distance, marching feet echoed between the buildings.

And here comes part two.

"If anything is missing from this wagon when I come back to get it, you and I are gonna have a problem," Zaina warned as she and her crew were herded away to whatever back exit the mansion was equipped with.

The stomping boots drew closer. A whole mass of people had gathered in the empty space between the building and the walls before it. I could only see their legs from my position under the wagon but I was pretty sure they were all carrying weapons and all waiting for their leader to appear. At last, the crowd before the door parted to allow a pair of slim legs to pass. I shifted my weight and got ready to make my move.

"Don't attack unless I give the word," the Rat King growled as he stalked through his gang and towards the gate set into the stone walls. "Anyone who fires without permission will be flayed alive."

The approaching force must have finally reached the courtyard before the walls because the sound of marching feet disappeared. Everyone in the Rat King's gang seemed to be holding their breath.

"High King Shade," the Rat King said. "What is the meaning of this?"

"I have come to ask you the same," Shade replied, his voice cold and hard as steel. "A few days ago, a whole swarm of armed underworlders surrounded the walls of Blackspire. Was that meant as an act of war?"

Placing my palms on the dusty stones, I slid off the metal bars and down onto the ground. Pebbles pressed into my hands and knees as I crawled towards the front of the wagon and then rolled to the side.

"An act of war?" the Rat King replied. "Of course not. Those people weren't mine. They were the Oncoming Storm's people. I thought she was an acquaintance of yours so you should question her instead. Maybe she has betrayed you."

With very slow and careful movements, I climbed to my feet in the tight space between the wooden wall of the building and the wagon.

No one looked in my direction. Every pair of eyes on this side were focused on their leader as well as the High King and his army outside the gate. Satisfaction coursed through me when I noticed that the Rat King's left arm was still braced by a sling after the damage I'd caused during our fight. Grinning slightly, I slunk towards the front door.

"Watch that tone," Shade said. "Your job is to control the Underworld. If you can't control it all, then perhaps you are not the right man for the job."

Though I couldn't see him right now, I knew what he looked like when he used that voice. A dangerous calculating glint in his dark eyes, arrogance playing over his lips, and authority dripping from his whole being. People usually found themselves wanting to retreat a step when that happened. He had used that voice on me more than once, so I should know.

While the Rat King's crew was busy fighting the urge to step back, I tiptoed the final bit behind their backs and reached the door.

There was no way to know if there were still people inside the house, but I couldn't risk anyone turning around and finding me out here so I just slipped inside and hoped for the best.

No one stabbed me. Sending a quick prayer to Nemanan, I continued into the hallway made of dark wood. So far so good.

According to the map we'd pieced together, the entrance to the basement where the vault was located was in the middle of the building. The route I had memorized would take me past two living rooms, one sparring room, and finally into some kind of strongroom that led down into the vault. And I would have to get through all of that and get back out again before Shade ran out of reasons to keep the Rat King occupied. Right. Piece of cake.

Shaking my head, I crept out of the corridor and right into a room full of armed men.

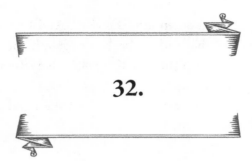

32.

The gasp caught in my throat and I threw myself back into the corridor. Pressed against the wall just outside the doorway, I waited for the alarm to be raised. Nothing happened. Still trying to slow my racing heart, I peeked back around the corner.

Men with crossbows lined the east wall. They were split into groups of four and all of them had their attention fixed on the view outside the windows. *Damn.* I had expected that Shade's maneuver would've drawn most of them outside but apparently, the Rat King was smarter than that. He had left them here so that if an enemy made it inside the walls, these people could shoot them before they reached the building. Smart. But incredibly annoying.

After carefully checking that no one was looking in my direction, I started forward again. Staying low, I snuck towards my first hiding place. With my pulse smattering in my ears, the wide sofa I had picked felt as though it was much farther away than it really was. I cast a worried glance at the east wall. The man closest to me shifted his weight. I resisted the urge to sprint away and instead forced myself to continue my slow sneaking pace.

Brown fabric finally appeared next to my shoulder. I released a soundless sigh of relief as I crouched down behind it and pressed my back into the soft material. Now I needed to cut straight across the room to get to the south side of the building but there wasn't a lot of cover between me and the next doorway. I sent another prayer to Nemanan, and one to Cadentia as well, for good measure. *And... now!* I sprang forward.

Wood groaned under my feet. Screeching to a halt, I jerked back and ducked behind the sofa again. *Oh Cadentia, you can be such a bitch.*

"What was that?" a man said.

"Didn't hear nothing," someone else replied.

"I heard it," a third man said in a gruff voice. "But it's probably just the house settling."

Leather creaked and soft footsteps sounded. *Oh, shit.* He was coming this way to check. I pressed my back further into the brown couch while flicking desperate eyes across the room. There was nothing else to hide behind, nowhere else to go without him seeing me. He drew closer. My heart slammed against my ribs as I tried to figure out something that didn't involve me having to fight twelve people with crossbows. Boots thudded against the floorboards. He was right on the other side of my cushion-covered hiding place. One more step and he would see me.

"He's moving," the gruff voice snapped from the window. "The Rat King's going out to meet him."

Feet slapped against wood as the man who'd been hunting me rushed back to the window. I dared one peek over the back of the sofa to make sure that their attention was otherwise occupied before I darted forward. No time to be sneaky. I knew how to move quietly, even at high speed, so unless another floorboard betrayed me, I would make it out.

The doorway grew bigger. On my back, the spot between my shoulder blades itched from the thought of a crossbow bolt burying itself there any second, but I didn't dare waste even one second by turning around. And then I was through the door.

Forcing myself to draw soft shallow breaths, I stopped by the wall just inside the next living room. Dust swirled in lazy circles inside a tastefully decorated room but other than that, it was empty. I allowed myself another soundless sigh of relief. Still staying light on my feet, I snuck along the wall full of paintings in gilded frames and towards the next doorway.

With no one to hide from, I made it out of the expensive living room much quicker than I had the other one. Casting a swift glance around the corner, I checked for potential enemies.

A long narrow hallway awaited me on the other side. Golden light streamed in through the windows and painted the dark wood in warm hues. Unlit candles were mounted on the walls but other than that, it was empty. I snuck forward.

So far, my map had been true. In the middle of this corridor there would be a door leading to the sparring room and then at the end, right before it ended in another living room, would be the door to the strongroom. I was almost there now.

Boots thudded against the floor up ahead. Panic crackled through me. *Shit*. They were coming this way. I couldn't retreat to the living room again because I would only be spotted and trapped there and there was nowhere to hide inside this corridor. My heart thumped in my chest. The footsteps were drawing closer and would be rounding the corner into the hallway any second now. I darted forward.

It had to be unlocked. It had to. Because if it wasn't, I wouldn't have time to pick it before I was spotted. Skidding to a halt, I shoved down the handle of the door to the sparring room. It slid down without resistance. I flung myself into the room and pushed the door shut right as the approaching men reached the corridor.

Heaving a deep sigh, I leaned back against the door. Something nagged me. There had been a clanking noise right when I had slipped inside and I was pretty sure it hadn't come from the people in the hallway. I swept my gaze over the sparring room. My heart sank. *Shit.*

A young man blinked at me in surprise. He was lowering the sword he had been swinging against a practice dummy made of wood.

"Please don't tell anyone," he said. "I won't be doing much good out there anyway and I never get to practice because everyone just says that it's their turn and that I have to–"

"If you don't get out there this instant, I'll call everyone in here right now and tell them about your insubordination," I snapped in an authoritative voice. "Hurry! Before I yell for them."

"What? Why would you...? I mean... don't you know the room is soundproof?"

Of course the room was bloody soundproof. Gods damn it. Well, in hindsight, it made sense. Kind of hard to sleep to the sound of clashing swords. If I'd really lived here, I would've known that. How was I supposed to explain my way out of this?

"How could you not know..." He trailed off and the frown on his face deepened. "Hey, aren't you...?" Alarm flashed over his face and he raised his sword. "You're the Oncoming Storm."

I rolled my eyes. "Put that thing away before you get hurt."

"No." He raised his chin to match the weapon he was now pointing straight at me. "I will capture you and then the Rat King will notice me. Then everyone will stop making fun of me." His hand trembled as he took a step towards me. "So just stay there."

"Listen, *kid*."

I called him kid even though he was probably only a year or two younger than me, but after everything I'd been through I felt as though I was four times his age. His nervous gray eyes flicked over me as he took another step. I yanked out two throwing knives and poured every bit of wickedness in my soul, which was a considerable amount, I might add, into my voice. If I'd had my powers, my eyes would've been black as death by now.

"If you know who I am, then you know what I am capable of," I said. My voice came out sounding like shards of glass scraped over ice. "I have slaughtered droves of your friends already and they came at me ten at a time. Do you really think you'll be able to get within fifteen strides of me unless I allow it?"

His knuckles were turning white from how hard he gripped the handle of that ridiculous sword but he took another step towards me. I threw the first knife. A hiss echoed through the air as it clipped his cheek, and he sucked in a shocked breath. Pressing a hand to his bleeding face, he stared at me with eyes wide with fear.

"You have two choices," I growled at him. "Drop the sword, hand me the handcuffs you've got on your belt, and sit your ass down in front of that pillar." A wolfish grin flashed across my teeth as I spun the throwing knife in my hand. "Or the next time you take a step towards me, I'll put this through your throat. Choose."

Metal clattered against wood as he dropped the sword as if it had burned him. While snatching the handcuffs from his belt, he hurried sideways until he reached the indicated pillar set into the floor and dropped to his knees in front of it. Brown hair fell into his eyes as he lowered his head.

"Please, I don't want to die," he whispered.

"Good choice."

I stuck the throwing knife back in its sheath and stalked towards him. His hands shook as he offered me the manacles. They were cold against my palms as I took them and skirted around to the other side of the support beam.

"I don't want to die. Please, I don't want to die," the young man repeated as I came to a halt behind him.

"You're not going to die if you do as I say. Now shut up and give me your hands."

He flinched as I shoved his wrists in place and locked them together behind the wooden pillar. Once the handcuffs had clicked shut, I retrieved my missing throwing knife and then strode back towards the door. Right as I was about to slip into the corridor again, his soft voice stopped me.

"Why?" he whispered. "The Rat King says you kill everyone. So why not me?"

"Because I don't have time," I muttered and turned back towards the door. But then I paused for a second with my hand on the handle. "And because, despite what people say, I don't actually like killing people who aren't a threat to me." Twisting slightly, I fixed him with a withering glare. "But if you tell anyone I said that, I'll come back and gut you."

Without waiting for him to reply, I yanked the door open and disappeared back into the hallway. It had been the truth.

Both reasons. I didn't have time to get into a lengthy fight because I didn't know how much more time I would have before Shade had run out of excuses to keep the conversation going. But I was also tired. Tired of killing people who didn't actually want to come after me.

Yes, I know, I have left a trail of bodies behind me so long that I can't even see the end anymore and I don't even feel particularly guilty about that. But I don't actually enjoy killing people. I kill to stay alive or to keep my friends alive. To me, there is a difference there.

The corridor was still filled with golden light but was now empty of approaching underworlders, so I reached the door to the strongroom without any more unexpected trouble. Placing a hand on the handle, I pushed it down. Locked. I knelt before it and studied the contraption while taking out my lockpicks.

It was more complicated than the standard locks on most doors so my ego took a couple of hits when I couldn't get it open straight away. I was about one second from letting out a lengthy string of curses when it finally clicked open. Casting a quick glance around me to make sure that no one was watching, I pushed down the handle and slipped inside.

Two pairs of glowing eyes met me.

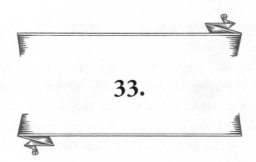

33.

A gasp escaped my throat. I fumbled for the handle but didn't make it. The first hound lunged for me. Darting to the side, I barely managed to avoid its snapping jaws as it crashed into the wall where I'd been standing only a fraction of a second before. The second dog watched me with calculating eyes from a few strides away. I had time for one quick sweep of the room before the first animal flew at me again.

Of course there were bloody hounds watching the entrance to the vault. If I'd had time to actually scout out the place properly before breaking in, I wouldn't have had to run blind into every damn room. But time was slipping away with each wasted breath and I didn't have any more seconds to spare to properly check every room before I entered. Sometimes, you just have to dive head first in and hope that the Goddess of Luck has your back. But I really should've learned by now that the fickle mistress known as Cadentia *never* had my back.

Leaping through the air, I evaded the next bite by scant margins. There were a few candles burning on the walls and I had half a mind to rip one down and wave it in the dog's face until he backed off but I discarded that plan as soon as a memory popped up. Last time I'd waved fire in an animal's face, I'd burned down an entire forest. Torching the Rat King's headquarters might be fun. But not with me in it.

The second dog snarled and now they fell into a synchronized hunting pattern. *Shit.* There were no desks or other furniture to take cover behind. Only the door at the back that I assumed led to the basement, the burning candles, and the stuffed heads of dead animals that decorated the walls. The two beasts barely gave me time to think at the speed they moved. Panic clawed its way up my throat when I saw them getting ready for a joint attack. I leaped onto the wall.

The antlers of some kind of deer I had never seen before creaked in alarm at the sudden weight but both it and the head of a boar held. I had used them as handholds to scale the wall and get out of reach of the charging hounds. Growling and snapping made me yank my feet even further up.

Now that I had a few seconds of breathing room, I could finally reach into one of my belt pouches and pull out some weapons I was sure would work. Dog anatomy wasn't high up on my list of skills but I figured that no matter where I hit with these, they'd get the job done. I shifted my weight on the boar head and twisted around until I could get a clean shot.

Throwing darts wasn't exactly something I was adept at since I had almost never done it before but I figured that the technique was about the same as throwing knives. Vania had insisted I take them and I was actually pretty sure I was supposed to blow them out of a tube, but *that* I had no frame of reference for, so I went with what I knew best. A throw.

After one more second to aim, I hurled the first dart. It struck the wilder of the two dogs straight in the back. A startled yelp came from it but before the second one could figure out what was happening, I threw the next projectile. It flew further back than I had intended but still lodged itself in the second hound's hind leg. One more second passed. And then both beasts collapsed on the floor. I stared at them.

Paralytic darts. Why had I never used things like this before? They were really convenient. Unless other people used them on you. Like they had done on me and Shade two years ago and I'd had to drag his paralyzed ass across the city while dying of some weird poison because a windmill of a woman had cut me. Then, they're really inconvenient.

Now that the dogs were immobilized, I let go of the dead animals on the wall and dropped back to the floor. While throwing a quick glance over my shoulder to make sure no one had heard the ruckus, I strode towards the door in the back. This one also had a rather complicated lock but it was the same kind as the door behind me, so I managed to pick it without too much effort. I knew that I was running out of time so as soon as the lock clicked, I pulled open the door to reveal a darkened stairwell beyond.

Stone steps led down into the basement but I couldn't make anything else out. I darted back into the room and snatched a burning candle from the wall. Every minute was borrowed time at this point. I had to finish this fast. Keeping the flame well away from the rest of my equipment, I hurried down the steps and into the darkness.

Fire danced over rough stone walls until the narrow stairwell emptied out in a small rectangular landing. The temperature dropped with each step underground and when I reached the landing, a refreshing coolness enveloped me and helped slow my racing heart.

Only a few steps away from the stairs rose a sturdy wall of solid metal. Something that looked kind of like a doorway was visible in the middle but it didn't look like any door I'd ever seen. The metal was cold to my touch as I drew a hand over the strange surface. I couldn't see inside but this had to be the vault. Now, I just needed to find the lock. I frowned at the wall. And the handle.

There was nothing that looked even remotely like a normal handle or lock. Only ruts and ridges set into the metal in strange patterns. Uncertainty flashed through me and I cast a glance towards the stairwell. They could be coming any minute now.

Shaking my head, I pulled my focus back to the problem at hand. I couldn't pick the lock on a door if I couldn't *find* the lock. Tracing my fingers over the cool metal, I tried to discover any hidden openings. Nothing. My heart slammed in my chest. I drew my fingers down random ruts and over ridges in difference sequences. Still nothing.

There had to be some kind of trick to this. If I could just figure out what, then I could get the door open. Panic pulsed through my body as I stabbed at different parts of the wall.

A metallic whirring filled the air. I blinked in surprise as a section of the wall parted above me to reveal a small rectangular window. Lifting the candle, I peered into the glass-covered opening. The flickering flame in my hand danced over stacks of gold, silver, gleaming pearls, and glittering gems. I sucked in a sharp breath and yanked out a hunting knife. Flipping it over in my hand, I rammed the hilt into the glass. A dull thud sounded. My mouth dropped open slightly when the glass across the window didn't so much as sport a single crack. That metallic whirring started up again.

"No, no, no," I blurted and slammed the hilt of my knife into the glass again while the metal rapidly closed back over the window.

Despite my rather forceful pummeling, the glass didn't shatter. I kept trying anyway until a sharp click sounded and the window had disappeared once more.

Setting the candle down on the floor while returning the blade to its sheath, I tried desperately to remember what I'd done to make the window appear. My fingers swept and stabbed across ridges and ruts in tune with my steadily rising panic. Nothing happened.

"Oh come on!" I half cursed, half pleaded and threw my weight against the wall.

A jolt spiked through my shoulder at the impact but the thick metal wall refused to move or reveal any more of its secrets. I cast another glance up the stairs. Time was running out. The treasure was in there but if I couldn't get the door open then all of this would've been for nothing. Without actually getting inside, I wouldn't be able to complete my mission.

Taking a running start, I once again threw myself against what I hoped was the door. Only a heavy thud echoed between the stone walls. Gods damn it.

Something whizzed through the air. On instinct, I jerked to the side. A crossbow bolt dinged against the metal wall right in the space I'd been standing only seconds before.

"Idiot! Watch the bloody door," a man snapped from atop the stairs. "No crossbows. The Rat King will flay us if we damage the mechanism."

My heart sank. *Shit*. Time was now officially up and I was still stranded in a basement with the stairs blocked and no other way out. Boots thudded against stone as the Rat King's crew started down the steps. I yanked the hunting knives from the small of my back. How was I supposed to magic my way out of this?

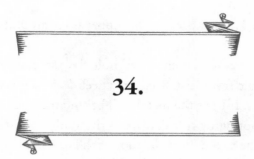

34.

Flames from the candle I had placed on the floor flickered across the narrow space. I swept my gaze over it, calculating the possibilities. The staircase was too narrow for me to slip past them and get upstairs. That meant I had to fight every single one of them until there was no one left and then make my way up the steps once they were all dead.

Weariness washed over me at the mere thought but I could see no other alternative that didn't also involve my involuntary suicide. At least the narrow staircase gave me one advantage as well. They would have to come at me one at a time. Slipping behind the wall, I spun the knives once in my hands.

Two legs appeared on the steps next to the wall. I slashed with trained precision. A howl reverberated through the cold air as I cut the attacker's hamstring. He tumbled down the steps in a flailing of limbs while the next person reached the same step. I severed his hamstring as well.

Cries of pain echoed between the metal and stone surrounding us as the two of them crumpled to the ground at the foot of the stairs. Unfortunately, it appeared as though the element of surprise had been spent because the next attacker didn't make the same mistake as the others. Without stepping in reach of my knives he leaned his upper body around the corner and fired.

I jerked back. The crossbow bolt flew so close to my face that the draft from it stroked my cheek as it whooshed past. I had to move. If I put the metal wall behind me, they'd be forced to stop shooting or risk damaging the vault door. Groans still rose from the two men at the foot of the stairs. Diving forward, I rolled behind them for cover while flicking my wrists. Their moans ended in startled gurgling as I slit their throats.

Now that I was directly below the stairs, I could get a clear view of what I was up against. A mountain of a man filled the narrow space and behind him I could make out a whole line of people waiting for him to descend the stairs. Whatever else happened, I couldn't let them do that. If they reached the landing, they could easily overwhelm me. Steeling myself for the onslaught to come, I launched myself at him.

Since he was so damn tall and I was standing below him on the steps, reaching something vital to stab was a lot more difficult than I would've liked. I slashed upwards but my knife met empty air as he jumped back and pulled the sword from his back. It cleaved the air as he swung. *Shit.* I ducked.

A metallic ringing filled the air. Both of us blinked in surprise at the noise and for a moment no one moved as we stared at the source. His sword had gotten caught against the wall as he tried to swing it in the narrow passageway. Thank Nemanan for shorter blades. Panic bloomed in his eyes as he tried to free his sword before I struck. He didn't make it.

In a swift motion, I swiped across his thighs. A hiss escaped between his teeth and his left knee buckled right as he got his weapon loose. I dove for cover as he tripped down the stairs with his sword in front of him. Steel and body parts slammed against stone but I didn't have time to look at it because the next man was rushing down the steps.

Leaping onto the stairs again, I slashed wildly to keep him from reaching the landing. He retreated a few steps upwards to escape the lethal blades right as a roar came from behind me. The huge man was struggling to his feet among his dead comrades and swung his long sword at me. I jumped just in time.

It cut through the air where my ankles had been and smacked into the stone wall next to me. The man above me attacked again. Ducking his thrust, I kicked backwards at the same time. A crunching sound rose behind me as my boot connected with something in the huge man's face. He released another roar and discarded his inconvenient weapon in favor of a barehanded assault. *Crap*. I couldn't keep fighting with an attacker both in front and behind.

Throwing my arms out, I whirled around in a few fast spins. Steel sliced through skin when the man behind me was too slow to jump back. He doubled over from my slash across his stomach. This was my chance. While the man above had leaped away and the one below was crouching down, I pushed off the stairs and arched my back as I threw myself backwards. Time seemed to pass in slow motion as I vaulted over the injured man before the world tilted back to its rightful place at the bottom of the steps.

The stones were slick with blood from the dead men so I completely botched the landing. Slipping in a crimson puddle, I slammed into the metal wall behind me with a force strong enough to jar my bones. My left hunting knife clattered to the floor. Still trying to right myself after the impact, I almost missed the coming attack.

Survival instinct shoved out the shock and I rammed my remaining blade forward. A grunt sounded. I yanked it out and slashed it across the hulking man's throat before he could figure out that I had just stabbed him in the chest. I pushed his dying weight aside and snatched up my other knife.

The fourth man was darting down the stairs. I shot forward. Metal ground against metal as our blades clashed. *Damn*. This one was also a knife-wielder. I ducked under his swipe and drove a blade towards his gut but he parried it with his other hand. Pain burned through my face.

I sucked in a sharp breath between my teeth as his knife came back red after delivering a shallow cut to my cheek. Blood slid down my face but I ignored it because another attack was coming. He stabbed at my throat. Twisting aside, I evaded the strike while also making him stumble towards me when the movement carried him forwards.

Surprise flashed over his face as his foot continued into the air above the next step. I jabbed my knife into his throat as he passed and then shoved his dying body aside. It thudded to the floor on the landing next to the stairs.

Tiredness washed over me. How many more? How many more people would I have to kill before I had a shot at the stairs? I wiped the blood from my cheek with the back of my hand but I had a feeling that I was just smearing it out even more.

Another attacker thundered down the steps with his sword raised. Calculating the trajectory, I didn't even bother ducking because I already knew it would get caught against the stone wall the same way the others had. Without having to worry about evading his blow, I could easily get inside his guard. Steel clanged against stone as the sword got stuck, just as I had predicted. I slashed my knives across his chest and stomach.

He tumbled towards me. Throwing my arms under his armpits, I caught his falling body and used it as a shield to block the axe-wielder who came after him. The heavy axe caught my human shield right between the shoulder blades with a nauseating crack. I heaved him to the side, taking the weapon buried in his back with it. His body thudded down on top of the other corpse on the side of the stairs while his sword bounced across the stones.

I rammed my knife up through the ribs of the now suddenly unarmed axe-wielder. He gasped but it died quickly as I slit his throat. Stepping to the side, I let his dying weight tumble down to join the others at the foot of the stairs.

And suddenly, everything was quiet. No one made a move to attack me because the other men had retreated to the top of the stairs after their six friends had fallen one by one to the demon in the basement and now lay dead on the stone floor below. Blood and swords littered the narrow space and that thick coppery tang hung heavy over the room.

Still gripping my knives, I didn't waste a second as I darted towards the top of the stairs and the freedom that lay beyond. The light from the doorway drew closer. Taking the steps two at a time, I blinked as the light seemed to be getting smaller again all of a sudden. Dread sank like a block of ice in my stomach. They were closing the door. I pushed my legs to go faster.

Right as I reached the final few steps something sailed past my head from the narrow gap in the doorway. And then it banged shut. Unable and unwilling to stop my forward momentum, I slammed into the door. Pain vibrated through my shoulder but the door didn't move. Glass shattered on the stones below the stairs. I whipped around.

In the flickering light of the candle I had left on the landing below, I couldn't really make out what had made the sound. I stuck my hunting knives back in their sheaths and snuck down the stairs until I could see the space below clearly. Apart from the six dead men and the candle, there didn't appear to be anything there. Except... I squinted at the pile of broken glass in the corner.

Dark mist rose from it. Slowly at first but then growing larger at a steady pace. Alarms went off in my head. I sprinted back up the stairs and threw my weight behind another shoulder tackle. Whatever that mist was, I should not be breathing it in.

I planted my palms against the cold metal and shoved with everything I had. My boots slipped on the stones but the door refused to open. I threw a glance over my shoulder. The dark mist was rising. Releasing a panicked howl, I banged my fists on the door. It remained shut.

Dark tendrils snaked up the stairs now and the whole landing was already filled with smoke. It wouldn't be long before it reached me as well. Worst case scenario, it was poison and I would die a failure here in this underground vault. Best case scenario, it was some kind of chemical that would just knock me out. But that would leave me defenseless, captured, and at the complete mercy of the Rat King. Wait... which one was supposed to be the best case scenario again?

Pressing my back against the unmoving door, I tried to think of anything that would save me. There weren't any windows so I couldn't get the mist out that way, or escape that way myself. What if I held my breath? How long could I even hold my breath? I had a feeling that the people on the other side of the door would wait until they were certain that I had breathed it in before they opened the door. Gods damn it. I pounded my fists against the door again as the dark mist rose before me. This was it. I was done for.

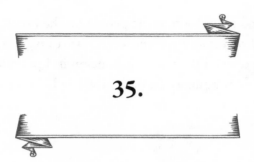

35.

My heart slammed against my ribs as the dark mist rose in the stairwell before me. If I could just find a way to breathe without having to breathe in those chemicals, then I would survive. An idea flashed into my mind like a lightning bolt. Something to breathe through. It couldn't possibly work, could it?

I stuck a hand into one of my belt pouches. My fingers fumbled as I tried to locate the item while keeping the panic at bay. The mist now reached my thighs. Finally, I found what I was looking for and yanked it up.

The flat green blob flapped from side to side as I turned it over. This was insane. This was, without a doubt, the most ridiculous thing I had ever done in an entire life filled with absolutely, positively, ridiculous things. I put the leaf over my nose and mouth and breathed through it.

Dark haze continued flooding the stairs while I used the, hopefully magical, leaf I had gotten from Vilya as protection. When the mist finally billowed over my head, I closed my eyes and sent a prayer to any god who would listen. The seconds ticked on. Opening my eyes again, I came to the conclusion that I was still conscious.

The whole basement was now blanketed by what looked like dark smoke but I was still standing there at the top of the stairs. Breathing through a leaf. Apparently, I *was* some kind of toad.

Another minute passed. Then two. Then three. And then finally, the mist dissipated and the flickering candle below the stairs grew brighter. I took the leaf from my face and heaved a deep sigh of relief. Okay, I had survived that. Now, all I needed to do was slip past them while they were busy looking for my unconscious body.

The leaf was now purple instead of green, and probably useless since Vilya had said it could only be used once, but I rolled it up and stuck in back in my belt pouch anyway. I swept my gaze across the room. Where could I hide where I would be out of sight but also close enough to make it out of the door? I cocked my head. That could work. It would be awfully difficult and would be a race against the clock, but it would work. It had to work.

Wiping my bloody hands on my pants, I got ready to move at the first sound of the door being opened. Another minute passed. Then, something clanked faintly on the other side of the door.

I leaped onto the wall and scuttled up the rough stones like a startled spider. The door creaked below me. With my heart thumping madly in my chest, I closed the final distance to the ceiling, stretched my legs until I reached the top of the doorframe, and braced my arms on the walls. The support from the doorframe under my toes made the maneuver possible but it still required a lot of strength to remain in the ceiling over the door.

At last, light spilled into the stairwell from the widening crack. Voices sounded. A man poked his head through and swept his gaze around the space as if to check that the mist was truly gone.

Something wet slid down my cheek. Blaring alarms went off in my head all at once when I remembered that I was covered in blood after the fight. If it dripped now, they would find me. Twisting my head slightly, I wiped my cheek on my shoulder while willing the rest of my blood-soaked body to keep it together for another minute.

The man below strode forwards. He was followed by another couple of men and they descended the stairs in tight formation.

"She's not here," the first man whispered.

"Of course she is," someone snapped from the room outside the door. "Check under the other bodies."

My arms still shook with the exertion of keeping myself hidden in the ceiling above the door but I pushed the pain and weariness to the back of my mind. Just a few seconds more.

"Bloody idiots," the irritated person muttered again and stalked forwards.

As soon as his mop of dark hair had disappeared down the stairs, I let go. The rough landing jarred my bones but I didn't have time to stop. With a small song of victory in my heart, I yanked out my hunting knives and sprinted through the door into the strongroom.

The two men on either side of the door were dead before they realized that I wasn't one of their companions. On the floor, the two paralyzed dogs still lay. I darted past them and set course for the door. Yanking it open, I skidded into the hallway beyond.

A pair of brown eyes blinked at me in surprise.

"She's here! She's getting awa—"

The rest of the warning died on his lips as I slashed open his throat. While he thudded to the ground behind me, boots stampeded towards me from the other side of the corridor. I took off in the other direction.

All I had to do was get to a window and then I'd be okay. Shouts rose as I flew into the next room. While the occupants of the room shot to their feet, I was already halfway to the other door. No chance of reaching those windows. I had to put some distance between myself and everyone else.

A staircase appeared at the end of the room. I bounded up it, taking the steps two or three at a time while trying to block out the slapping feet behind me. Another corridor waited atop the stairs but I had no time to figure out which direction I should be running in so I just picked a random room and yanked open the door. Something whizzed through the air.

I dove forwards and barely escaped the sword someone had swung at me. Without looking, I threw out the hunting knives I was still gripping and slashed blindly. A scream rang out. The man who'd been in the room when I barged in crumpled to the floor as my blade cut through the muscles in his left calf. I shot to my feet and shoved the knives back in their holsters while boots thundered on the wooden planks outside.

Putting all my weight behind it, I shoved a large dresser in front of the door in a panicked frenzy. Someone crashed into the door a scant second after my temporary blockade was in place. Wood vibrated as they pounded on it. On the floor, the man kept screaming and sweeping his sword in a mad arch towards me.

"Shut up!" I snapped as I raced to the window. "I can't fucking think!"

The shutters banged against the wall as I threw them open while yanking out a knife again. Twisting it up and down, I caught the golden rays of the setting sun on the polished blade.

Behind me, the dresser was groaning and scraping against the floor as the people on the other side of the door heaved. The injured man on the floor kept yelling and crawling towards me with his sword slashing back and forth across the dusty floorboards. Blood rushed in my ears. *Come on, Elaran, where are you?*

A whizzing sound split the air. Followed by a sharp thud. Relief flooded my chest and I backed away to get a running start before leaping out of the window and gripping the rope Elaran had just secured between the mansion and the building across the street. Because of the force behind his shot, the arrow was buried deep in the wood but the rope still creaked as it had to bear my whole weight.

Twisting around, I swung my legs up until I could hook them around the line from below while I kept putting one hand in front of the other. Since I was facing the Rat King's mansion, I had no idea how far it was to the next building but I hoped it was close because my pursuers had finally broken through the door. They shoved each other aside until one man claimed the spot and leaned out through the window.

He tilted his head up to look at the arrow that secured the rope to the wall above his head. And then he pulled a knife. Malice flashed over his lips as he raised the blade towards the line. *Shit*. I scrambled faster towards the other side.

The rough rope burned my palms as I hurried away from the mansion at a much higher speed than was safe. In the window, the man put his knife to the line and started sawing. The rope wobbled underneath me as I climbed faster and faster. I was past the stone wall. It couldn't be that much further now.

The line snapped. My stomach lurched as I plummeted towards the stone street below. Something dark streaked past me. I threw out a hand and grasped desperately for it. A sharp thud sounded just as my fingers closed around another rope.

A scream tore from my throat and I thought my arm was going to rip from its socket but I managed to keep my grip on the second rope that Elaran had shot. With shaking muscles, I swung myself back on the line and scrambled towards safety again.

Something whizzed through the air next to me. Throwing a panicked glance at the window, I found the source. Now that the rope was out of reach to them, they'd brought out another weapon. Crossbows. By all the gods, could I never catch a godsdamn break?

People were milling onto the courtyard inside the stone walls while the men in the window got ready. Crossbows were raised from every direction. My heart slammed so hard against my ribs I thought they would crack. I climbed faster.

And then the arrows flew.

While shoving out a very intense urge to close my eyes, I braced myself for the impact. But it didn't come. Still scrambling along the rope, it took me a second to realize that the arrows hadn't come from the mansion. They'd come from the building across the street. Sleek black and brown shafts hailed down on the Rat King's people from atop the roof on the other side.

Screams rose as they all ran for cover while I continued my mad climb.

Strong hands wrapped around my shoulders and yanked me away from the rope. I let out a yelp as I was heaved up and over the edge of the roof before I fell backwards again. A body made of packed muscle broke my fall as I landed on top of someone's chest.

Shade rolled over until he was on his hands and knees above me. I blinked into a face that was tight with fury and... worry?

"That was the stupidest, most reckless thing I've ever seen," he growled in my face.

Sitting up, I shoved him aside. "Run now. Yell later."

When a chuckle filled the air, I suddenly realized that Elaran and Shade weren't the only people here. Haela, Haemir, Zaina, and Liam were all crowded on the roof as well. Bending down, the grinning Haela helped me to my feet while Elaran did the same for Shade.

While the elves secured their bows to their backs again, I shifted my gaze to Elaran and then nodded towards the twins. "You brought them too?"

"I told them where I'd be going and they came along because apparently no one has any say in what Haela does," Elaran grumbled and sent a scowl in the indicted elf's direction.

She grinned back at him. "Correct." While securing the last fastening on her bow, she narrowed her eyes at me. "And I am super offended that you didn't come to me with this. Didn't I tell you not to get into any fun mischief without me?"

Before the exasperated laugh could leave my lips, Liam cut in. "Didn't we agree to run now and yell later?"

"Right." I cleared my throat. "Shall we?"

On the street below, the Rat King's gang was braving the stones again now that the rain of arrows had stopped. The seven of us took off across the roof as the sound of pursuit once again rose behind us.

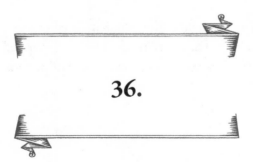

36.

My exhausted muscles screamed as we raced over the roof tiles but it wasn't that far to the hiding spot I had picked out. Zaina, who was the least experienced at this mode of transportation, kept up surprisingly well as we jumped the gap between two buildings. I swerved left. Pushing the weariness to the back of my mind, I continued putting one foot in front of the other until a spacious rooftop garden finally came into view.

When I planned this attack, I had taken into account that I would need to disappear fast. The Black Emerald was too far away to be a reliable safe spot so I had picked another one as a temporary shelter where we could lay low until we lost our pursuers.

Leaves rustled as the seven of us jumped the wooden fence covered in vines and landed on the other side. Thick plants and drapes in different shades of green covered the whole area and made it very difficult to see in from the outside. I had come across this rooftop garden a while back when I was still mapping out the city and marked it as a potential hiding place. My current hunted self thanked my past scheming self as I slipped towards a cluster of wicker divans in the middle.

I flopped down on a divan while my friends made for seats of their own. My chest heaved. For a moment, I just lay there with an arm draped over my eyes and breathed until the thumping in my chest lessened. Holy fuck. Had I really just survived that?

A yelp ripped from my throat as someone hauled me up by the front of my shirt. I only had time to blink at Shade before he shoved me backwards. The tall wooden frame filled with climbing vines that sectioned off the seating area rattled in distress as I slammed back first into it. Terrified leaves fell from the vines above.

Flicking my gaze from the falling greenery to the man in front of me, I found a furious Master Assassin staring down at me. I raised my hand to push him back but his hand shot out and snaked around my wrist before I could.

"That was the most reckless thing I've ever seen," he repeated.

I glared at him. "You said."

"Yes, I did. And I've also made it abundantly clear that when I give people orders, I expect them to obey." Shade leaned down until he was so close that our breath mingled. When he opened his mouth again, his voice came out sounding even more like a growl. "I told you to get out of there alive. You were cutting it *way* too damn close."

"But I did get out of there alive, didn't I?"

The lightning dancing in his black eyes didn't let up. "If you hadn't..." He shook his head. "I would've killed them all. Every single one of them. Every. Single. One."

"What happened to not plunging the Underworld into chaos and civil war and having a united city when the star elves attack so that the rest of the world–"

"To hell with the rest of the world," Shade growled.

Letting go of my wrist, he put a hand behind my neck and yanked me towards him. His hard body pinned me against the wooden frame while he pressed his lips to mine. I raked my fingers over his muscled back and lost myself in a kiss so desperate that it made the ice around my cold black heart crack a little.

After what could've been years for all I knew, Shade drew back and rested his forehead against mine. With his eyes still closed, he whispered against my lips.

"Don't ever do that again." He drew soft fingers from the back of my neck towards my collarbone. "Don't ever do that to me again."

Not trusting my voice right now, I gulped back a breath and nodded.

Zaina cleared her throat. "Yeah, you do remember that we're still here, right?"

"Like, come on, kids, get a room," Haela added.

Heat flashed over my cheeks as Shade and I tore our gaze from each other to glare at the rest of our friends.

"Shut up," we muttered in unison.

Haela threw back her head and let out a loud cackle. She was joined by Zaina, and then Haemir, and finally Liam who giggled with unrestrained merriment. From the corner of my eye, I could've sworn I saw even Elaran smile but when I shifted my gaze to the grumpy elf, it was gone.

He crossed his arms and drew his eyebrows down. "He's right. That was unnecessarily risky. You could've gotten killed."

"I know. But I didn't." Emotions that couldn't be adequately put into words burned behind my eyes as I swept my gaze between my friends. "Because of you. All of you. Thank you."

Liam shot me a beaming smile while Elaran just drew his eyebrows down even more and muttered something under his breath.

"Alright," Haela said, a thoughtful expression on her face, "because of that, I might be able to forgive you for not including me in this plan from the beginning."

A wicked grin spread across Zaina's face. "And because of your intimate little show with Shade just now, *I* might be able to forgive you for bursting into my sister's bedroom at the wrong time."

"Zaina!" I gaped at the grinning pirate.

"Wait, what?" Haemir asked, shifting his gaze between me, Zaina, and Liam.

A deep red color flushed Liam's cheeks as well once he realized that everyone had put two and two together. I picked up a green pillow from the divan next to me and hurled it at the amused smuggler. She ducked and the cushion slammed into the wooden plant frame behind her instead. Dark green leaves rustled in annoyance at being flattened by flying décor but stayed on their vines.

Laughter echoed throughout the rooftop garden. Tipping my head back, I let out a long sigh while a lot of the tension from the near-death experience at the Rat King's mansion left my body. Leave it to my friends to know exactly what to do to pull me back from the edge. When I looked back down, their expressions were serious again.

"It didn't work, did it?" Liam said.

It was more of a statement than a question but I gave him a tired smile and replied anyway. "No."

Haemir's face was filled with worry when he looked at me. "What will you do now?"

I raked my fingers through my hair but then remembered that my hands were covered in blood. With a slight shrug, I decided that it didn't really matter because so was the rest of me, so I finished smoothing my hair before saying, "I've gotta find some other way to get rid of the Rat King's fortune. Especially after today, I have a feeling that's the only thing keeping him in power right now."

Zaina arched a dark eyebrow at me. "You have a plan?"

I grinned. "Always."

My friends smiled back at me but I was pretty sure they all knew it was a lie. I had put everything into this plan and now that it had failed, I had no idea what to do. Since I'd already shown my hand, I wouldn't be able to break in again. Exhaustion washed over me. After flashing my friends another tired smile, I told them I was just going to lie down for a bit while we waited for the heat of the pursuit to die down.

Seated on the comfortable furniture around me, they talked softly among themselves but I just kept staring at the rapidly darkening sky above. What was I supposed to do now?

When a half hour had passed and we deemed it safe to leave the rooftop garden, I still hadn't figured out an answer to that question. I met each of their eyes in turn as we got ready to split up.

"Drinks are on me next time," I said.

Zaina and Haela grinned in unison. "We'll hold you to that."

And with that, we split up and went our separate ways. Shade heading back to Blackspire, Liam and Zaina to the school, and the elves to their barracks. Countless thoughts swirled in my mind while I jogged back towards the Black Emerald. I was so lost in thought that I blinked in surprise when my tavern suddenly rose before me.

Shaking off the confused thoughts, I jumped the final gap between the buildings and used the window to break into my own room. After this pathetic failure, I didn't want to face my gang just yet. And besides, I was covered in blood. Vania would subject me to a stern lecture if I walked through the door looking like that.

My feet had barely touched the floor before I started stripping off my knives, tools, and clothes. Once I had washed off the dirt and blood, I donned a new set of clothes and redid my braid. My stomach grumbled.

"Yes, yes, I know," I muttered at my discontented abdominal organ.

After pulling on my boots again, I stalked down the stairs in search of something to eat. It was only when I descended the stairs that an uneasy feeling slithered up my spine and I realized what had been bothering me since I got back. Everything was quiet. Way too quiet for a tavern, especially during the evening. I hadn't bothered to strap on all my knives again but as I reached the final staircase, I shot my stiletto blades into my palms.

Creeping down the stairs, I listened for any kind of sound. Only deafening silence met me. When I finally reached the bottom and stepped onto the floor, my heart stopped.

Overturned furniture lay scattered across the room, along with chips of wood that had been hacked loose. Crimson drops dotted the planks. And not a soul in sight.

"What the hell happened here?" I whispered as I snuck forward.

Signs of struggle were everywhere but whoever had broken in here must've had an overwhelming force. Or something that knocked people out. I shook my head. Because there was no way they would've been able to defeat my whole damn gang otherwise.

Scraping sounds drifted from the kitchen. I darted towards the door and peeked inside. *Shit.* After checking that it wasn't a trap, I hurried towards the chair that had been left in the middle of the room and the woman who was tied to it.

Helena pulled at the ropes around her arms and tried to say something but only muffled grunts made it past the gag. In a few precise slits, I cut her ropes. She ripped off her gag and coughed.

"The Rat King," she said. "He came with his people. We fought back but... I didn't do so well. He dragged me in here and told me..." A shudder went through her. "He said that he was going to take everyone and that you were to come to his mansion at midnight and surrender or he'd..." She gulped down a breath. "He'd kill them all. And then he threw some kind of glass thing and dark smoke filled the room. I passed out and when I woke up, I was tied to this chair."

I closed my eyes while dread spread through my body like cold poison. "When?"

"A little after you left."

Slumping back against the counter, I closed my eyes. So that was why the Rat King hadn't personally come to oversee my capture outside his vault. Once he was done with Shade, he'd come here. To get *my* people. And his gang had found me far too easily in that basement. As if... As if he'd known all along that I would be breaking into his mansion today. How the hell had he known that?

"Helena," I said. "Go to Red Demon Rowan. In fact, go to all the gang leaders who've sworn support. Tell them I need help."

Determination settled on her face as she nodded. While she disappeared from the kitchen and out the front door, I stared unseeing at the empty kitchen wall. The Rat King had taken my people. *My* people. After I swore to protect them. And I only had the hours until midnight to figure out a way to stop that.

Well, at least I had that much, I suppose. He probably just told Helena that on the off chance that his people would be incompetent enough to actually let me escape his mansion. After all, it wasn't me as such that he needed. It was my submission. With every defiant act, I'd been pissing him off more and more but it was also what had secured my survival. The more I made him look weak, the less he could just flat out kill me. He needed to make me publicly bow to him to ensure that others wouldn't pick up where I left off.

Unfortunately, that had also dragged people I care about into this fight. People who were now in danger because of me. Shoving aside thoughts and feelings that would do nothing to help my current situation, I went in search of something to eat while I waited for Helena to come back.

After raiding the kitchen, I righted a chair in the tavern and slumped down in it. While shoveling cold stew into my mouth, I created and discarded plan after plan for how to solve this problem.

The front door creaked open. I jerked my head up to ask Helena what kind of support I could be expecting but drew back when I noticed who had walked through the door. Putting down my spoon, I frowned at the man who slunk through the door and approached me. What the hell was he doing here?

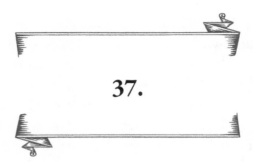

37.

Floorboards vibrated as Red Demon Rowan stalked across the tavern. Behind her, the other gang leaders who had pledged support to me followed. A smile began spreading across my mouth but then disappeared and was replaced by a frown as I studied Rowan's face. A jagged scar ran down her forehead, through her eyebrow, and ended on her cheek below the eye but that wasn't what made me pause. It was the expression on her face. She looked pissed. And so did the other gang leaders. I was just about to ask why when Rowan cut me off.

"They took Lind," she spat out. "And a handful of my other high-ranking members."

"Same with my gang," Kessinda said. The tall dark-haired gang leader snatched up an overturned chair and dragged it over to my table. "My Second and four others of my top people."

"Mine too," the other leaders confirmed.

"Shit," I swore. Shifting my gaze to Helena, who had trailed in behind them, I addressed her. "Thanks. Go somewhere safe where you can lie low until this is over."

She nodded and slipped out the door while the irritated gang leaders plopped down in chairs around my messy table.

Rowan's green eyes locked on me. "We all got the same message afterwards. You surrender to the Rat King before midnight, or he kills all our people."

Leaning back in my chair, I drew my fingers through my hair and let out a long sigh. Oh, the Rat King was good, I had to give him that. This had been complicated enough when it was just my people on the line but now that he was using other gangs as leverage as well, he could put even more pressure on me. Their members were in danger because of me and if I didn't surrender, they would be killed. Talk about high-level peer pressure.

After tipping my head back down, I met each of their gazes with steady eyes. "And what are your thoughts on that?"

"You know I like you," Rowan said. "And I owe you. But you don't know the Rat King like I do. At the first sign of a rescue attempt, or literally anything other than surrendering to him, he *will* kill them all." She blew out a sigh. "Loyalty to my own people must come first. I can't sacrifice my core crew for something that might never actually become reality." Her eyes softened. "Even if that is an Underworld free from the Rat King's messed-up worldview."

Kessinda flicked her black eyes between me and Rowan. "Same. I'd love to see the Rat King's empire crumble, which is why I threw my support behind you. But... if I can't protect my gang in the process, then what's the point of destroying him?"

The other gang leaders backed them up with a nod.

What they were saying was basically that they wanted me to bow to the Rat King so that their own gangs would be safe. Even though that meant they would rather sacrifice me, it actually made me respect them even more. *This* was what I wanted for the

Underworld. Loyalty. People who would die and kill to protect their own.

"I get it." I gave them a genuine smile. "More than you know."

Paper rustled as I shifted the rolled-up scrolls on the table before me. Leaning down, I snatched up two fallen mugs from the floor before straightening again. I unrolled a scroll and placed the mugs on either side to make it stay open. Fire flickered as I moved the crooked candle closer and pointed at the hurried drawing and scrawled notes on the thick sheet.

"Here's the plan," I began.

Chairs creaked as the room full of gang leaders shifted in their seats to see better while I explained the resources I could pull together on short notice and hopefully use to free all our people. When I was done, the tavern fell silent.

"You really think that'll work?" Rowan asked at last, a slight frown on her face.

"The only reason the Rat King is still in power is because he can buy their loyalty." I lifted one shoulder in a lopsided shrug. "Until he can repair his reputation, he's gonna need an unending stream of money to stay in power. I know it. He knows it. I'm counting on that need."

Kessinda tapped a slender finger to the tabletop. "And if this doesn't work?"

"Then I will do whatever I have to, to make this right and keep all our people safe."

"Even if that means kneeling in front of the Rat King and publicly bowing to his authority?"

I met each of their gazes in turn before replying. "Yes. Whatever it takes."

It was the truth. I didn't know how many of my gang members had been taken by the Rat King and how many had managed to escape or hadn't even been at the Black Emerald when shit hit the fan. There were way too many of them to even fit inside this building all at once so there had to be lots still out there. Safe. But it didn't matter. Even if he had only taken one person, I would've come for them. Because they were my people. And no one touched my people.

"You're a special kind of crazy, you know that?" Rowan barked a laugh. "Maybe that's why this'll work. What do you need us to do?"

The moon rose higher in the sky while I explained what I'd need their help with. Time was running out. Fast. But with this many people, we'd be able to get everything together before midnight.

Once I was done, we all hurried out into the night. I had already pulled off the impossible today by escaping the Rat King's mansion alive, so what was one more ridiculously dangerous and highly improbably feat?

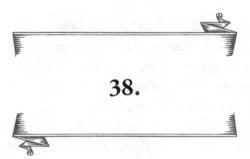

38.

Countless boots stalking forward in unison sent an ominous echo bouncing between the buildings. Marching at the head of the force, I held my head high and my eyes fixed on the square at the end of the street. On the stones beside me strode Red Demon Rowan, Kessinda of the Black Waves, and all the other gang leaders who had sworn to take down the Rat King. The collective army we had managed to muster after leaving the Black Emerald followed us like a wall of leather and steel that filled the whole street far behind us. Weapons gleamed in the moonlight.

Up ahead the road emptied out in a wide square, and on the other side of it lay the Rat King's mansion. I squared my shoulders as we passed through the final set of buildings and into the open space. Leather creaked and feet thudded as my allies fanned out behind me until we took up the whole short side. Then, the starlit night fell silent.

About three quarters of the way down, along the buildings on my right, were clusters of people. They were all seated on the ground with their hands shackled in front of them. The largest of the groups, I recognized instantly. Yngvild, Vania, Kildor, Yua, and a good portion of my gang sat motionless on the dusty stones but they watched me and the army I'd brought intently.

In one of the other groups I found Lind, so I assumed the other gang leaders' people were there as well.

"The Oncoming Storm," the Rat King called across the square. He cast a glance at the clock tower visible over the houses to my left. "And with a whole half hour to spare."

The King of the Underworld was standing in front of the stone walls to his mansion. A mass of people stood at attention in long lines behind him. None of them had any weapons out but in every single window of his headquarters stood dark shapes with crossbows.

"You made a mistake," I said. "When you took my people and my allies' people." A smirk spread across my lips while I raised my arms in a cocky motion. Rustling and clanking sounded as the army behind me lifted their weapons. "You're about to pay for that mistake."

A loud thud echoed into the night as we all took a collective step forward. The Rat King cocked his head but made no move to stop us. Only when we had reached the middle of the square did he open his mouth again. A derisive laugh drifted into the night. Expecting a trap, I held up my hand and motioned for everyone to stay where they were.

After making a show of dabbing his eyes, the Rat King cleared his throat and fixed me with a scornful stare. "You are so predictable. This is how you solve every problem, isn't it? By trying to stab it until it goes away."

"Well," I lifted my shoulders in a nonchalant shrug, "it's worked so far, hasn't it?"

"Then allow me to crush that foolish notion. Brute force won't work this time."

"That right?"

"Yes." The Rat King raised his arms to indicate the building behind him. "If you try anything, these people will fire on your shackled friends over there."

Metal clanged faintly against stone as the groups seated by the walls on my right shifted uneasily. Yngvild's attentive eyes continued to sweep back and forth across the area while Vania kept her gaze fixed on me. I wanted to tell them both that everything would be fine but I couldn't. Both because there was no way to tell them that without everyone hearing, and because I wasn't even sure if it was the truth. So I broke her gaze and shifted my eyes back to the Rat King.

"Hmm. Yes, but see, there's a problem with that." I lifted a finger and made a show of counting the people standing in the windows of his mansion. "If my calculations are correct, you'll only be able to hit one person per group before your archers have to reload, and during that time, I will already have crossed the courtyard and rammed a sword through your throat."

"Such arrogance." His beady eyes glinted in the silvery light as he looked at me. "I'll enjoy beating that from you when you're kneeling at my feet."

I snorted. "Yeah, good luck with that."

Irritation flashed over his face but when he opened his mouth again, his voice was calm and collected. "I already told you that brute force won't work this time. I expected you to try something like this, so earlier today I acquired something especially for you. Poison." He motioned at his headquarters again. "The reason that there is only about one archer for every group is that tied to each crossbow bolt is a glass vial. When the vial shatters, it releases a deadly poison that will kill everyone close to it."

A ripple went through the captive men and women by the wall. Three of the groups huddled closer together but the others seemed to suddenly find themselves wanting to separate from the others. The thick chains that connected their manacles made that impossible, though.

"So you see," the Rat King pressed on. "Before you can make it two steps towards me, all these lovely hostages will die." Malice shone on his face. "Can you imagine? Every Second and high-ranking member of all those gangs behind you... dead, in one fell swoop."

Clothes rustled as my army shifted nervously. I clicked my tongue. Well, it had been worth a shot. Just as the Rat King had expected me to try to take him out with brute force, I had expected him to counter like this. Which was why I had made other arrangements as well.

Raising my arm, I flicked my hand in the air a couple of times. Wood creaked and metal jingled softly as the crowd behind me parted to let several people through. Showing up with an army at my back had mostly just been to buy me some time and to pave the way for my actual plan. After all, having a host of armed underworlders behind me went a long way if I wanted someone to take me seriously. The people lugging large chests between them passed me and continued towards the Rat King.

"If this is some kind of trick, everyone dies," the Rat King warned as they drew closer.

However, both of us knew that it wasn't. He had already discovered my secret, that I actually cared about my people, so he already knew that I would never risk their lives in this way. Though he kept his hand raised to give the signal to shoot, he let the men and women approach with the wooden chests. After they had placed them before him, they withdrew to our side of the square again.

With a flick of his wrist, he sent some gang members forward to open them. Wood banged against stone as they fell open. A gasp reverberated through the air. The Rat King's eyes widened as he flicked them between the now open chests.

Precious metal and flawless gems glittered in the moonlight. Every single chest was filled to the limit with expensive necklaces, bracelets, earrings, and other pieces of jewelry. Counterfeit jewelry of this kind of otherworldly quality did not come cheap and this was my entire stock that I had smuggled from Keutunan to Pernula to sell. It was worth a fortune. If Zaina didn't kill me for this, then Lady Smythe surely would. Oh well, one death threat at a time.

"Here's the deal," I said.

"A deal?" The Rat King tore his gaze from the invaluable treasure before him and let out a derisive laugh. "Do you really think you are in any position to make deals?"

"Yes. Because we both know that a full-scale war will only hurt our people and businesses in the Underworld." I swallowed my pride and pressed on. "So I've come to make you an offer."

He smiled like a vulture. "Do tell."

"I will buy their freedom." I swung an arm towards the shackled people on my right. "The contents of those chests are my entire current stock. I will also give you every shipment of smuggled jewelry to come for free for you to sell at a profit. You can have it all, for their freedom."

The Rat King raised his eyebrows. "And what about our other disagreement?"

"After I give you this and you give us back our people, I will back off." My eyes hardened. "But so will you. I will go back to being a small player and you can go back to doing whatever it is that you do without my interference. I won't challenge you for power and you will stop trying to make me bow. We'll both just stay out of each other's way."

"A most generous offer." He gave me a patronizing smile. "But I think I'll decline."

"You're seriously gonna turn down *that* kind of fortune and risk an Underworld war because of what? Spite?"

"No. I'm turning it down because there is only one thing I want." His eyes glittered with malice. "Your submission." Raising a hand, he snapped his fingers at the people behind him. "But I think I will keep these trunks too. For the inconvenience you've cause." He jerked his chin. "Take them to the vault."

"The hell you will." Yanking out my hunting knives, I took a threatening step forward as the Rat King's people lifted the chests containing all my jewelry and hauled them inside. "If you think I'm gonna just let you–"

The King of the Underworld held up a hand. "Ah, ah, ah," he warned while wagging a finger in the air and then pointing it towards the archers in the windows.

With blades gripped tightly in my hands, I glared at him. He just continued smirking at me as my treasure disappeared into his mansion. Spitting out a curse, I rammed my hunting knives back in their sheaths. Yep, Zaina and Lady Smythe were definitely going to kill me.

A strong night wind kicked up a cloud of dust and made the shutters on the buildings around us rattle. I continued scowling at the Rat King in silence. Behind me, leather creaked and clothes rustled as my allies shifted nervously now that my offer of a truce had been rejected.

"Now what?" the Rat King called into the fragrant night air. "Are you going to attack? Blow us all away with your powers and try to force your way to the hostages?"

Still glaring at him, I said nothing.

"No?" A victorious smile spread across his lips and he raised his voice further even though everyone could already hear him. "Have you noticed something strange? For weeks now, there has not been a single report of the Oncoming Storm using her powers. Not even when she was trapped and almost captured inside my mansion did she use her Ashaana powers even once. Why?"

The square remained silent.

"Could it be because she doesn't have them anymore?"

A buzz went through the crowd on both sides. From my right, I could feel Yngvild and Vania seeking eye contact but I kept my stare focused on the Rat King.

"I never knew for certain because all my people were dead when I got there, but this seems to confirm the fact. That I managed to strip the Oncoming Storm of her powers."

Several gasps rang out and eyes from the army behind me were burning holes in my back but I kept my chin raised and didn't break the Rat King's stare.

"You wanted to make a deal." He flicked a nonchalant hand. "Fine, I'll make you a deal. Use your powers right now. Just once. And I will let all the hostages go. No strings attached." His malicious smile deepened. "Go on then. Do it."

No one dared breathe as the Rat King waited for me to summon the darkness. I forced my heart rate to slow and resisted the urge to flick my gaze around the square. Seconds ticked by. Then, a cackle echoed between the buildings.

"See," the Rat King said. "The powerful Ashaana you supported is no longer powerful at all. Her powers are gone. By my hand." Raising his voice and his arms, he addressed the people behind me. "Now, I have an offer for you. I will give you all another chance. Come back to me and I will forgive your transgressions."

"Don't listen to him," I growled.

"Join me," he pressed on. "Recognize me as the undisputed leader of the Underworld once again and I will no longer have any reason to hurt your people."

"He's lying."

"Every gang leader who sends their part of this army away and then comes back and pledges their support will get their people back safe and unharmed."

Clothes rustled behind me.

I ripped out my hunting knives. "Don't you dare."

"The Oncoming Storm can't protect them. Her negotiations have failed and her powers are gone. She has nothing left. I am your only choice if you want to keep your people alive."

Boots thudded against stone. And then copper hair flowed in the night air next to me.

"I'm sorry," Rowan said as she walked past me and towards the Rat King.

Kessinda followed. And then the muscled gang leader with the scarred face. And then another. And another.

My eyes darted around the square.

Behind me, the force I'd brought was dissolving and disappearing back into the shadows after being given orders to disperse. The gang leaders who had once stood behind me formed a long line as they strode across the square. In front of them, the Rat King's eyes glittered.

I was on my own.

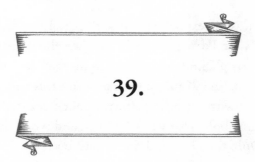

39.

Gripping my knives tightly, I watched as my allied gang leaders came to a halt and once again dropped to a knee before the Rat King. He didn't even look at the line of kneeling men and women. His eyes were focused solely on me and they were filled with triumph and malice so strong I could feel it from across the square.

"And you too," he said and shifted his gaze to the side of the courtyard. "You have now finally earned your way back to your gang."

I frowned at him but then slowly turned my head when I realized that he hadn't been talking to me. Following his gaze, I found a slim but wiry figure gliding out of the shadows.

Raising my eyebrows, I shook my head and spit out a disappointed sigh. "So, you were a spy?"

Helena avoided my gaze as she pushed her dirty blond hair back behind her ears and slunk towards the Rat King. The woman who I'd seen get kicked out of her gang that first night had been a traitor all along. Once I became a threat, the Rat King had probably approached her and offered her a way back to her gang if she joined my crew and spied on me. I should've seen it coming. Man, I was becoming way too trusting.

But at least it explained a few things. Like, how the Rat King knew when I'd be gone and which warehouse to steal from. Or when I was planning to break into his mansion. Helena had tended the bar. She would've been able to eavesdrop on a lot of conversations without much effort. Sudden realization hit me like a lightning bolt. *That* was why Liam and Norah hadn't been attacked. Only the elves and Shade had been to see me at the Black Emerald, so Helena would only know about my friendship with them and not about my relationship with Liam and Norah.

Shaking my head, I gave myself an internal slap. I had a lot to learn about being a gang leader. Like, how to properly screen people before they joined. Vania had done most of that after the gang was officially formed, but Helena had been there from the start and had slipped through the cracks. I was such a fool.

Yngvild and Vania were staring daggers at the blond woman crossing the square but she kept her eyes on the stones until she reached the Rat King's side and disappeared into the throng. Rowan and the other gang leaders were still kneeling in a long line before the Rat King. At last, he twitched his fingers. They climbed to their feet and moved to stand to the side that was closest to their shackled Seconds.

"Everyone has abandoned you," the Rat King called across the silent stones.

I swept my gaze across the square again. A mass of people faced me while my side was completely empty apart from me. My heart pattered in my chest.

"Now, then." The King of the Underworld raised his chin and spread his arms. "Are you going to fight me all alone?"

Earlier today, I had broken into his mansion, snuck past a room full of archers, threatened a man with a sword, evaded two bloodthirsty hounds, fought and killed six men while trapped in a basement, breathed through a leaf to survive a cloud of poison, hid in a ceiling, raced through an entire building filled with enemies, hurt more people, climbed a rope across two buildings, nearly fallen to my death, been yelled at by a Master Assassin and a grumpy elf for being reckless, and then finally gone back to my home to find that my entire gang had been taken hostage. I was tired. In fact, I was exhausted. I had absolutely no interest in fighting the Rat King's crew on my own, but since the damn Goddess of Luck could never let my schemes proceed exactly according to plan, I didn't have much choice.

After heaving a deep sigh, I twisted my face into a cocky grin and spread my arms. "Yeah, I am."

"I shall enjoy this." The Rat King flicked his wrist. "Go play."

A portion of his crew broke off from the rest. While pulling out weapons, they advanced on me. I scraped together every smidgen of energy I had left and braced myself for the battle to come. My attackers spread out in a semicircle as they drew closer and lifted their weapons towards me. This was going to hurt.

I snapped my hunting knives back in their sheaths and yanked out four throwing knives. Surprise was the only emotion that had time to register on their faces as I hurled the blades into the throats of the four closest men and women. They went down in a tangle of limbs.

While the rest were busy recovering from the shock, I'd thrown four more knives. Eight attackers dead within a matter of seconds. It evened the odds a little but... Oh who was I kidding? It didn't even the odds at all. They still outnumbered me like twenty to one.

Drawing the hunting knives from the small of my back, I crouched into a defensive position. I just needed to buy some time. If I could just buy a little more time then I could–

They charged. Ducking under a sword, I threw out both arms and spun in a quick circle. Clothes tore and flesh split as the knives found their marks. At least one advantage of fighting this many attackers was that no matter where I sliced, there was always an enemy there to hit.

Metal dinged as I blocked a strike to my ribs while swinging a blade towards the neck of another man. He redirected the thrust and I stumbled to the side just in time to miss another blow coming for my chest. A hiss rose into the night air as I slashed across his arm while bending backwards to escape yet another sword. It whizzed past in the air over my head.

My only other advantage in this incredibly unfair fight was that I knew they weren't actually trying to kill me. The Rat King just wanted to humiliate me a little before he made me bow. I decided to make the most of that fact.

Kicking out a leg, I caught a sword-wielding woman to the side of her knee. She let out a grunt as she stumbled into the man next to her. While their blades blocked each other, I flicked my wrists and cut both of their throats. Whirling around, I got ready for the next strike but found the immediate area around me empty.

All my attackers had backed away a few steps. Damn. They had just figured out that coming at me all at once like this only benefitted me since they just got in each other's way all the time. Well, it had been a nice advantage for as long as it lasted.

"Stay back," a heavyset man with a longsword growled. "She's mine."

The others hung back while he advanced on me. Steel sang as he swung at me with everything he had. I jumped back and twisted away because that blow would've broken my knives if I'd tried to parry. When he roared and swung again, I started to doubt my earlier conclusion that the Rat King didn't want them to kill me. If that sword hit me, it would cleave me in two.

Air vibrated in front of me as the heavy blade hurtled past. While his whole torso twisted with the missed strike, I flipped both hunting knives to the same hand and snatched a throwing knife from my shoulder. It left my hand as soon as I gripped it. The man's head snapped back. Loud thuds boomed across the stones as he toppled to the ground with a blade sticking out of his eye. I switched my hunting knives back to both hands just as another man charged.

Panic flared through me. He was much faster than the last and he also wielded two daggers. I threw up both arms to block his strikes. Steel ground against steel as he shoved my blades away. While ducking, I slashed towards his chest.

I sucked in a sharp breath as pain burned through my arm. Sidestepping my attack, he had drawn his dagger across my forearm in a swift strike. Black flashed past at the edge of my vision. I whipped around to face it and barely managed to catch another sword that had been swung at me from behind.

More pain shot through my body as a dagger cut across my left shoulder blade. I shoved the sword away and made as if to turn back to the knife-wielder behind me but I didn't make it. Something hard slammed into the back of my knees.

I crashed to the ground with enough force to send a jolt through my bones. Rolling with the motion, I slashed at the pair of legs closest to me. A man went down screaming as I severed his ankle tendon. His cries died as I rammed my knife through his windpipe.

A boot connected with my chest. With my knife still in the dead man's throat, it was ripped from my grip as I was flipped around and landed back first on the stones. Swinging blindly, I caught someone else across the shins before another heavy boot kicked the remaining hunting knife from my fist.

My fingers throbbed in pain but I reached towards my final throwing knife just as a face bent down over me. Spitting out a battle cry, I hurled the blade into his face with all my might. The knife slammed into his forehead with a sickening crack and he toppled to the side. I rolled away to avoid his falling corpse.

Air exploded from my lungs. I gasped in a breath to refill them while the boot that had stuck me square in the chest and stopped my escape drew back again. Pain flared through my body as someone else landed a kick to my back. Shooting a stiletto blade into my palm, I stabbed it into the first brown boot I saw. A shriek tore through the night above me.

Leaving the blade trapping the foot to the stones, I pushed onto my knees and got ready to climb to my feet. One gloved fist gripped the front of my shirt and hauled me forwards while the other one slammed into my cheekbone.

Black stars danced before my eyes as my head lolled back. As the man who had struck me pulled me towards him again, I threw out my hand against his chest to stop him. It made contact but didn't make a difference. While still trying to clear my vision, I shot my other stiletto from my sleeve. It disappeared into his chest with a wet sliding sound.

The hand on my shirt lost its grip and I slid down on the ground again. I was vaguely aware of a body crashing to the ground in front of me right before someone else planted a foot on my chest and shoved me the final bit down. My back hit the stones with a loud thud while my arms flopped down to my sides. Heavy weights pressed down on my wrists but even without the two boots keeping them trapped against the ground, I wouldn't have been able to lift them. Exhaustion and pain rolled over my body like tidal waves.

A sword appeared above my heaving chest. The sharp point was positioned right above my heart but I was too busy getting my eyes to focus again to care much about that. Once the last of the black spots finally disappeared and I could once again see my surroundings clearly, I became aware of the fact that everything was very still and dead quiet. Then, a satisfied laugh echoed between the buildings.

"Oh, I did enjoy that," the Rat King's voice came from somewhere on my right. "The dread in your eyes when you realized you had no hope of winning and the pain on your face when you received strike after strike. Exquisite. And worth losing a few men over."

He must've flicked his hand or something because the men around me suddenly retreated. I stayed on the ground and sucked deep breaths in and out of my lungs for a while before pushing myself to my knees. My body screamed in pain at the movement. Shoving it to the back of my mind, I struggled to my feet and swept my eyes across the square again.

The area around me was slick with blood and fourteen dead bodies lay sprawled across the stones. Fourteen. Well, at least I'd given them a run for their money.

Eyes stared at me from every direction while the surviving half of the group trailed back to the Rat King. I deliberately avoided looking at Vania and Yngvild as I stepped out of the circle of corpses and moved towards a clear spot. Blood dripped from my arm.

"Would you look at that?" the Rat King said. "You still have five more minutes."

The large clock on the clock tower showed five minutes to midnight. I sucked in a shuddering breath.

"Kneel before me and I will let your people live." A wide grin spread across his narrow features. "I gave you explicit instructions. If that clock strikes midnight and you haven't surrendered to me, my archers will fire and your people will die."

Every instinct in my body was screaming at me. While drawing another quivering breath, I flicked my eyes across the square yet again. Both Yngvild and Vania were watching me intently now. I broke their gaze and shifted it back to the Rat King.

The smile on his face disappeared when I didn't move immediately. "Fine. I'll just kill them all right now and show you what hesitation costs you."

"No!" I yelled. My very soul was still screaming at me but I steeled myself and took a step forward. "You win. Okay? You win."

A ripple went through the mass of underworlders as I slowly made my way towards the Rat King. My body throbbed in pain with each step but I kept my chin high. I had sworn never to bow to anyone again. On that ship sailing away from the City of Glass I had realized that the one thing I wanted most of all was freedom, and in that throne room in the Red Fort I had promised myself that I would make sure no one ever looked at me like I was a piece of property again. And yet here I was, about to get on my knees and bow to the Rat King.

Bile rose in my throat. Shallowing it, I cast a quick glance at Vania, Yngvild, Kildor, Yua, and the others. The things we do for the people we care about.

I came to a halt a few steps from the Rat King and drew a bracing breath before shifting my eyes to his face. His beady little eyes gleamed.

"Bow to me," he said.

At four minutes to midnight, I got down on my knees before the Rat King and bowed my head in submission.

The silence across the square was so loud it was deafening. Then, a triumphant voice cut through the night air.

"See!" the King of the Underworld called. "See the mighty Ashaana, the Oncoming Storm, kneeling at my feet."

Every fiber of my being was screaming at me to get up and punch his teeth down his throat but I just balled my fists and kept my eyes on the ground in front of me.

"This is the fate of anyone who tries to defy me." He lowered his arm and twitched his fingers in front of my face. "Look at me, because I want you to see this."

Slowly raising my head, I met his gaze. Wickedness burned in his eyes as he raised a hand in the air.

"Treachery will not be tolerated," he called in a loud voice. "Disobedience will not be forgiven. Remember this day when someone dares speak of rebellion."

He jerked his fist down.

"No!"

Gasps and cries cut through the night as the archers in the windows fired and crossbow bolts loaded with poison vials hurtled towards the hostages.

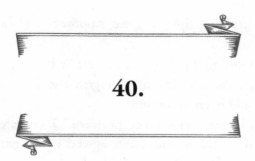

40.

Glass shattered and purple mist exploded around the shackled underworlders by the wall. Yngvild and Vania disappeared from view in a quickly spreading cloud. Metal clanged against stones and shrieks filled the night as all the Seconds and other captive members from every gang tried to get away. I stared at the Rat King. Victory blazed on his face as he looked from them to the gang leaders who had been promised mercy for their members and then finally to me.

Silence fell over the square once again. And then the purple mist cleared. Across the stones, all the hostages were flicking terrified eyes between one another while waiting for the first person to start dying.

"What?" the Rat King blurted out.

While the befuddled King of the Underworld stared uncomprehending at the shackled underworlders who were all still very much alive, I climbed to my feet and took a few steps back. When he still didn't turn to look at me, I cleared my throat. Confusion swirled in his eyes when he finally shifted them to me.

"It was a solid plan, really," I said. "And it would probably have worked if not for one teeny tiny detail that you, of course in all honesty, couldn't have known, but that turned out to be crucial." Lifting my shoulders in a light shrug, I let an innocent smile drift across my lips. "You see, Apothecary Haber and I go way back."

Understanding flooded his eyes. While backing away a few more steps, I flashed him another grin and held up a finger before he could open his mouth.

"Ah, and now you see the problem." I retreated another couple of steps. "Haber has never agreed to sell exclusively to me, which is why you've no doubt been able to buy those inconvenient glass chemical things that knock people out. But you see, when you went to him today and told him you needed enough poison to kill my whole crew and then some..." I shot him a knowing smile. "Let's just say that he was reluctant to lose his best customer."

"Get her!" the Rat King screamed, apparently having finally snapped out of his stupor, and then swung an arm towards the hostages. "And kill them!"

The people behind him scrambled for their weapons and started forward but I had already managed to put some distance between us. My grin turned feral as I raised my arms.

"Oh, and we discovered something else." I slammed my arms forward.

Dark clouds shot out around me and hurricane winds crashed into the Rat King's ranks. With eyes that had gone black as death, I watched them fly backwards before coming to an abrupt halt against the stone walls. The archers in the windows disappeared as the blast knocked them off their feet as well.

Rage and insanity danced in my eyes as I leveled them on the King of the Underworld who was now struggling to his feet on shaking legs.

"Since you tasked Haber with creating a potion that would block magic months before I even returned, and I never actually told him that I had lost my magic..." I frowned. "Or that I even had magic, for that matter. Well, because of that, we didn't put two and two together until just this evening when he came by my tavern to inform me that he had sold you what's basically just colored water vapor instead of real poison vials. And like any good apothecary would, he had of course also created an antidote for his magic blocking potion."

"You insolent little–" he began but I cut him off.

"To think, both parts of your plan ended up depending on someone who actually likes me and doesn't want me dead. I'll have you know that *that* part of the population is a lot smaller than the ones who hate me and do want me dead. The odds really were in your favor but..." I threw a glance at the clock. One minute to midnight. "What a small world, huh?"

The Rat King and his crew had finally gotten to their feet again. Hatred radiated from the graying king's eyes as he locked them on me and stabbed a hand in my direction.

"Kill her!" he screamed. "Kill them all."

Putting a finger to my mouth, I tapped my lips before raising it in the air as if I had just remembered something. "Oh, and there was one more thing."

The clock struck midnight.

And then his mansion blew up.

Throwing up my hands, I sent a blast of wind to keep the fire and the falling debris from hitting me or any of the people by the wall on my right. The Rat King and his crew, on the other hand, were on their own.

Broken planks, roof tiles, bits of metal, and furniture flew through the air as the Rat King's headquarters was torn apart from the bottom up and scattered to the wind. Thudding and clanking rang out as debris sailed through the starlit night and hit buildings and streets alike. Black tendrils twisted around my arms as I looked at the carnage.

I raised my voice and shouted across the screams and falling building. "This is the man you served. He promised to spare their people if the other gang leaders joined him again but he broke his vow and tried to kill them all. And he is constantly hiding behind others. No loyalty. Only weakness."

Previously, Rowan and the others had been the only ones moving as they hurried to pick the locks on our shackled gang members. But now, the surviving parts of the Rat King's crew were struggling to their feet as well. I swept mad black eyes over them.

"And all of who served him for money..." Flicking a hand, I motioned at the smoldering pile where the great mansion had stood. "Well, that's all gone now."

Uncertainty began replacing fear on the faces surrounding the Rat King as they realized that the man they'd followed didn't really have much to offer them anymore. Pushing aside planks and bits of furniture, his former gang members advanced on him. The Rat King stabbed an arm towards me.

"Not me, you idiots," he snapped. "Kill her!"

They continued towards their former leader.

A disinterested look settled on my face as I flicked a nonchalant hand at them. "He's all yours."

"What are you...?" the Rat King blurted out. "Stop."

A shocked gasp rang out. His eyes widened as he stared down at his chest. The sharp point of a sword had been shoved through his back and was sticking out on the other side. Wet squishing sounds mingled with the crackling fire behind as the blade was pulled out to reveal the determined face of the young man I had let live and handcuffed to a pillar earlier today. Huh. How about that?

Strained gurgles escaped as the Rat King reached up to claw at the hole in his chest. Blood bubbles popped on his lips. Then, his knees buckled and he crashed to the ground in an undignified heap. There he was. The King of the Underworld, stabbed in the back by his own gang member and dying in front of his ruined mansion after his empire had been torn apart. All because he wanted an arrogant selfish thief to bow to him. Seriously, when would people learn? I did not bow to anyone.

I watched the light dim in the Rat King's eyes until they glazed over completely. Then, I yanked out one of the knives strapped to my thighs and climbed up on the ruined remains of the stone wall. My voice boomed across the area as I pointed the blade towards the burning building. Black smoke snaked down my arms and over the glinting steel.

"This is the old Underworld," I shouted. "It dies tonight. When the sun rises over the horizon, a new Underworld will be born."

Yngvild, Vania, and the rest of my gang, as well as Rowan and the people from the other gangs, were drifting towards me as soon as they were free of their restraints. On the stones below the wall, the Rat King's old crew stared at me, transfixed.

"There will be no more ratting each other out and selling out your own people just to survive another day." I slashed the knife through the air. "We are underworlders. Our gang is our family. Loyalty, to our gang and to our world, comes first."

A bang punctuated my words as a heavy beam crashed to the ground behind me. Smoke and smoldering embers rose in the air.

"From now on, we will respect our gangs and we will respect the Underworld. We will *protect* our own because that is what we do." Moonlight glinted off the blade as I slashed it through the air again. "We will stand united against anyone who would dare threaten our people or our way of life. *We* are the Underworld."

A cheer that was more like a desperate shout rose until it spread across the whole square. Every underworlder still breathing raised their fists or weapons towards the darkened heavens and let out a battle cry so full of conviction and relief that it rattled the walls.

From the mass of people below me, a woman with copper hair strode forth. While Rowan made her way to the front, the other gang leaders followed until they formed a long line. As one, they drew their blades.

"A new Underworld is born," Red Demon Rowan repeated. "And we will protect our people and our way of life from anyone who would seek to destroy us." Flames danced over the fierce expression on her face. "A new Queen of the Underworld rises. And we will follow you." Still keeping her eyes locked on mine, she drew a cut across her palm. "By this blood oath, I so swear."

"By this blood oath, I so swear," was echoed through the whole line as all the other gang leaders drew a shallow cut across their palms as well.

"Do you accept our allegiance and your responsibility to lead our world with strength and cunning?" Rowan called.

I swept black eyes blazing with determination across the gathered underworlders. "I accept your allegiance and my responsibility to lead our world with strength and cunning."

Blood dripped from their clenched fists as the gang leaders raised them in the air. "Strength and cunning!"

Hoisting my blade in the air, I screamed the words into the silver-speckled heavens as well. "Strength and cunning!"

With the promise still ringing in my ears, I stuck the knife back in its holster and leaped down from the wall.

"This'll have spread across the whole Underworld before the night is over," Rowan said with a knowing smile. "Get ready to do this again once all the other gang leaders show up to swear blood oaths to you as well." Her smile widened. "Queen of the Underworld."

"Yeah." A tired chuckle slipped from my lips. "Being in charge still sucks, though."

She threw her head back and laughed. "It sure does."

After giving her a grateful nod, I started out. Rowan, Kessinda, and the others clapped me on the back as I passed. Vania and Yngvild were moving towards me but I slipped through the crowd before they reached me. The darkness pulled back into the deep pits of my soul.

Despite my screams about strength, the truth was that power was draining from me like blood from a severed limb. On my way past the circle of fourteen dead bodies, I stopped to retrieve all my missing knives before slinking into a darkened side alley.

Then, I slumped down on the ground and heaved a sigh so deep I thought it would never end. I could barely believe that I had actually pulled off this insane scheme.

The hardest part of my plan, by far, had been the timing. When Haber had come to the Black Emerald to tell me that the Rat King had tried to buy poison to kill my crew, I had picked his brain about possible counterattacks. While Helena was out fetching Rowan and the others, we had drawn up plans until we finally settled on something I specialized in. Hurting, destroying, and burning things to the ground.

Rigging the explosives inside the chests and then filling them with enough jewelry to hide them had taken most of the night. Well, that and giving Haber enough time to actually set up his new time released bombs.

From the very beginning, my plan had been to blow up his vault. After all, how was I, being only one person, supposed to have been able to carry his entire fortune out the door? I had brought explosives with me when I broke into his mansion and my plan had been to plant them inside the vault but unfortunately, I hadn't been able to get through the door. Since the ordinary explosives I carried then wouldn't have been able to tear through the thick metal wall, my mission had been a failure.

So this time, I had the Rat King deliver the bomb for me. I knew he wouldn't accept my proposed truce but I also knew that he wouldn't be able to resist taking the trunks of jewelry anyway. As I'd explained to Rowan and the others, he was dependent on a steady stream of money. They hadn't been entirely convinced that it would work but had agreed to play along and pretend to switch sides, if it came to that, in order to buy me time.

Which brings me back to the hardest part of my plan. Timing it correctly. Well, that and constantly looking at the clock tower without anyone realizing that *that* was what I was doing when I kept sweeping my gaze across the square all the time.

But back to the timing. I had to get here early enough to give the Rat King time to move the treasure chest into the vault. Since I had no idea how long it would take them to get through that strange vault door that had neither lock nor handle, I had to err on the side of caution. But leaving enough time to make sure the exploding jewelry made it into the vault also meant that I had to stall much longer before I could play my hand.

Until the bombs went off, I had to keep him distracted. Unfortunately, since I couldn't reveal my connection to Haber, that also meant that I couldn't use my powers until I finally showed my hand and blew up his mansion. Which especially sucked when I had thirty people beating the shit out of me.

I also had to prevent him from realizing that the poison was fake until the last minute, since that would have revealed my connection to Haber just as clearly as me using my powers. When he threatened to fire a few minutes early, I had to play along and pretend to submit to keep him from figuring it all out until I was sure there was no time left to stop the bombs from going off. Not being able to tell Yngvild and Vania that they were in no risk of dying had tugged at my cold black heart, and Rowan and the others hadn't been happy about it either, but they'd understood the need for secrecy.

So yeah, arriving early, convincing the Rat King to take my explosive jewelry and move it into the vault, keeping him distracted by talking and pretending that my allies abandoned me, fighting thirty people without revealing that I had regained my powers, buying myself the final few minutes by pretending to submit, and all while constantly checking the time without anyone catching on had definitely been the most difficult part of my plan. The rest... Piece of cake. Wait... was there anything left of the plan after that?

"That was the craziest thing I've ever seen. And I've seen some crazy shit."

Looking up, I found Yngvild beaming down at me. Beside him, Vania matched his smile. When the muscled warrior reached down a tattooed arm, I took it and let him help me to my feet.

"A heads-up that the poison was fake would've been nice, though," Vania added.

"Yeah, you should've seen her," Yngvild said. "She looked like she was about to cry when that glass broke."

"Me? You're the one who looked like you were about to piss yourself." Vania raised her eyebrows in outrage but when she saw the grin tugging at Yngvild's lips, she just shook her head and slapped his muscled bicep with the back of her hand.

"Yeah, sorry I couldn't warn you," I said.

Vania waved a hand in front of her face and then narrowed her eyes as she scrutinized my appearance. When she spoke, her voice was much softer than the no-nonsense tone she usually used. "How are you feeling?"

"Like someone threw me out the window and then ran me over with a horse cart. Repeatedly."

Yngvild crossed his massive arms and nodded with a thoughtful expression on his face. "You look like it too."

I snorted. "Thanks."

"The others are waiting," Vania said. "Let's go home, shall we? So you can have our doctor take a look at your wounds."

Yngvild poked my blood-soaked shoulder. "And a bath."

"And sleep," I added with a tired chuckle. "In that order."

A satisfied smile spread across both Yngvild and Vania's mouth. "Whatever the Queen of the Underworld wants."

I shook my head as we made our way out of the narrow alley. Fire still crackled over ruined remains on the other side of the square and the smell of smoke blanketed the whole area. The other gangs were in the process of leaving too. As we reached Kildor, Yua, and the others and started towards the Black Emerald, I couldn't stop the incredulous laugh that bubbled out of my throat.

When I first got back, I hadn't even wanted to be a gang leader and now I was the bloody Queen of the Underworld. If someone had told me that then, I would've laughed. Or stabbed them. Queen of the Underworld. Me. It really was a rather ridiculous notion, when you thought about it, given what a selfish bastard I was.

But after all these weeks of constantly thinking that someone needed to change how things worked in the Underworld, I had realized something. If I wanted to live in a world that worked the way I wanted it to work, then *I* would actually have to help create that world. Shocking, right? So, here I was. The Queen of the Underworld. I shook my head as we strode through another empty moonlit street. Who would've thought?

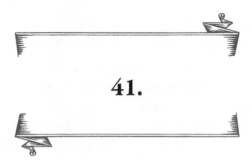

41.

"Every time." Elaran shook his head in disbelief. "Every bloody time."

I frowned at him as I made my way down the final steps and reached the tavern floor. "What?"

"Every time you go somewhere, *something* blows up."

Boisterous laughter echoed across the room as my gang members saw the truth in the grumpy elf's words. I shook my head. Idiots.

After getting back to the Black Emerald, having a bath, and getting my wounds dressed, I had collapsed in my bed and slept the rest of the night. And the whole day after that as well. When I'd woken up an hour ago, I'd finally felt like a living human being again. I was starving, though, so I'd gone down to raid the kitchen. And, apparently, to be yelled at by elves.

"Yeah, well, maybe I like blowing shit up," I countered.

Haela rubbed her hands. "You and me both."

While both Elaran and Haemir were busy rolling their eyes at us, I made my way over to their table. They were seated in the open space at the front, which someone had taken the time to put back in order while I was out like a light, so I wove towards them. No sooner had I pulled out a chair and plopped down than a plate full of food was placed before me. After a nod of thanks to the cook, I started shoveling delicious beef stew into my mouth.

"You just gonna inhale that then?" Haela said, nodding at the mounds of food before me.

With my mouth still full of stew, I looked up at her and then nodded. She chuckled and took a large swig from her mug of ale. Gulping down the mouthful of beef and spiced rice, I did the same.

"I mean, you're always welcome here but..." I glanced suspiciously at the three elves. "Any particular reason you're here?"

"Elaran was worried about you," Haemir said.

Panic flashed over Elaran's face before he turned to scowl at the black-haired twin. "I wasn't worried about her." Shifting his gaze back to me, he crossed his arms and drew his eyebrows down. "I just heard that something blew up and... wanted to make sure you hadn't gotten yourself blown up as well this time."

A wide grin spread across my mouth. "Uh-huh."

"Shut up," he muttered.

"We came by this morning but they said you were sleeping," Haemir filled in. "So we came back after our training with the army but they said you were still sleeping."

Haela shrugged. "So we helped ourselves to some ale while we waited."

I waved a hand over our table filled with mugs, plates, and candles by way of saying that they were more than welcome to it. Wood creaked as Haela threw herself back in her chair with a conspiratorial grin on her face.

"We also heard that there's a new Queen of the Underworld," she said. "Care to comment?"

A sly smile spread across my lips. "I have no idea what you're talking about."

She matched my grin. "I knew you had it in you."

"But so, with the Rat King dead–"

The door banged open. I jerked up and my gang was halfway to their feet when a dark-haired woman sauntered into the room.

"Zaina?" I said.

"There you are." Zaina shook her head. "I've been looking for you at the warehouses."

While I waved my gang back in their seats, the striking smuggler strode forward, revealing two more people behind her. My eyebrows shot up.

"Lady Smythe?" I blurted out.

The talented jewelry forger from Keutunan inclined her head. "Come on, Charles," she said to the child, looking to be about eight years old, that held her hand as she followed Zaina towards our table.

For a moment, I just sat there gaping at them. Zaina dragged over three chairs from another table and plopped down in one while Lady Smythe and her son lowered themselves gracefully into the other two. I pulled the burning candle closer to my side of the table so that it was out of reach. After eyeing the child suspiciously for another second, I shifted my gaze to his mother and the smuggler beside her.

"What are you doing here?"

Leaning back in the chair, Zaina crossed her ankles and rested her hands behind her head. "I told you. They arrived this afternoon and we were looking for you at the warehouses but you weren't there so we came here."

"I meant, what is Lady Smythe doing in Pernula?"

Lady Smythe's dark eyes met Zaina's for a moment before she turned to me. "Zaina always speaks so well of her home country so I wanted to see it for myself."

"Yeah, I figured we could show her how the business is set up over here." The smuggler narrowed her eyes at me. "But we can't seem to find any of our wares. I found the pistols but where's the jewelry?"

Shit. From a table on my right, I could feel Yngvild grinning at me. Zaina and Lady Smythe looked at me expectantly while I tried to come up with some kind of excuse. Screw the Rat King and his army. *This* was probably the most dangerous situation I'd been in for quite some time. Those two were definitely going to kill me.

"They're currently... not available for, uhm, inspection."

"What does that mean?"

I was dead. I was *so* dead. Elaran and the twins studied me curiously as I cast my gaze around for something to distract them with so they wouldn't find out that I had blown it all up.

"Did you come here alone, Lady Smythe?" I said, trying to change the subject. "Or where is your husband?"

"Dead."

Blinking, I sat back in my chair. "Oh, uhm, I'm sorry to hear that."

"Don't be." She drew a hand over the dark orange skirts of her dress. The exquisite jewelry she wore glittered in the candlelight as she moved. "That is what tends to happen when a man marries a woman twenty-five years younger than himself."

"Twenty-five years?" Haela frowned. "That's not a lot."

Haemir coughed pointedly and gave her leg a smack under the table.

She cleared her throat and grinned sheepishly as if she had just remembered that we were humans and not elves. "I meant, sorry he's dead."

I could almost hear Haemir's internal groan as he rolled his eyes and slapped his forehead. But Lady Smythe's gorgeous features just drew into a secretive smile.

"Oh, do not weep for me. I do not need a husband to support me. I have been the mistress of my own fate for quite some time now." Her intelligent eyes flicked to me. "As you well know."

A chuckle shook my chest. "Yes, since before I was old enough to join a guild, if I remember correctly?"

"Exactly." She stroked an affectionate hand over her son's dark hair. "And besides, the current Lord Smythe does what I tell him to." When Charles grinned up at her, she smiled back. "Mostly, anyway."

Laughter rose around our table. Thinking I had managed to divert their attention, I picked up my mug and took a large gulp of ale. From across the flickering candle, Zaina watched me intently.

"You still haven't answered my question." Her observant eyes bored into me. "Where's the jewelry?"

A coughing fit racked my body as I choked on the last mouthful of ale. Wood rattled as I slammed the mug down and gripped the edge of the table while still trying to get the alcohol out of my windpipe. Haela and Elaran exchanged a glance.

"She looks nervous, doesn't she?" Haela said.

Elaran studied me with the practiced gaze of a hunter assessing his prey. "She does."

My chair scraped against the floorboards and wobbled precariously as I shot to my feet. "You know what, I just remembered that I've gotta do something."

The elves all arched dubious eyebrows in my direction but before they could say anything, I waved an arm around the tavern.

"But you can stay as long as you like. Drinks are on me." Mischief crept into my eyes as I shifted them to Zaina. "And maybe you could show Lady Smythe some other parts of town. Like, the Lemon Tree Café." The grin on my face widened as I strode towards the door, putting a safe distance between us. "Or some other more... intimate locations."

Her mouth dropped open but before she could spit out whatever retort, or threat, she had loaded up, Haemir beat her to it.

"Where are you going?"

"Oh, uhm, I'm just gonna..."

Haela's eyes glittered as she flashed me another conspiratorial grin. "Or, *to who*, might be the better question."

Yanking open the door, I grimaced at her but didn't reply. Why did she have to be so perceptive? Damn elves.

"I'll see you soon," I called over my shoulder as I took a step across the threshold.

"Don't burn anything else down!" bounced off my back in the form of Elaran's muttering voice. Laughter followed it.

Blowing out a deep breath, I closed the door behind me and leaned back against the carved wood. Well, I had survived Elaran, Lady Smythe, *and* Zaina. If that didn't bode well for the rest of the night, then I didn't know what did.

Pushing off the door, I strode down the steps. Silky night air full of spices and warmth caressed my face as I took off down the street and slipped into the darkness. I had a Master Assassin to see.

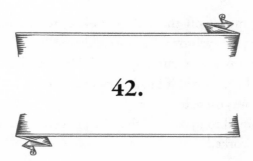

42.

Intense black eyes stared straight at me as I slipped through the door. I pushed it closed behind me and leaned back against the wall just inside the door while Shade studied me from behind his desk. His muscles shifted under his black shirt as he rose and moved around the elegant piece of furniture to lean back against the tabletop.

"Yet another late-night visit in my bedroom." Candlelight cast gold glittering shadows in his eyes. "One might almost think this was becoming a habit."

I gave him a quick rise and fall of my eyebrows. "At least I didn't bring any handcuffs."

He matched the sly smile on my lips. "Pity."

A soft breeze blew in through the open window and made the candles flutter. Firelight danced over the neatly decorated room in black and red while Shade and I continued watching each other.

"I came to tell you that you don't have to worry about a divided city when Queen Nimlithil makes her move," I said. "The Underworld is back under control now."

"I know." He pushed off from the desk and took a step forward. "I saw."

Peeling myself off the wall, I took a step forward as well while raising my eyebrows. "You were there?"

"Yes. It was a very cunning plan." His gaze locked on me. "One I would've ruined if I hadn't run into Haber."

"Haber was there too?"

"He wanted to make sure that the plan you two had cooked up actually worked."

"And you?"

Shade took another few steps forward. "I would've slaughtered them all when they were beating you up if Haber hadn't explained what the plan was. And when you knelt before the Rat King and bowed..." Steel crept into his eyes. "You couldn't have told me what you were planning?"

"There wasn't time." I shrugged. "And besides, I didn't think you'd find out until afterwards."

"This is my city, remember?"

I rolled my eyes. "As if you'd ever let me forget."

Papers rustled by the desk as another night breeze drifted through the room. After my one step away from the wall, I had remained rooted in place so there was still half a room between the two of us. Silvery moonlight fell in through the open window and illuminated the patch of dark floor between us.

"But from what I hear, it's your city too now." A satisfied smile spread across his lips. "The Oncoming Storm. Queen of the Underworld."

I shot him a teasing grin. "It does have a nice ring to it, doesn't it?"

"It does." His eyes were so intense when he locked them on me that I almost forgot to breathe. He took another step forward. "You, standing there atop the smoldering ruins, covered in black smoke and blood and glinting steel. The other gang leaders swearing blood oaths to you. You looked glorious. Striking."

Heat crept into my cheeks and I suddenly didn't know what to say or where to look or what to do with my hands. Shade closed the distance between us. Placing a hand on my jaw, he tilted my head up to meet his eyes while his thumb caressed my cheekbone.

"Now that we both have what we wanted, maybe it's time we revisited that conversation we had on the ship outside the City of Glass."

"Yes, maybe we should. But let's get something straight." I held his gaze steadily. "I will not be wearing poofy dresses and trailing demurely behind you in this castle. You might be the High King of Pernula, but I am the Queen of the Underworld. I bow to no one."

His pleasant laugh filled the room. Crossing his arms, he arched an eyebrow and shot me a knowing look. "If I liked women who trail demurely behind me, do you really think I would've fallen for your stubborn ass?"

"Stubborn? Me?" I grinned up at him. "I don't know what you're talking about."

"Uh-huh."

"But I'm being serious." Letting out a long sigh, I met his gaze again. "I can't be an upperworlder here with your lords and ladies. It's not who I am. I might be a somewhat..." I tipped my head from side to side. "Well, I wouldn't go as far as saying *pleasant*, but I can be a somewhat *tolerable* person from time to time. But I also come home covered in the blood of my enemies every now and then."

Once again, Shade's rippling laughter bounced off the smooth black walls. "I know."

When he tilted his head down again, there was so much emotion in his eyes that I drew in a soft breath in surprise.

"There is light in you," he said. "That fierce devotion to the people you love. And yes, there is also darkness. A fire-breathing demon that will never be subjugated." His penetrating gaze held me firmly in place as he moved closer. "I love your light *and* your darkness. And all the morally gray bits in between. You won't ever have to change for me."

Feelings I didn't know I was capable of burned like wildfire inside me. "You infuriating, arrogant, dictatorial assassin with your intelligence and your strength and your cunning and your honor and that unbreakable survivor's soul of yours. Gods help me but I love *everything* about you too."

Shade pushed me up against the wall. His breath was ragged as he planted a hand on the smooth obsidian next to my head and leaned towards me. I shot a stiletto blade from my sleeve.

Before his lips reached mine, I stopped them by placing the cold edge of steel against his throat. "If you ever betray me, I will kill you."

"I know." His black eyes glittered as he reached up and, with a firm grip on my wrist, moved the blade back against my own throat. "And same."

After exchanging a knowing look, we both let out a dark chuckle because only a thief and an assassin could find death threats romantic. And because we both already knew that neither of us would ever betray the other. Not for anything. We might be murderers and liars and godsdamn demons in human flesh but we would never, *ever*, betray our own.

Releasing my hand again, Shade tilted his head to the right. "So, no threatening and blackmailing each other while we do this?"

A sly smile spread across my lips as I retracted the blade into my sleeve again. "No *excessive* threatening and blackmailing each other while we do this."

Shade released a dark laugh. "The two of us together. Gods help anyone who dares cross us."

"Oh the world doesn't stand a chance."

Black fabric rumpled under my fingers as I gripped the collar of his shirt and yanked him towards me. He put a hand behind my neck and knitted his fingers through my hair while drawing me tighter. As he pressed his hard body against mine, his greedy lips worked their way from my collarbone, up my throat, and towards my lips. I sucked in a shuddering breath and ran my hands over his back and then towards his stomach.

My heart slammed in my chest as I reached the edge of his tightfitting black shirt and pulled it upwards. A slight moan escaped Shade's lips as my fingers brushed over his abs on their way upwards. Releasing his tight grip on me, he grabbed his shirt and yanked it over his head. Firelight played over his lean muscles as his shirt hit the floor.

Stepping away from the wall, I placed my hands against his muscled chest and pushed him backwards before yanking my own shirt over my head. Another black garment hit the floor as I backed Shade across the moonlit obsidian and towards the bed. Steel clattered as we stripped off the hidden blades we had carried strapped to our bare skin below our clothes. I kicked off my boots.

"Remember when you handcuffed me to the bed and told me you'd make me beg for it?" I asked. It had been in an entirely different context but I'd still sworn I'd get him back for that. A wicked smile flashed across my lips. "I'm the one who's gonna make *you* beg for it before the night is over."

Still backing towards the bed, he took a firm grip on my chin and stole a kiss from my lips. "We'll see about that."

When we reached the black silken sheets of the bed, I shoved him backwards. His hand shot out and snatched at my belt, pulling me with him. The mattress creaked as he twisted and threw me down on the bed underneath him. I sucked in a shuddering breath and drew my fingers down his ripped stomach towards the top of his pants. A dark moan that sounded more like a growl came from his throat. His strong hands snaked around my wrists and moved them towards me.

Pinning my hands against the mattress above my head, Shade leaned down over me until his lips were so close our breath mingled. Both strength and vulnerability the likes of which I had never seen before swirled in his black eyes as he locked them on me. When he spoke, his voice was raw with emotion.

"I love you, my black-hearted thief."

My heart felt like it was going to burst and be consumed by raging wildfire. "And I love you, my cold-hearted assassin."

Another growling moan escaped his lips before they ravaged mine. Then, they moved downwards. Over my jaw, my throat, and then over my collarbones. Bolts of lightning shot through me. I pulled against the hands forcing my arms to stay locked above my head. He moved my wrists further down so that he could reach better but kept them trapped against the cool silk sheets. I wanted to touch him, to run my fingers through his thick black hair and down his back, trace the ridges of his abs. But against the strength in those sculpted arms, I had nothing. His soft lips reached my chest.

Arching my back, I pushed my hips against his as he worked his way down my chest. The sensation made me feel like my brain was shutting on and off with each brush of his lips. My pulse pounded in my ears. I once more pulled against the strong hands keeping my wrists trapped but his hard muscles kept me pinned to the bed until I was on the verge of actually begging him to let me touch him back.

Shade's black eyes glittered as he smiled in victory and finally released my arms. I raked my fingers through his silky hair and down over his back before locking them behind his neck and pulling him harder against me. A shiver coursed through his body as I kissed him in that sensitive spot where his neck met his shoulders. With my lips against his skin, I breathed him in. He smelled like the night. Dark and alluring.

Lightning crackled through me as he traced his fingers down my body. His skin was warm against mine. I arched my back and pushed my hip bones into his and then smiled in satisfaction when that dark growl came from his throat again.

My breath hitched as his fingers finally reached the top of my pants and started unbuckling my belt. Not being able to endure the wait any longer, I sat up and got to work on his as well. The rest of our clothes sailed through the air and hit the floor with a rustling sound. His breathing was ragged as he reached up and brushed back strands of hair from my face with his calloused hands.

Emotions so raw my heart almost stopped shone in his eyes when he guided me back against the black silk sheets. Drawing a desperate breath, I leaned into his touch as we lost ourselves in each other. Lost ourselves in knowing that we had found someone in the middle of this messy adventure called life who was like us. Another survivor. Someone else who had scars on both skin and soul. And a cold black heart. Someone who didn't shy away from the darkness inside us but instead embraced it and loved it. Someone who would have our back. Always. Someone like him. And someone like me.

NIGHT AIR SMELLING like spices on a warm summer day drifted in through the open window. Leaning my back against the cool obsidian frame, I shifted my weight on the windowsill and gazed out across the darkened city.

Stars decorated the heavens like glittering silver dust and the moon shone bright above the tall city walls. Out there, somewhere, the star elves were getting ready for battle. War would soon be here.

I shifted my gaze to the darkened city below, where Elaran and the twins, Liam and Norah, Zaina and Lady Smythe, Yngvild and Vania, Rowan, Haber, and everyone else I cared about were staying. I had to make sure they survived. All of them. They had to survive.

Turning my head, I looked back at the figure sleeping on the bed. Shade's muscles shifted as his ribcage expanded and contracted with each deep breath. Moonlight played over the scars on his bare back and arms. *He* had to survive.

By all the gods, I would wade through rivers of blood and sell my soul to every demon in hell if I had to. He would survive.

They would all survive. Steel seeped into my blackened heart as I tilted my head up to look at the glittering stars above. War was coming. And I would make damn sure we won. Black smoke twisted around me as I squeezed my hand into a fist. It was time for the world to learn, once and for all, not to mess with the Oncoming Storm.

Acknowledgements

A nd there we go. Our stubborn thief and assassin finally took things to the next level. I know, I know. It took six books. Six. That's roughly half a million words, in case you were wondering. And if you weren't, now you know anyway. But yeah, for those of you who have been waiting for this, thank you for persevering. It's not as if I've been sitting here laughing like a villain while you've been screaming into the abyss every time Storm and Shade almost got together but didn't. Muahaha. Ahem. Wait, what was I saying again? Oh, right. Thank you for enduring my evil whims. And I hope you have found or will find your own black-hearted thief or cold-hearted assassin one day. Here's to not threatening and blackmailing excessively! And to love. Of course. Yes. To love!

As always, I would like to say a huge thank you to my family and loved ones. Mom, Dad, Mark, thank you for the enthusiasm, love, and encouragement. I truly don't know what I would do without you. Lasse, Ann, Karolina, Axel, Martina, thank you for continuing to take such an interest in my books. It really means a lot.

Another group of people I would like to once again express my gratitude to is my wonderful team of beta readers: Deshaun Hershel, Jennifer Nicholls, Luna Lucia Lawson, and Orsika

Petér. Thank you for the time and effort you put into reading the book and providing helpful feedback. Your suggestions and encouragement truly makes the book better.

To my amazing copy editor and proofreader Julia Gibbs, thank you for all the hard work you always put into making my books shine. Your language expertise and attention to detail is fantastic and makes me feel confident that I'm publishing the very best version of my books.

Dane Low is another person I'm very fortunate to have found. He is the extraordinary designer from ebooklaunch.com who made the stunning cover for this book. Dane, thank you for the effort you put into making yet another gorgeous cover for me. You knock it out of the park every time.

I am also very fortunate to have friends both close by and from all around the world. My friends, thank you for everything you've shared with me. Thank you for the laughs, the tears, the deep discussions, and the unforgettable memories. My life is a lot richer with you in it.

Before I go back to writing the next book, I would like to once again say thank you to you, the reader. Thank you for being so invested in the world of the Oncoming Storm that you continued the series. If you have any questions or comments about the book, I would love to hear from you. You can find all the different ways of contacting me on my website, www.marionblackwood.com. There you can also sign up for my newsletter to receive updates about coming novels. Lastly, if you liked this book and want to help me out so that I can continue writing books, please consider leaving a review. It really does help tremendously. I hope you enjoyed the adventure!

Printed in the USA
CPSIA information can be obtained
at www.ICGtesting.com
LVHW041318090923
757485LV00011B/30